A Fatal Collection

— A KEEPSAKE COVE MYSTERY —

MARY ELLEN HUGHES

MIDNIGHT INK
WOODBURY, MINNESOTA
MIDNIGHT INK

FIRST EDITION
First Printing, 2017

Book format by Bob Gaul
Cover design by Ellen Lawson
Cover Illustration by Mary Ann Lasher-Dodge

Midnight Ink, an imprint of Llewellyn Worldwide Ltd.

Library of Congress Cataloging-in-Publication Data
Names: Hughes, Mary Ellen, author.
Title: A fatal collection / Mary Ellen Hughes.
Description: First edition. | Woodbury, Minnesota: Midnight Ink, [2017] |
 Series: A Keepsake Cove mystery; #1
Identifiers: LCCN 2017030283 (print) | LCCN 2017039136 (ebook) | ISBN
 9780738753096 | ISBN 9780738752198 (softcover: acid-free paper)
Subjects: LCSH: Murder—Investigation—Fiction. | GSAFD: Mystery fiction.
Classification: LCC PS3558.U3745 (ebook) | LCC PS3558.U3745 F38 2017 (print)
 | DDC 813/.54—dc23
LC record available at https://lccn.loc.gov/2017030283

Midnight Ink
Llewellyn Worldwide Ltd.
2143 Wooddale Drive
Woodbury, MN 55125-2989
www.midnightinkbooks.com

Printed in the United States of America

For Edna Rogers Hughes, one of the best, with thanks.

One

$\mathcal{O}$h, you're here!" Callie's Aunt Melodie, a pretty, middle-aged woman in a blue shirt-dress, ran around the counter of the music box shop to give Callie the best hug she'd had in ages. It felt wonderful.

"How was your drive? Did my directions make sense? Are you hungry?" The questions came rapid-fire, giving Callie no chance to even think of answering. Then her aunt stepped back, still holding on to her niece but at arm's length, to look Callie over head to toe. It was in such a totally loving way that Callie felt confident her rumpled clothes and her blond hair gone limp from the long, hot drive mattered little. She knew her strong resemblance to her father, Aunt Melodie's brother, still shone through in her slim build, blue eyes, and freckled upturned nose.

"Goodness!" her aunt said. "You've grown up since I last saw you at your dad's funeral in California. You were in college, then. How long ago was that? Eight years?

"Ten," Callie said, aware that her grimace revealed that they weren't exactly great years. She'd spent a total of three semesters in college before dropping out. Her first bad decision. The second was falling for a struggling country-western musician.

"I'm sorry it's been so long, Aunt Melodie. After I moved to Nashville, then West Virginia a couple of years ago, I really thought I could make the drive to Maryland much sooner. The time just, you know, slipped away."

"No worry," Aunt Melodie said, dismissing Callie's words with a loving hand squeeze. "You're here now. That's all that matters."

Callie noticed that her aunt didn't bring up the fact that Hank hadn't come with her. In her more recent emails, Callie had hinted at problems between them. She was hoping that this two-day visit to Maryland's Eastern Shore would help clear her mind about what she was doing with her life. Maybe, at twenty-nine, it was time to figure out what she really wanted?

"Come on in," Aunt Melodie said, interrupting Callie's thoughts. "Let me show you around the shop. We can head over to the cottage in a few minutes to give you a chance to rest up."

Her aunt had changed little since Callie had last seen her. She must be in her mid-fifties, Callie guessed, but looked and acted much younger, with a trim figure and light brown hair with just a hint of gray. Why had she never married? Had there been any relationships? There was a lot Callie didn't know about her aunt, who'd always lived so far away. Letters and emails were fine, but they didn't tell you everything.

"These are my quick-sale music boxes," Aunt Melodie said, waving her hand over a grouping of small music boxes clearly designed for children. Twirling ballerinas, boys or girls posed with praying hands on flower-trimmed pedestals, and a pink and sparkly unicorn covered a small table. "They're priced low and appeal to customers who are looking for a gift on their way home from Ocean City. We're right off the main route, you know, for vacationers heading back to Baltimore or DC. Over here," Melodie continued, leading Callie to the shelves against the wall, "are my music boxes for serious collectors."

Those boxes, Callie could instantly see, were of higher quality and the variety was wider. Her aunt lifted the lids of a huge silver Hershey's Kiss, a round pill box, and a ceramic flower-topped box, flooding the shop with music.

Callie laughed with delight. "I thought you'd named your shop *House of Melody* after yourself. But it really is a house of melody!"

"I simply carried on the family tradition," her aunt said, smiling. "Daddy—your Grandpa Reed—started it all. He loved music boxes and named me Melodie because of that. He was the one who suggested your name—Calliope—to your mamma and daddy. He always had music on his mind, and Calliope, you know, was the Greek goddess of music."

Callie winced. "I much prefer Callie. But I appreciated—eventually—the sentiment."

She felt a twinge of sadness thinking about her parents. She still missed her father, and her mother had recently remarried. Callie liked her new stepfather and was truly happy for her mom, but she was aware of a sense of loss as her mother became immersed in her new life, which included much travel.

The shop's door opened as a plump, forty-something woman in an ankle-length cotton dress came in. "Is this your niece, Mel?" she asked, her face beaming. She turned to Callie. "I spotted the West Virginia license plate on the car out front. Delia Hamilton," she said, taking Callie's hand in both of hers. "Mel's been talking about nothing but your visit for days."

"Delia has the shop next door," Aunt Mel explained. "Collectible salt and pepper shakers."

"*Shake It Up!*" Delia said, naming her shop with a cheery grin. "Do come over when you have a minute."

"Are all the shops at Keepsake Cove one or another kind of collectible?" Callie asked. She remembered her aunt mentioning something about that in one of her emails, but it hadn't fully sunk in.

"Just about," Delia said. "This part of Mapleton is like a collector's mall, except not under one roof. We're a little town within a town."

"Keepsake Cove developed over time," Aunt Melodie further explained. "One or two collectible shops set up first and became hugely popular. That drew more businesses to the area. Before you knew it, just about every shop in the two-or-three-block square had become a collectible shop of one kind or another."

"Except for the café," Delia added.

"Right. And the name Keepsake Cove simply evolved—because of the collectible shops, of course, and because of the little bay we back up to, turning the area into a destination."

"What I've seen so far is charming," Callie said, meaning it. "The storefronts look like something out of a Dickens novel."

"Wait till you see your aunt's cottage."

Aunt Melodie smiled. "It's not half as nice as yours, Delia. But I am rather proud of it." She glanced at the clock on the wall. "It's just about closing time, so why don't I finish up here and I'll take you over? Want to join us for dinner, Delia?"

"I wouldn't dream of barging in, Mel, but thank you. I hope you'll stop over tomorrow," Delia said warmly to Callie before taking her leave.

"She's a dear person," Aunt Melodie said as the shop door closed behind her friend, "and a wonderful neighbor. Unlike ... well, we won't get into that now. Let me close up and we'll head out back. I've had a Crock-Pot simmering most of the day, so dinner should be ready as soon as I toss a salad together."

As her aunt got busy behind her counter, Callie wandered about the shop, delighting in the variety and beauty of the music boxes she saw, until Aunt Mel turned the front door lock and flipped the *closed* sign. She led Callie to a small office at the back, where she stopped at an old desk that looked vaguely familiar.

"Remember this?" Aunt Mel asked. "It was Grandma Reed's."

Callie suddenly remembered the secretary desk, with its drop-lid desktop, sitting at one end of her grandparents' living room. She'd loved the many cubbyholes, which, as a child, she'd thought were perfect for hiding secret messages.

"It's full of nicks and scratches, but it's the perfect size for this room. And I like being able to lock up a few things in it." To demonstrate, Aunt Mel logged out of her laptop and closed it. Then she slid the compact computer to the back and lifted the drop lid to shutter the desk. She locked the lid with a ring of keys she'd retrieved from a lower drawer, then turned off the lights and led the way out the back door. There she stopped to let Callie take in the view of the cottage that stood about twenty steps away.

Callie saw a greenery-framed little house that whispered—no, cried—"English countryside" to her. All her favorite books sprang to life as she gazed at her aunt's red-painted cottage. A steep-pitched roof hugged a second floor dormer window with a flower-filled window box beneath. A large, multipaned window sat to the right of a sage green door that was reached by passing under a white, rose-trimmed trellis. Varieties of blooming flowers edged the cottage foundation. All that was missing, Callie thought, was thatching on the roof. "Aunt Melodie, it's wonderful!"

Aunt Melodie smiled. "You should have seen the place when I bought it. A run-down disaster. It's been a loving work-in-progress for several years. I still have a project or two in mind. Come," she said, stepping onto the brick walk and leading the way, "I have something special to show you inside."

Callie followed, catching the sweet perfume of the roses as she passed beneath the trellis. The bland entrance to her apartment building back in Morgantown came to mind, dreary in comparison, but she brushed that thought away. She had two days to enjoy this fairyland before she needed to return.

Stepping through the door, she entered a blue and white living room as pretty as a piece of Staffordshire china. As she moved to the middle of the room and gazed around, something suddenly swooped down from the top of a bookcase and landed at her feet. Callie screeched and jumped back, falling into a cushioned rocking chair as a flash of gray zipped past her and into the kitchen.

"Jagger!" Aunt Mel scolded. "That wasn't nice! Are you okay, Callie?"

Callie stopped rocking and grinned. "I didn't know you had a cat."

"Jagger thinks it's the other way around. It's his dinner time. He assumes I need daily reminding."

Aunt Melodie followed her cat to the kitchen, and Callie pulled herself up to join them. Jagger sat next to an empty white bowl and blinked benignly at Callie, who saw no remorse in those round eyes for his attack-style greeting. Aunt Mel filled the cat's bowl and watched fondly as he dug in.

"I got him from a shelter," she said. "His previous owner was obviously a Mick Jagger fan. I kept the name when I saw how he strutted around the place like a rock star. Well, now we'll have a little peace for what I first intended to do." Aunt Mel waved Callie back to the living room and to a roll-top desk tucked in the corner. As she unlocked the desk top and opened it, Aunt Melody turned to watch Callie's reaction. "Remember this?"

Callie gasped as she recognized the square music box that sat in the middle of the desk. Its polished wood gleamed, showing off a beautiful inlaid design on the lid.

"Grandpa Reed's music box!"

"It was his favorite. Yours too, when you were little."

"I remember him winding it up to play, over and over."

"And you'd waltz around the room—"

"My version of a waltz," Callie said, laughing. "I was pretending to skate."

"Of course you were!" Aunt Melodie said, smiling. "Since the tune is *The Skaters' Waltz*." She lifted the lid, and the familiar music played as a figure of a miniature skater twirled inside.

Callie sang softly along until the music finally wound down. She tilted the box, exposing the key beneath. "May I?" she asked. "Grandpa Reed never let me wind it myself."

"He wouldn't let me touch it either, until he judged I was old enough to be careful. His music box collection, after I inherited it, provided the start-up for my shop. But this one has never been for sale."

"I'm glad you held on to it."

"I was as fond of it as you were. I'll keep it safe, and it'll be yours next."

Callie gazed at the box, as happy to see and hear it again as she was to be with her aunt. Possessing the box for herself, she was sure, lay far in the future. For now, it was wonderful simply to know it was in good hands and treasured.

Callie woke the next morning, uncertain for the moment where she was. Then she saw the sun peeking through the muslin curtains at the dormer window as it lit the taller blooms in the flower box below, and she smiled. Aunt Mel had insisted on giving up her room to Callie, claiming she had a little work to do in the guest bedroom that doubled as her home office.

Callie stretched and gazed around, taking in the pretty watercolors on the walls that echoed the greenery outdoors. Her puffy comforter fairly floated above her, adding to the airy lightness of the room. Aunt Mel's touch shone in every detail.

They had spent hours talking the evening before, closing the gap of years between them easily and making Callie wish she'd visited much sooner. Maybe today she'd bring up her concerns about her future. Hank or no Hank, that was the question. Or part of it. But for now, she thought as she pulled herself up to a sitting position, coffee was the question.

A glance at the bedside clock told her it was seven thirty, and Callie listened carefully for sounds that her aunt was awake. All was silent, so she eased out of bed and tiptoed to her door as she wrapped her robe around her. She was surprised, then, as she stepped into the hall to see the door to the guest room open and the bed rumpled and empty. Aunt Mel must be up. However, after Callie trotted downstairs, she found the lower rooms unoccupied except for Jagger pacing near his empty bowl.

"Didn't get your breakfast?" Callie asked. She checked through the window, expecting to see her aunt in the garden, but all she saw were scampering squirrels and chickadees. She hesitated, but after Jagger began mewing and looking pointedly at his bowl, she found a box of cat food and shook some out for him. When he dug in, obviously hungry, Callie felt uneasy. Aunt Mel wasn't one to neglect feeding her pet. Callie hadn't spotted any note to explain a hasty departure, but she shrugged. Aunt Mel must have had a good reason to run out and most likely would be back in minutes.

Still wanting that coffee, Callie set up a pot to begin brewing, then went back upstairs to get dressed, listening with one ear the whole time for sounds of the front door opening and her aunt calling out cheerily. When that didn't happen by the time she returned to the kitchen, she began to feel anxious. But, she told herself, Aunt Mel could have simply gone in to her shop. Deciding that must be the explanation, Callie filled a mug and carried it with her out the door to head over there.

It was a beautiful morning, and Callie breathed in the fresh air tinged with rose perfume. She stepped carefully along the brick walkway that was wet with dew until she reached the back door of the music box shop. When she tried the knob, it turned easily, and Callie smiled with relief. She had guessed right. Her aunt must be inside.

"Aunt Mel?" she called as she entered the shop's office. It was dim, and she could see that the shop beyond was also dark, which seemed odd. "Aunt Mel?"

Callie froze as a feeling of dread washed over her. She tried to shake it off, telling herself she was being silly. Aunt Mel simply hadn't turned on the lights for whatever she'd come over to do. Still, Callie stayed in place, unwilling to go further. Why wasn't her aunt answering her?

She tried one more time. "Aunt Mel?" When all she got back was the ticking of a wall clock, she forced herself to move forward.

Callie first saw the pale hand, outstretched on the floor. Then the pushed-up sleeve of a blue robe. When she saw her aunt's face, eyes open and mouth slack, lying in a pool of dark red blood, Callie screamed.

She'd forgotten she was holding a mug of coffee until it went crashing to the floor.

Two

*D*elia came running within moments of Callie's screams. White-faced, she checked for signs of life in her friend, then hustled Callie out while calling 911.

"There's been a bad accident," Callie heard her say. A few more words of explanation, then a shaky, "No, I don't think so." Callie understood what that meant. Aunt Mel was dead. She sat numbly in the back of Delia's shop, motionless except for her shivers, and waited.

There were sirens, of course, followed by streams of countless people, both official and onlookers, then endless questions from all. Finally, after what seemed like hours, everyone around her seemed satisfied.

"Accident," they all concluded. It was all so overwhelming that Callie wasn't able to think, so she nodded automatically without really agreeing. Aunt Mel was dead. That was all she knew for sure.

Eventually things around her calmed. Delia's shop emptied, and she asked Callie if she'd like to stay with her that night. "I imagine you'll want to go home for a few days before the funeral."

Funeral! Callie hadn't even thought that far. " I don't know. Everything's been so … "

"Yes, it has." Delia squeezed her hand sadly. "But there's nothing for you to worry about. Mel pre-arranged everything long ago—the service, the reception, everything—something she urged me endlessly to do. I've never been as organized"—Delia paused, smiling sadly at Callie—"or as considerate as your aunt. All you need to do is show up."

Callie nodded. That was some small relief, at least. What did she know about arranging funerals? But then, that was Aunt Mel, she thought with a wince. Considerate to the end.

∽

The service, Callie felt, was beautiful. The mourners were numerous, and she shook hands with so many Keepsake Cove shopkeepers, customers, and friends of Aunt Mel's that faces and names quickly blurred. Brian Greer, however, was one whose face and name became familiar. Part of Aunt Mel's pre-arrangement was for the Keepsake Café to handle the food for the reception, held in the church hall. Callie had been surprised at their first meeting, having expected a motherly, or perhaps a grandmotherly, person to be the Café owner. Brian was definitely male and, she guessed, in his early thirties, not your usual cozy café proprietor. But his food, which was simple—sandwiches, cut-up veggies, assorted cookies—was tasty and clearly enjoyed by all.

"I rounded up a few helpers for Brian," Delia told Callie. "Ladies from the church. Brian doesn't have the staff. But he was determined to do his best for Mel."

Callie made a point of seeking Brian out as the reception wound down. "Everything you provided was wonderful," she told him sincerely and saw his face light up in appreciation.

"Mel was a special person," he said. "We're all going to miss her. I didn't have a chance to say so earlier, but I'm so sorry for your loss."

Callie had heard those words at least a hundred times that day, but they sounded particularly genuine coming from Brian. His face, not quite handsome but definitely pleasant, was filled with sympathy and understanding. Quite a contrast to Hank, who, unsurprisingly, had found an excuse not to come back with her. "Hey," as he'd so artfully said, "it's not like your aunt will *know!*"

Swallowing the lump that threatened to rise, Callie said, "Thank you, Brian."

They were interrupted by a woman who came over to say good-bye, and Callie walked her to the door, learning as she did that the woman owned *Stitches Thru Time*, a vintage sewing shop just two blocks down from *House of Melody*. As she left, Callie glanced around and saw that her new acquaintance, Dorothy, had been the last. She spotted Delia gathering up the sympathy cards and went over to thank her for all her help and support.

"Would you like another cup of tea before you meet with George Blake?" Delia asked, referring to Aunt Mel's lawyer, who had asked Callie to stop in immediately after the funeral.

Blake had apologized for the timing, explaining that he had to leave town that evening for several days. "There are things that need to be settled before I go," he'd said.

Callie knew Aunt Mel had made a will and assumed Grandpa Reed's music box had been left to her, as her aunt had mentioned. Perhaps Mr. Blake intended to hand it over right away, which would save a little trouble later.

She turned down the tea. "I should head on over," she said. She'd decided to leave for Morgantown right after the meeting, and it was getting late.

They hugged, shed a few more tears over the special person they'd lost, then waved goodbye. Callie drove to Blake's law office in the center of Mapleton, only a ten-minute trip. She found a parking spot across the street, in front of the red brick bank, and crossed over to the office, remembering the brisk, efficient manner with which the white-haired lawyer had paid his respects earlier.

"Ah, you're here," he said when his assistant ushered her in. He took her hand, offered a few more words of condolence, then waved her to a seat.

Callie glanced around the tidy office as he shuffled the papers on his desk. She was looking for Grandpa Reed's music box but snapped back to attention as Blake cleared his throat.

"Your aunt, Melodie Reed, died, as you know, without issue," he said.

Callie blinked, then realized the lawyer meant Aunt Mel had no children. She nodded.

"Nor were there surviving siblings."

"Yes," Callie said, also aware that her late father was Aunt Mel's only brother, as she was his only sister.

"Ms. Reed therefore named you as her sole heir."

Callie stared for several moments. "You mean ... ?"

"It means you inherit all your aunt's material goods and wealth, which includes *House of Melody*, her cottage, and all their contents. Plus any and all funds left after outstanding bills are paid. Oh, and her cat." He held out a copy of the will. "It's all there. There'll be paperwork, of course, but as her executor I will handle most of it. I'm also authorized, since you're here, to hand over the keys to her property immediately, if you'll simply sign these papers."

He pushed the papers forward to the edge of his desk along with a pen. Callie, however, had become frozen. "Me?" she squeaked. "Everything?"

Blake nodded and edged the papers a little closer.

"I ... I thought I was getting one music box. Not the entire music box shop!"

"And the cottage, as I've explained." He glanced at his watch.

"But ... Aunt Mel never said anything about this. I had no idea!"

"Your aunt, I'm sure, expected to survive much longer than she did. Her sudden death was a shock to us all." He paused to look properly somber. "Perhaps she intended to tell you in time. Now if you would ...?" He held out the pen.

Callie took the pen, still struggling to believe what she'd heard. "Everything to me?"

Blake nodded, a bit impatiently this time. "As I said. Now, I really have to be going ..."

"Of course." Callie scribbled her name on the line with an *X* next to it, plus on a few more that Blake pointed out, after which the lawyer gathered the papers and stood.

"Here are the keys," he said, holding out a ring. "They're all labeled and should be in good order. If you have any urgent problems during the next week, you may call my office manager, who can get in touch with me. After that I'll be back and happy to answer any questions."

He stepped around his desk, ready to usher her out, but Callie, who had automatically started to follow his lead, suddenly stopped.

"I do have a question, Mr. Blake."

The lawyer pulled up. "Yes?"

"My aunt's death. Did it seem right to you?"

"Her death? You mean the fall?"

"Yes, it was ruled accidental. Did that make sense to you?"

The lawyer's thick eyebrows pulled together tightly. "There was nothing to suggest foul play, if that's what you mean. Is it?"

"I don't really know what I mean," Callie said. "It's just ... my aunt, you know, wasn't that old. She was strong and healthy. Why should she slip and fall so catastrophically? What could have caused that?" Callie realized she was voicing for the first time thoughts that had slipped in once she'd recovered from the shock of finding Aunt Mel. She'd agreed, at the time, that her aunt had taken a terrible fall. But she'd developed reservations the more she'd thought about it.

"The report didn't mention anything like water or objects on the floor that would have triggered a fall," Blake said. "But it was late at night. Your aunt could have merely stumbled in the dark."

That was another thing Callie was having trouble with. Why had Aunt Mel gone to the shop at three a.m.? They knew the time of her death by the musical clock that had been broken during her fall. Aunt Mel had been in her night clothes and her bed had been slept in. But Blake didn't look like he had any answers. He'd clearly accepted the official conclusion of an accidental death. Obviously Callie needed to do so as well.

"Thank you, Mr. Blake," she said. "The news of this inheritance has been pretty overwhelming. It'll take me a while to get used to it."

"Understandable. As I said, I'll be back in a week. I'll have more papers to go over with you at that time. In the meantime, your aunt's cottage is now yours to stay in, if you wish. Take some time to decide if you want to sell it and the shop."

Sell *House of Melody*? The idea sounded shocking to Callie. But the idea of keeping the shop was just as staggering. She shook George Blake's hand and left, a ring of keys in her hand and a million thoughts buzzing through her head.

She climbed back into her car and somehow got herself safely to *House of Melody*, considering her minimal focus on the traffic. After she pulled up in front and switched off the ignition, she simply sat and stared into space. The shops in Keepsake Cove had all shut down for

Melodie's funeral, and the area was quiet—no pedestrians strolling and few cars driving by. Callie's phone dinged, signaling a text. It was from Hank.

Bought a great guitar! U on UR way back?

Callie sighed. She pocketed the phone, then noticed evening had fallen and climbed out of the car, clutching the ring of keys George Blake had given her. She found the key for the shop's front door and unlocked it.

Stepping into the dim, empty shop felt eerie. She hadn't been in it since returning from Morgantown, and she felt like a trespasser. The figurines on the music boxes seemed poised, as though waiting to see what she was going to do—something Callie didn't really know herself. She wound slowly between the tables and shelves, her fingers gently brushing the beautiful collectibles. Aunt Mel had put so much thought into choosing these special things. What was she going to do with them?

She entered the little office at the back of the shop, passed the file cabinets and desk, and opened the back door. The fairy-tale cottage looked even more magical in the fading light. Callie followed the brick walkway to the rose-covered trellis, where she again shuffled through the keys to unlock the front door.

Jagger came running toward her as she stepped inside. Delia had been looking after him, so he hadn't been neglected, but the gray cat wound through Callie's ankles with such joyful purring, as if to say "At last! You're here."

Callie scooped him up, and the cat rubbed his cheek against hers with rumbling purrs. Though she knew he must have been lonely, his enthusiastic greeting seemed to come from more than that, as though he understood Callie and his late mistress's relationship and felt he'd been properly transferred. Callie smiled at the thought but felt a similar affection spring from her, aware as she was of her aunt's fondness for the large cat.

16

Could she take Jagger with her to Morgantown? How would Hank react? Callie suddenly realized she didn't care. She'd been living her life according to Hank's choices for so long and had too rarely considered what she herself wanted. But she was no longer a starry-eyed, naïve girl. She'd grown up.

She set Jagger down gently and wandered through the downstairs, the cat at her heels. She left the living room and climbed the narrow stairs to the second floor. Callie glanced into the guest room first, with its pillow-plumped single bed, small desk, and calico-covered chair. She then crossed the hall to Aunt Mel's lovely room, the one she'd spent one night in, wrapped in its cozy warmth. She sank, now, onto the pale green and white bed and pulled out her cell phone to press in a familiar number. She counted the rings.

Hank picked up after four. "Hey, how'd it go? Get my text?"

"I did. The funeral had an amazing turn-out. Aunt Mel had a lot of friends."

"Yeah, I figured I didn't need to show. You heading back now?"

"No, I'm not."

Hank was silent for a few seconds. "Yeah, okay. That Delia woman should be willing to put you up, right? No use wasting money on a motel. Get an early start tomorrow. I'll call your office, let them know you'll be in late."

"Hank, I'm not coming back at all."

"Huh?"

"Aunt Mel left her place to me."

"No kidding! Hey, great! Sure, stay a while. Grab onto some good real estate people. Tell them to get top dollar for it. Hallelujah! At last! The windfall we've been waiting for."

"No, Hank. No windfall. I'm not selling. Not the shop nor the cottage. I've decided to keep it all and stay here."

There was a long pause as Hank digested this. Then Callie let him have his say, feeling she owed him that much. But she held firm. Their relationship was over. She intended to move forward with her life.

When she'd had enough, Callie said goodbye in the middle of an increasingly nasty rant and disconnected. Then she turned the phone off and sat holding it in silence.

Had she made the right decision? What did she know about running a shop? What did she know about music boxes other than that they were charming and beautiful? Come down to it, what did she know about Maryland's Eastern Shore in general and Keepsake Cove in particular? Had she just gone crazy, or had she become crazy-smart?

Jagger jumped onto the bed, and Callie scratched his head absently as those questions worried through her head. At some point she became aware of a faint tinkling, and she turned, listening. What was it?

Jagger's ears had perked, and Callie stood, pinpointing the sound. She realized it was coming from downstairs and followed it, gradually recognizing the tune as she closed in. The music came from inside Aunt Mel's roll-top desk in the corner of the living room. Callie went over and curled her fingers under the lid to lift it, but she couldn't. It was locked.

Aunt Mel, she remembered, had unlocked the desk with a key from the ring George Blake had handed over. She retrieved the ring from the end table where she'd dropped it, then fingered through the bunch to find the right one. There was one unlabeled key. Callie slipped it into the small lock, which turned easily. She lifted the roll top to find Grandpa Reed's music box, whose *Skaters' Waltz* continued to play. Callie stared in bewilderment.

The music box had been silent when she'd first entered the cottage. It had been locked inside the desk and would need to be wound in order to play. Who, Callie asked herself as she continued to gape, had wound it up?

Three

*C*allie spent a restless night in the cottage due to an ongoing flood of worrisome thoughts. She was standing a bit groggily in the kitchen the next morning when she heard a tap at the door and answered it to find Delia on the doorstep.

"I came to feed Jagger," Delia Hamilton explained, "but then I saw the light on. So you stayed over? I'm glad. Yesterday must have been draining."

"You could say that," Callie said, smiling weakly as she pushed a limp strand of hair from her face. "I've just made coffee. Want some?"

"I'd love a cup." Delia stepped inside, looking ready for her work day in an ankle-length dress similar to the one she was wearing when Callie first met her. Her light brown hair was pinned to the top of her head with an enameled barrette. "If I'd known," she went on, "I would have brought over some breakfast things. Brian whips up a mean omelet at the café, among other things, if you're hungry. He opens early."

"I'll have to stop in and say hello," Callie said. She pulled out an extra mug from an upper cabinet, having already found a jar of powdered creamer as well as a partially filled sugar bowl. "But I'll probably head to the supermarket and stock up first."

"Stock up?"

"Yes." Callie drew a deep breath, not sure how Aunt Mel's friend would take the news that she herself was still struggling with. "George Blake informed me yesterday that I've inherited everything—the shop, this amazing cottage, everything."

"And you're staying?"

When Callie nodded, Delia threw her ample arms in the air. "How wonderful!" She grabbed Callie in a tremendous hug then stepped back, grinning. "Welcome to Keepsake Cove!"

"Thank you—I think. I've never run a shop before, so I'm not really sure what I'm getting in to." Callie poured out two mugs of coffee and handed one to Delia.

"What did you do before?" Delia added sugar to her mug before carrying it into the living room. Callie followed, guessing that morning coffee in Aunt Mel's cottage had been a familiar routine for her neighbor.

"I'm an administrative assistant at a small law firm." Callie paused. "Was."

"You'll do fine," Delia said, flapping a hand. "Anyone who can handle lawyers can probably handle anything. You can ask for help from any of us, except"—Delia paused to take a sip—"probably not Karl."

"Karl?"

"Karl Eggers. He owns *Car-lectibles*, the model car shop." She turned toward the window and pointed. "It's on that side of *House of Melody*. He and Mel didn't get along so well."

Callie remembered her aunt hinting at a strained relationship, but she hadn't shared details. Taking the seat across from the rocking chair Delia had settled into, Callie asked, "What was the problem?"

"Karl wanted Mel's shop."

"What?"

"Well, not the music boxes. Just the shop. The premises."

"Why?"

"He wants to expand—to add collectible model trains to his business. Karl has a nephew who's in need of a job and would have run it for him. But Karl wanted the train shop close by—to be an extension of the model car shop, but also so he could keep a close eye on things. Mel's place fit all his requirements."

"But Aunt Mel didn't want to sell."

"Right. And with *Car-lectibles* being on the corner, hers is his only neighboring building."

"Well, that's unfortunate for him, but he can't expect someone to sell just because he wants them to," Callie said. Jagger padded over and looked ready to jump into her lap. She lifted her mug safely out of his way.

"Most people would agree with you. Karl, however ... " Delia shrugged and downed a swallow of coffee.

"I don't think I've met him. Was he at the funeral?"

Delia made a face. "Nope. That's how badly he holds a grudge. You should be prepared for your first encounter, which is bound to happen soon and is sure to be unpleasant. But however poorly he behaves toward you, Callie, don't take it personally. On the other hand, if you should change your mind about staying, you'll have a ready buyer."

Though the tone of Delia's last comment was neutral, Callie caught the hint of apprehension. "I won't change my mind," she assured her new neighbor. "Once I made my decision, I knew it was the right one." She gave Delia the short version of having decided to end her long-term relationship and received a warmly sympathetic response with no questions, which she appreciated. When she got more used to the idea, Callie was sure she'd feel like talking about it more, but not just yet. "So you see, I've burned my bridges. Aunt Mel made it possible for me to start my life over. I'm going to try my darnedest to do it right this time."

The mysteriously playing music box nudged into her thoughts, but she didn't mention it. Why jeopardize a budding friendship by sounding wacko from the start? There surely was a good explanation for what set the music off. A slip in the mechanism? A minor earthquake—which nobody in the entire area happened to register? She grimaced inwardly. Whatever.

"Well," Delia said, getting up, "I should head over to my shop. I'm expecting a shipment of salt and pepper shakers with a Christmas theme and need to make room for them."

"Christmas?" Callie asked as she followed Delia to the door, thinking summer had just begun.

"Oh, yes! They'll be big sellers. We get a lot of beach traffic, you know, since we're just a quick jog off Route 50. Vacationers love to shop, and they love to shop ahead for Christmas. You'll have to keep that in mind with your own place."

"My first bit of helpful advice," Callie said. "Thanks!"

Delia grinned, then grew serious. She took hold of both of Callie's hands. "I'm truly delighted you're going to stay and continue Mel's business. I didn't know what was going to happen to it and confess I was a bit worried. Now it'll feel like Mel's here in spirit, although I'm sure you'll put your own stamp on the shop, once you get going."

"Thank you, Delia. That means a lot to me." Callie watched as Delia headed down the brick walkway to a well-worn footpath that ran between the two properties. It cut through an opening in the thick bushes that hid Delia's cottage from her own except for the roof and chimney. Knowing she had such a welcoming neighbor and potential good friend was a comforting start to her new life.

As she stood at her doorway, Callie heard a door slam and caught movement to her left. A man had come out of the back door of *Car-lectibles* and stopped at the opening of a tall wooden fence to stare in her direction. He was fifty-ish and burly, and Callie realized this glowering man was most likely the person Delia had just told her about. Thinking she might as well introduce herself, she took a deep breath and stepped forward.

"Hello! I'm Callie Reed. Are you Mr. Eggers?"

The man, dark-haired and sporting a full beard, stared a moment longer, then nodded. "I am. Reed? You're related to her?" His head jerked toward *House of Melody*.

"Melodie was my aunt," Callie said, hearing her voice catch and wincing. Though she'd just had a comfortable chat about Aunt Mel with Delia, something about Karl Eggers brought back her feelings of loss.

Eggers glanced toward the cottage. "Clearing out her things?"

"Actually, I'm settling in. My aunt, it turns out, left everything to me."

"Everything? What about the shop? Will you be selling?"

Callie shook her head. "I plan to keep *House of Melody* running."

"Then we have nothing more to say to each other," Eggers growled. He slammed back into *Car-lectibles*, leaving Callie standing, open-mouthed. Despite Delia's warning, his reaction stunned her. She'd run into her share of rudeness, but nothing as blatant. But Delia had also advised against taking it personally, so Callie turned back to her cottage, repeating that mantra to herself several times. Jagger met her at the door and she scooped him up to stroke his soft fur and concentrate on good thoughts. When she felt calmer, she released the cat and went about picking up the coffee mugs and tidying up in the kitchen. Time to move forward.

She began by checking her supplies. They were limited to anything in a can, bottle, or box, so Callie made a list of fresh items to run out for. A meow at her feet reminded her to add cat food to the list—*was Jagger able to read minds?* Then she grabbed her purse and car keys and headed out the door.

The supermarket was a few blocks outside of Keepsake Cove, in the "other" part of Mapleton. As she drove, Callie couldn't keep her thoughts off her encounter with Karl Eggers. His ongoing anger over not getting what he wanted was too disturbing. She hadn't said anything to Delia about questioning the "accidental" ruling of Aunt Mel's death—George Blake certainly hadn't encouraged any thoughts in that direction. But Callie was unable to put them aside, and having met the person who continued to hold such bitterness against her aunt magnified them.

Could Eggers have had something to do with Aunt Mel's death? Had he thought her death would make the music box shop available to him? Callie grimaced. That seemed like a weak motive for murder.

Murder! It was the first time she had actually formed the word, after days of skirting around it. She hated even thinking it. But if it wasn't accidental, murder was exactly what Aunt Mel's death had been.

The supermarket loomed ahead, and Callie turned her focus toward navigating the parking lot without mowing down pedestrians. After that, she concentrated on finding her way around the store. She gathered the food items she wanted—milk, bread, fruit, a few frozen entrees—and then remembered that all she'd brought with her from Morgantown were enough toiletries to freshen up with before the funeral, so she picked up a few more. She would need to shop for clothes, too, to tide her over until she could retrieve her own things.

And she needed to call her former bosses, of course. Callie could recommend a replacement, but should probably check with the person first about whether she wanted the job.

Her head began to spin with all these *must do* thoughts. "One thing at a time," she cautioned herself, not realizing she'd said it aloud until a woman with her back to her turned around.

"Huh?"

"Oh! Sorry. I was talking to myself."

The young woman, who had long chestnut hair and a sixties-style beaded headband, nodded. "I do that a lot. Especially when I have a lot on my mind, like you must have. I mean, having just lost your aunt."

Callie looked more closely at her. The woman looked vaguely familiar, though Callie was sure she hadn't been wearing a tie-dyed shirt and flower-embroidered bell bottoms when they'd met. "You were at the funeral?"

"Yup. Tabitha Prosser. Don't feel bad about not remembering. There were a lot of us there." Tabitha paused, then asked, "Will you be re-opening the shop soon?"

Callie blinked. "How did—?"

Tabitha shrugged. "Deductive reasoning. I knew you were Melodie's only relative—I've worked with her, off and on—so I figured you'd inherit the shop. And here you are, still in town and stocking up on supplies." She grinned. "Plus, I'm psychic."

Callie grinned back, but she wasn't totally sure her new acquaintance was joking. "I remember your name now. Aunt Mel mentioned you, but you weren't at the shop during my visit."

"I worked for Mel part time. I make and sell beaded jewelry the rest of the time, but the sales for that have been somewhat unpredictable."

Callie bit back the comment that perhaps a psychic should have foreseen that. Instead, she studied the younger woman thoughtfully.

"I could really use someone who knows *House of Melody* better than I do. Would you be interested in coming back?"

Tabitha grinned. "I knew there was a good explanation for my sudden craving for rice-milk chocolate. I just hadn't put my finger on it. It must have been so we could run into each other. I'd love to be back at the shop. How soon? Tomorrow?"

Callie paused, thinking, why not? "Yes, tomorrow would be perfect."

"Great! See you then." Tabitha took off, carrying her rice-milk chocolate to the checkout counter as Callie mused once again about how quickly things seemed to be falling into place. It was almost as if—no, she wasn't going to go in that direction. One "psychic" in the music box shop would be more than enough.

❦

When she got back to the cottage, Callie put away her groceries, then headed upstairs to the guest room where Aunt Mel's second laptop sat on the small corner desk. It occurred to Callie that she'd hired someone that she knew very little about, and she hoped she might find something in Aunt Mel's records that would tell her more.

She booted up the laptop and was immediately asked for a password. Uh-oh. Callie thought for a moment, then remembered her aunt had grabbed a folder when she'd wanted to show Callie an unusual music box she'd recently ordered from an online wholesaler. Melodie had needed a password to enter the site, and she'd checked a printed sheet inside a folder.

A wire desktop organizer filled with papers and folders sat beyond the laptop. Callie fingered through the collection, looking for the dark blue one she remembered Aunt Mel holding. Of the three dark blues, only one was unlabeled. Inside was a printed sheet of passwords. Hooray!

Callie typed in the laptop's password and watched with satisfaction as the screen colors changed and *Welcome* appeared. The menu page offered many familiar icons, and Callie clicked on Quicken. A few more clicks pulled up employee information, and Tabitha Prosser's name was there. Two more names were also listed, but the dates of their employment were much earlier. Tabitha had begun working for Aunt Melodie eighteen months ago, part time, and her most recent paycheck had been only three weeks ago. So she seemed to have been an employee in good standing, which reassured Callie. She also saw Tabitha's salary, which answered her other question.

She closed the program and opened up Word, interested to see what files her aunt had stored. Hopefully plenty of in-depth information on music boxes, which she could certainly use. She browsed through the titles of saved documents. Many did deal with music boxes, one way or another, and Callie resolved to read through them later on. But at the moment she felt herself drawn to another section of her aunt's computer. She left Word and opened up her aunt's emails.

Fighting off guilty feelings of snooping—she was, after all, the heir to her aunt's estate, and the more she knew about it the better—Callie clicked on several received emails. Many of them had to do with shop business, so she read through them. One recent message came from a customer who'd asked Aunt Mel to find him "the music box we discussed." Callie checked the *sent* box and, finding no response to that email, made a note to contact the man for more information

She then noticed that a message was stored in *drafts.* She opened it, expecting to find an email to the customer. She was surprised to find instead the draft of an email addressed to her.

Dear Callie, it began. *I've debated about writing to you about this, not wanting to unnecessarily worry you. But something has come up lately that I think you should know about, in case anything happens.*

The message stopped there and had no signature. Aunt Mel had typed it a few days before Callie's visit. What had she intended to share? Why didn't she finish? Had she perhaps decided to talk to Callie instead, in person, during her time there? Callie stared at the screen until she began to hear a familiar sound. She turned slowly toward the doorway.

Grandpa Reed's music box, still downstairs and inside the roll-top desk, had started to play.

Four

Callie left her cozy cottage the next morning with a stomach full of butterflies, carrying a mug of chamomile tea she'd fixed for its soothing properties. After setting Aunt Mel's mysterious draft email aside to mull over later, she'd spent a portion of the previous day on the phone with her now-ex employers—the lawyers in Morgantown—who were wonderfully understanding about her sudden resignation after hearing about her unexpected inheritance. Surprisingly, most of the office was also pleased to learn of her split from Hank. Jubilant, in fact. Though she was glad for the reassurance, Callie wouldn't have minded hearing a word or two from them a bit earlier, when she could have used a nudge in the right direction. But she accepted everyone's good wishes and promised faithfully to keep in touch.

The rest of that day, and much of the night, she'd spent studying Aunt Mel's shop records and music boxes in general. Today she would open *House of Melody* for business for the first time, and she really didn't want to mess up.

What could go wrong? Callie asked herself in an effort to calm the butterflies as she unlocked the rear door of the shop. The music boxes were tagged with prices; she knew how to ring up sales; and, if questions from customers came up, there was a handy reference book sitting behind the front counter to help her out. Plus, Tabitha would be showing up to resume her part-time job. That last fact gave Callie the most confidence. If she found herself floundering, at least she knew reinforcements were arriving.

Setting down her mug, she raised the shade on the front door, turned the lock, and flipped on the lights. Done! She was now officially open for business. All she needed was a customer.

Callie looked up and down the sunny street and saw little activity—not surprising, she supposed, for nine a.m. Except that the Keepsake Café across the street seemed to be bustling. She saw two women exit the Café and pause to glance her way. Callie felt her heart beat a little faster. Her first customers? She watched through her window as they consulted a list. Then the one in green pointed down the street, and the two took off in that direction. Callie's pulse slowed—whether in disappointment or with relief, she wasn't quite sure.

She turned from the window and picked up her mug to take a sip, telling herself to be patient. She wasn't, after all, offering fast food or quick-sale souvenir T-shirts. She'd be dealing mostly with specialty collectors, who would likely arrive in dribs and drabs. She'd better know what she had to offer, especially if she wanted them to come back. Callie carried her mug with her as she wound among the tables and shelves, studying, memorizing, and occasionally playing the tunes of the quainter music boxes. She smiled when she wound up a Winnie-the-Pooh globe and heard a tinkley "Happy Birthday" song, and when she lifted the top of an Elvis box to hear "Love Me Tender," minus the King's rich baritone, of course. The variety seemed endless, and she wandered about enjoying each and every music box. Then a very different tune startled her. The jingle of her shop door opening.

"Good morning!" a middle-aged woman with a cap of brown curls and an eager face called as she entered. "I saw your shade up and came right over. I've been coming here for years and was so sorry to hear that the previous owner passed away. She was really a lovely woman with a wonderful shop. I hated the thought that it might be gone. Are you the new owner?" she asked, glancing around and obviously expecting a more mature person, perhaps, to step forward.

"I am," Callie answered, and watched the woman's eyebrows jiggle in surprise. Callie introduced herself and explained her relationship to Melodie Reed. "I'll be continuing my aunt's business with her same love of music boxes, and I'm working hard to reach her level of expertise."

"Oh, how exciting! And aren't you lucky!" The woman caught herself. "I mean, of course, I'm so sorry about your loss. But to be handed a shop in Keepsake Cove! They're highly prized, you know. The Cove has an amazing reputation among collectors, and shop space is limited."

Thinking of Karl Eggers and how he coveted *House of Melody*'s premises, Callie nodded.

"Now"—the woman rubbed her hands together and looked around keenly—"what new items do you have that I would like?"

"Um…" Callie said as panic began to rise in her throat. "I, that is—" As the stammers threatened to paralyze her, the shop door flew open and a 1940s version of Joan Crawford swept in: shoulder pads, open-toed shoes, pompadour and all.

"Hi!" the Ms. Crawford look-alike called out cheerily, then focused on Callie's customer. "Mrs. MacDonald! How're you doing?"

Callie's customer studied her greeter a moment, then grinned. "Hello, Tabitha. I'm very well. Good to see you."

Tabitha? Callie stared as Joan-slash-Tabitha stepped casually behind the counter and slid her clutch bag underneath. She slowly recognized the facial features of the young woman she'd spoken to briefly at the grocery store, though it was a struggle to locate them under the heavily-penciled eyebrows, pancake makeup, and thick, dark lipstick. What had happened to yesterday's hippie in headband and bell-bottoms?

"Looking for a new music box?" Tabitha asked Mrs. MacDonald, then launched into a short list of ones the woman might be interested in. Callie stepped aside and watched in awe as her employee led her customer around the shop, picking up various items and discussing them knowledgeably. In the end, Mrs. MacDonald chose a lovely walnut box with brass hardware and a hand-painted lid.

"I love its tune," Mrs. MacDonald said as Tabitha packed up the box.

"'As Time Goes By' from *Casablanca*," Tabitha said, nodding. Her eyes turned upward thoughtfully; possibly she was picturing a future Ingrid Bergman look.

Mrs. MacDonald took off, looking happy, and Callie turned to Tabitha. "That was impressive. You seemed to know exactly what she wanted."

"Oh, Mrs. Mac comes by a lot. You get to know what people like. Mel kept a file on her phone. I'd see her refer to it when someone came in who hadn't been here in a while."

"I'll have to start doing that." As well as check Aunt Mel's phone, Callie noted to herself.

Tabitha had gone back to the area where she and her customer had last been when Delia bustled in with a smile on her face. "I saw Mrs. MacDonald leave with a package. Your first sale?" she asked Callie.

"Actually, Tabitha's," Callie said.

"Oh, Tabitha's back!" Delia scanned the shop to find the young woman, who was just standing up after having straightened boxes on a lower shelf.

Tabitha waved. "Hi, Delia!"

Delia gazed at the girl thoughtfully. "Joan Crawford?"

"Like it? I found the dress at *Second Thoughts*. It spoke to me."

"Love it."

As Tabitha disappeared into the back office, Callie leaned toward Delia. "So she does this a lot? I mean, the costumey thing?"

"Tabitha is very creative in her dress. Mel's customers got used to it. Some actually came by just to see who Tabitha would be channeling that day. She's quite a good salesperson."

"Yes, I noticed. I just didn't know what to make of—" Callie stopped as Tabitha returned with a polishing cloth in her hand.

"Fingerprints on the polished mahogany," she explained, holding up the cloth.

"I'd better get back," Delia said. "Great to see you again, Tabitha. You're in good hands, Callie, with Tabitha around. She'll be able to answer a lot of questions that come up."

Tabitha shrugged modestly but didn't argue, and Callie felt the worries that she'd arrived with that morning fade. Delia held the door for an entering customer as she left, and this time Callie took charge, welcoming, asking a few questions, and eventually walking the gray-haired woman toward a selection of music boxes that might interest her. She ended up making a sale, and even though it was only an inexpensive child's jewelry box—with figures that twirled to Disney's *Frozen*—her customer seemed delighted to have found the perfect gift for a young granddaughter. Callie felt pleased with herself as she rang up the sale, and a glance at Tabitha got her a thumbs-up.

More people wandered in after that, most browsing and some buying, and many of them carrying bags from other Keepsake Cove shops, which told Callie how useful it was to group collectible shops together. Now and then a customer asked for information on where to find other shops—which Tabitha quickly gave them—and Callie presumed *House of Melody* would be pointed out by other shopkeepers in turn. Except, most likely, by Karl Eggers. When things were quiet, she asked Tabitha about him.

"Karl?" Tabitha said, leaning back to straighten the seam on one stocking before pulling over a tall stool. She hooked one chunky-heeled shoe onto a rung as she sat. "Karl's been a pain, like, forever. It's a wonder he keeps any customers. Maybe model car collectors are just less sensitive than music box or salt and pepper shaker people?"

"Could be. Delia said he wanted Mel's shop for a nephew to run a model train shop. So Karl has at least one sibling. Does he have a wife?"

Tabitha snorted. "No way. At least not now. I'm guessing not ever."

Callie described her encounter with Karl the previous morning. "Delia warned me, but I thought being neighbors we could at least have a nodding relationship. I love Aunt Mel's cottage, and having Delia on one side of me is such a comfort. I'm not feeling as thrilled about Karl as my other neighbor."

"Well, there is that privacy fence between you."

"Yes. I guess he put that up?"

"Uh-uh. Mel did."

"Really!"

"Yup. She got tired of checking out her window to see if Karl was in his yard before going out to do her gardening. His constant dirty looks took all the pleasure out of it."

"Makes sense. There's no fence on Delia's side. Though the tall bushes do make a soft screen." Callie thought of the footpath that ran through them. That well-worn path said a lot, just as the solid wood fence on the other side did. "The fence between Karl and Mel's—that is, *my*—cottage does have a gap in it, close to the shops. That's where I saw Karl yesterday morning."

Tabitha nodded. "Mel did that on purpose. She could have run the fence all the way up. But she decided to leave that spot open. She thought it would signal that he was still welcome whenever he chose to change his attitude."

"That was generous of her." But might Aunt Mel's readiness to be open to her churlish neighbor ultimately have been a bad idea?

"Tabitha," Callie began hesitantly, "were you satisfied with the explanation of how my aunt died?"

"You mean that it was an accident?" Tabitha's heavily penciled brows pulled together. "No," she said. "I wasn't. I don't know what Mel was doing in the shop so late at night, but I guess she could have had a good reason. But to fall like that? So hard? I mean, why should she fall in the first place? We never left things around on the floor to slip on, and she wasn't, like, ninety and, you know, getting around with a walker."

"That's what bothered me. But George Blake, Aunt Mel's lawyer, didn't seem to have a problem with it, so I thought maybe I was way off base."

"Oh, George." Tabitha flapped a hand dismissively. "I guess he's a good lawyer. Mel used him, after all. But I've never seen him really look at anyone, you know? His mind is on cases, not people. But I'll tell you ... " She paused significantly, and Callie leaned forward. "The day before Mel died, I felt danger."

"You did? Why?"

"I saw it in my Tarot cards."

"Oh."

A customer pushed open the shop door at that moment, saving Callie from further comment. Which, she thought, was for the best.

❧

When things had quieted down again, Callie, whose stomach had been rumbling for a while, asked Tabitha if the Keepsake Café had carry-out.

"Sure, but why not take a real break and eat there?"

"I thought I could pick up something for both of us. I'm starved. How about you?"

"Uh-uh. Had a late breakfast, plus I always bring along something to nibble while I'm here, which is only four hours, during Mel's busy time. You didn't want me for the whole afternoon, did you? 'Cause I really can't. I need time to work on my jewelry."

"No, we can stick with that. So, if I go off for lunch you don't mind watching the shop a little longer?" As she said it, Callie realized how silly that sounded. *She* was the one likely to be nervous on her own, not Tabitha. But Tabitha, thankfully, didn't point that out.

After grabbing her purse, Callie took off across the street, knowing she could have gone back to her cottage and fixed a good lunch from her recently stocked groceries. But she wanted to say hello again to Brian Greer, who she'd been able to exchange only a few words with after Aunt Mel's funeral and hadn't seen since. He might not even know she was taking over *House of Melody*.

She'd purposely held off on eating until the lunch rush was over, and she was glad to spot a few empty tables at the Keepsake Café, as well as vacant stools at the counter. She headed over to the stools and slid onto one in the middle, setting her purse at her feet. She looked around for Brian but saw only a scattering of customers.

The café was modest—chrome and laminate-topped tables with center groupings of paper napkin dispensers and condiments. A small pellet stove hugged the corner nearest the front door, unused for now, but Callie was sure it added a cozy touch in the winter. The décor was simple and, she thought, reflected a man's practicality more than a woman's taste. But everything looked super clean, a quality topped in importance only by the food, which she already knew from Aunt Mel's funeral reception would be good.

A door at the back marked *Kitchen* opened and Brian stepped out. He spotted Callie at the counter and, much to her surprise, lit up. "Hi there! I heard you'll be staying. That's great!"

A few heads turned, and Brian explained to the place at large, "This is Mel's niece. She's going to keep Mel's shop going." Several oohs and ahhs, along with welcoming words, greeted Callie, and she responded cheerfully, though she was just as glad when it settled down.

"Sorry about that," Brian said, grinning. "I get a little carried away sometimes."

"That's okay. It's nice to feel welcome. I admit I wasn't sure how Aunt Mel's friends might feel about me trying to replace her."

"Nobody will think that, don't worry." His hand started to reach out for hers, perhaps for a friendly pat, but he seemed to think better of it and slid a laminated menu toward her instead. "I guess you came in for something to eat. We're out of pastrami, but we're good for everything else."

Callie wondered about the "we," having seen only one person—Brian—at work so far, but she studied the list of choices and asked for ham and Swiss on rye with a glass of iced tea.

"Coming right up," he said and disappeared into the kitchen.
"You'll like it."

Callie turned to her left to see an elderly woman with a face full of wrinkles that deepened with her smile. "One of my favorites," the woman continued. "Brian makes everything fresh and he doesn't skimp. Puts his heart into getting everything right."

"Has he been here long?" Since Brian was fairly young, Callie wondered if she would hear that he also had stepped into the business after a death in the family.

"A year or two, I guess. Maybe more. Gave up some kind of professional job, I heard, in DC. Something in government, I think. He probably chucked a big salary for the simple life. Back to the basics, that kind of thing. We're lucky he did."

Brian reappeared in a few minutes and set a plate in front of Callie. It held a sandwich piled thickly with thinly sliced ham and cheese, and garnished with a crisp-looking dill pickle, a handful of chips, and a scoop of creamy coleslaw. When Callie took her first bite of the sandwich, her eyes widened.

"It's great," she said after chewing and swallowing and dabbing a few drops of sauce from her lips.

"Didn't I tell you?" the woman to her left asked, looking indignant.

Brian laughed. "Hazel's my unofficial PR person. Also my marketing consultant."

Hazel cackled, but Callie said, "She didn't exaggerate." She took a sip of her tea, which was clearly freshly made, before returning to her sandwich.

The three of them chatted as Callie ate—Brian refilling Hazel's coffee cup—and were joined in the conversation by two more customers, an older couple who sat at one of the tables. Callie guessed that the locals timed their visits to the café to avoid the shopping crowd, just as she had. When Hazel bid them a good day and left,

Brian cleared her dishes and then lingered nearby, chatting about various things Callie might like to see and do in the area.

"Do you like biking?" he asked. "The Eastern Shore is so flat that a bike is a great way to get around and appreciate the scenery."

"In West Virginia, everything was hills," Callie said. "So, no bike riding there. I probably haven't been on a bike since high school."

"You could rent. I'd be glad to take you. Some evening when both our places are closed?"

Callie hesitated before shaking her head. "Thanks. Maybe sometime later. Right now, though, I've got an awful lot on my plate."

Brian nodded and casually changed the subject. They chatted a little more until new customers walked in, and Callie decided it was time to go. She finished up and promised to be back soon.

As she stood waiting to cross the street back to *House of Melody*, Callie thought about Brian's almost-date suggestion and hoped he was okay with her sidestep. He struck her as a terrific guy, but she wasn't the least bit ready to think about seeing anyone. Although he might have meant the bike excursion as a strictly friends kind of thing. Which was fine. And, really, kind of nice. She was sure she was going to like his being right across the street from her.

The traffic cleared and Callie stepped off the curb, thinking pleasant thoughts, when she happened to look over to the right. Karl Eggers was at his store window, his features thrown into shadow by an overhead light. He stared pointedly at her for a moment, then slowly turned away. Callie felt a chill slide over her and rubbed at her arms, but she shook her head and continued on to her shop. Too bad, she thought, that Aunt Mel hadn't continued her privacy fence all the way to the street.

Five

When Tabitha left at the end of her shift, Callie felt ready to take on the rest of the day solo. The stomach butterflies had long settled down, and she'd started to enjoy her first dip into retail. It helped immensely that the music boxes that filled her shop were so endlessly intriguing. Her pleasure in them probably equaled, if not topped, those of her customers as together they browsed through the shop, the discoveries often as much a surprise to Callie as to her customer. In the process, she was getting more and more familiar with the stock on her shelves.

Between a modest but still-satisfying number of sales, Callie looked over Aunt Mel's order records to see how her inventory would be replaced in the short term. She remembered Delia's suggestion to have Christmas-themed items on hand well before the season and was happy to discover that several Christmas-themed music boxes of varying prices were already heading her way. She also studied the wholesale catalogues but held off on placing any orders. She needed a better feel for what her regular customers were looking for, as well as the casual first-timers who tended to buy more impulsively.

By six o'clock, Callie was more than ready to close up shop, feeling an exhaustion that came less from the strain of being on her feet for hours than from the effort of storing a million details in her head. She looked forward to sitting back and enjoying some down time.

Jagger was waiting eagerly at the door, and Callie felt a twinge of guilt for having forgotten about him. Between lunch at Brian Greer's Keepsake Café and her total absorption in the music box shop, she hadn't been back to the cottage all day.

"Did Aunt Mel pay more attention to you?" she asked as she lifted the gray cat up and was rewarded with purrs and furry cheek rubs. She carried him into the kitchen, where she set him down next to his bowl, refilled it, and freshened his water. As Jagger went to work on his dinner, Callie considered her own. A long stare at the inside of her refrigerator resulted in a tired sigh, and she ended up pulling out the makings for a sandwich and opening a can of soup.

"It's a balanced meal, right, Jagger?" she asked the cat. "Hot and cold. The most I'm up to doing tonight." Jagger merely flicked an ear in response as he continued eating.

Quick and easy as it was, Callie found her meal more than satisfying as she dined at the glass-topped table set against the kitchen window. The chair was comfy, and the window provided a lovely and soothing view of greenery at the back of the cottage, with chipmunks scampering and birds flitting between branches. *Thank you, Aunt Mel*, she said silently for perhaps the hundredth time, still awed over the amazing gift she'd been handed. *But,* she added, *I still wish you were here.*

As sadness threatened to descend, Callie briskly gathered up her dirty dishes and loaded them into the dishwasher. She headed to her front door, flicking a glance toward the fence that separated her yard from Karl Eggers's before stepping outside. She wasn't sure what she would have done if she'd seen her grouchy neighbor scowling over the tall divide, but she felt better just knowing she had her privacy.

Callie strolled about her new yard for several minutes, enjoying the fresh air and Aunt Mel's flower garden even while knowing the upkeep would now be up to her. After a few minutes of pleasant down time, she thought of Tabitha's comment that Aunt Mel had kept notes on customers' preferences on her cell phone. She decided to check that out and went back inside.

She found the phone where she remembered having last seen it— in the drawer of the end table closest to the front door. Noticing that it was password locked, she trotted upstairs to consult the folder holding Aunt Mel's list. The password, she found, was the four numbers in *House of Melody*'s street address, and Callie typed them in. She gained entrance and soon tracked down the customer preference list in the Notes app.

She studied the list of names and the comments beside each. One customer wanted only Italian-made boxes, another searched for '50s music, while another preferred novelty boxes. Callie was intrigued to see that one person apparently was enthralled with fish-themed music boxes. Happily, the names were listed alphabetically, plus Aunt Mel had done cross-referencing, giving the type of music box followed by names of those who would be interested.

It was a good lesson in business practice, which Callie was glad to learn. She wondered if all shopkeepers did the same, or something similar, and thought that would be a good question to pose as she spoke with other Keepsake Cove shop owners. It might bring up other useful tips as well. She vowed to drop in on them all as soon as she could.

Callie sent the list to her own phone, then carried Aunt Mel's back to the living room. As she pulled the end table's drawer open again, she noticed something tucked behind a group of cork coasters at the back. It looked like another phone. Surprised, Callie reached for it. It *was* another cell phone, but a prepaid, disposable type. She turned it over, wondering why her aunt would have it. Was it an old one, bought before her smart phone? Callie pressed the power button and it came to life, indicating it was nearly half charged. She checked *Messages* on the phone but there were, oddly, none at all. *Contacts* showed no names and numbers. The charged battery implied recent use, but for what? Did it actually belong to Aunt Mel?

Curious, Callie returned the phone to the drawer, then went back upstairs to Aunt Mel's laptop. She scrolled through her aunt's inbox until she found what she was looking for: an email from Tracfone advising Melodie Reed that her pre-paid minutes were running low and she should buy more soon. It had been sent two months ago. The disposable phone, then, was hers. The question that remained was why? Why keep a second phone that apparently was being used but whose history appeared to be wiped clean? Callie leaned back in her chair and huffed, not having a clue.

❧

The next morning, Callie set aside the phone puzzle to focus on the new day. After a good breakfast, she crossed over to *House of Melody* and raised the front door shade, feeling much more confident than she had twenty-four hours ago, and in charge—kind of. She knew she still had a ways to go, but the path ahead was definitely less foggy. She flipped her sign to *Open* without a trace of nerves, then settled behind the counter, confident that customers would arrive in good time, and that when they did she would be ready for them.

Her customers wandered into the shop in ones and twos, that morning's bunch mainly browsers and seemingly in search of conversation as much as collectibles. Callie was happy to provide that as well, since it often meant learning more about the specialness of her new surroundings. The Eastern Shore—always capitalized, as she'd picked up early—was unusual because of its separation from the rest of Maryland by the Chesapeake Bay. With access to the area so limited from Colonial days until modern times, many outlying areas developed their own cultures and even accents over the years because of their isolation.

That changed dramatically with the construction of the Chesapeake Bay bridge, a graceful, four-mile-long span that Callie had driven over in awe on her first visit. The bridge had finally connected the Eastern Shore to the rest of Maryland in the 1950s and brought an influx of new residents to the long-established fishing and farming towns, as well as a flood of vacationers to the Atlantic beaches. Not surprisingly, this was viewed as a mixed bag by locals, and Callie heard differing opinions on the subject, though the input from her collectible customers tended toward the positive. Keepsake Cove, after all, wouldn't have sprung up if shoppers hadn't been able to travel there easily from Baltimore, Washington, and points north and west. The older towns remained picturesque, Callie was told, and she vowed to visit them soon.

She took a break for lunch and a little "Jagger time" at the cottage, leaving Tabitha in charge. Her assistant had arrived that day looking mod, in a red, long-sleeved, mini-skirted dress and black boots. Less surprised this time, Callie had simply accepted the look without comment. She'd just returned from her break when a man dressed in tan khakis and a green polo walked into the shop. He stopped to study Tabitha.

"Twiggy?" the man asked.

"Mr. Harman!" Tabitha tsked. "Don't you recognize Lieutenant Uhura? From *Star Trek*?"

"Uhura!" He slapped his forehead. "I should have known."

"I admit I don't match her look perfectly. After the hair, I didn't have time to do a lot of makeup."

"The impression is definitely there," he assured her.

Tabitha smiled and turned to Callie, who'd been privately thinking *Uhura*? "Callie, this is Jonathan Harman, one of Mel's long-time customers."

"How do you do, Mr. Harman?" Callie asked, stepping forward and holding out her hand. "I'm Callie Reed, Mel's niece."

"Callie inherited *House of Melody*," Tabitha informed him.

"Did you?" Harman said, shaking Callie's hand. "Let me extend my sincere condolences. I was unable to attend the funeral. But I was truly shocked and sorry to learn of Melodie's untimely passing."

"Thank you," Callie said. She was gradually getting used to accepting condolences, though they still brought a lump to her throat. Harman's manner, while obviously sincere, was matter-of-fact enough to allow her to keep her cool, and she appreciated that. She released his hand and stepped back, assessing the tall man. By the moderate crow's feet and the touch of gray in his hair, she judged him to be in his mid-forties, but a youngish, in-shape forties. "So you collect music boxes?"

"Passionately," he said, grinning. "Well, maybe not to that extent. But I've always had a thing for them. My grandparents liked them, and I enjoyed visiting their house once a year, where there was always a new music box to look forward to. I suppose they passed on their interest."

"It seems to run in my family, too," Callie said. "Did you inherit their collection?"

"No," Harman said, shaking his head. "They fell on tough times while I was still in school—health problems—and sold most of them off before any of us were aware of it."

"That's sad."

"It was. But," he said, brightening, "I've been making up for it ever since."

"You certainly have," Tabitha said, tucking in a loose strand of the long hair that she'd somehow managed to twist and pin into a reasonable facsimile of the space ship character's hairstyle. "Mr. Harman must have bought at least a dozen music boxes from Mel, that I'm aware of anyway."

Harman shrugged. "What can I say? It becomes an addiction. Well," he said briskly, glancing around, "I wish I had time to shop today, but I was passing by and saw you were open. Just thought I'd stop in and say hello. But I'll be back." He smiled. "You can count on it."

"We'll look forward to that," Callie said, walking him to the door.

Harman suddenly stopped. "Where's *the* music box? He was staring at the high shelf behind the counter.

Callie, puzzled, looked to Tabitha.

"Oh!" Tabitha said. "You mean the skater?"

"Yes. Mel always kept it up there."

"Why did she do that?" Callie asked, realizing which one they meant. "It was my grandfather's music box. It wasn't for sale."

"Oh, I know," Harman said. "Mel told me all about that. She just liked having it on display, didn't she, Tabitha?"

Tabitha nodded vigorously enough to have to grab at her hair. "She loved having that box around. She'd bring it down to show if someone asked about it. And she'd wind it up to play for people."

"You didn't sell it, did you?" Harman asked.

"Oh, no. It's just as special to me as it was to my aunt. It's at the cottage."

"Why not bring it back here?" Tabitha asked. "It was a good conversation piece. I'm surprised no one else has asked about it."

"Maybe I will," Callie said, thinking that though the mysterious music playing had stopped, she'd found herself listening for it a little too much. Bringing it out of the cottage and into the shop, where she'd be much busier, could put an end to that.

"Well, I'm off," Harman said. "Best of luck on your new venture, Miss Reed."

"Not Miss Reed, please. Callie."

"Callie, then. And I'm Jonathan." Harman smiled, lifted a hand to Tabitha, and left.

"It's great to see Mel's customers returning," Tabitha said after the door had closed. "You two seemed to hit it off," she teased. "First name basis right away."

Callie shook her head. "It's just because of our mutual interest. He does seem very nice, though. Does he live around here?"

"Somewhere outside of town, I think. Not too far. He works at home, but I'm a little vague on at what, exactly. Something financial?" Tabitha grinned helplessly.

"Not that important," Callie said. Tabitha's cell phone dinged, which reminded Callie of something that was of more interest to her. After Tabitha dealt with her text message, Callie asked, "Tabitha, do you have any idea why my aunt would keep a second, disposable cell phone around?"

"Disposable? An old one she never tossed?" When Callie explained about it being charged, Tabitha shrugged. "Maybe as a back-up? In case she lost her iPhone?"

"Except there's nothing on it—no contacts, no messages, nothing."

"Well, that's weird. Unless maybe she just got it and hadn't gotten around to doing anything with it?"

That wasn't the case, Callie knew, as the Tracfone email sent two months ago made clear. She decided not to get into that and only asked, "So you never saw her using it?"

"Uh-uh. But who checks out anyone else's cell phone?"

Nieces, Callie thought, who are poking through things that are probably none of their business. She let the matter drop.

Six

That evening, as Callie was finishing her dinner, she realized she was starting to feel at home in her new surroundings. It was a good feeling, and she savored it. Then she got a call from Hank. She groaned when she saw his number on the display and briefly debated answering. After two more rings, she picked up.

"Hey, babe." Hank's rich baritone, probably the only thing about him that she still appreciated, rolled out.

"Hi, Hank."

A long pause followed, and Callie wondered what Hank was waiting for. A rush of gratitude over his call? A confession of having finally come to her senses? She let the silence run on until he finally broke it.

"Been missing you."

"How've you been, Hank?" she asked, politely rather than solicitously. He seemed not to have noticed, as she heard a deep sigh.

"It's been rough."

"I'm sorry to hear that. Was there a reason you called, Hank?"

"Just … wanted to hear your voice. You okay?"

"I'm fine. By the way, I've arranged for a company to pack up my things and transport them here."

"You're letting strangers pack up your stuff?"

"Saves me a trip back. I'm pretty tied up here, what with all the things I'm trying to learn about the shop."

"So you're really keeping it? The shop?"

"Yes, Hank. As I told you."

"Yeah, but … I figured you'd change your mind. I mean, a music box shop? What're you going to get out of running something like that?"

Callie didn't like the put-down in his tone. She could have, in turn, pointed out the increasingly seedy places he'd been performing in lately, along with his steadily decreasing income, but she rose above it.

"I like the shop," she said simply and changed the subject. "I'm not having any of my furniture sent on. You can have whatever you want before Goodwill picks it up." It wasn't much of an endowment, she knew, since most of the things she'd acquired over the years were a mishmash of secondhand and cheap.

"So you're really staying there?"

"I am." There was another long silence. Callie, losing patience, broke that one. "Hank, it'll be fine. This will be a good move for both of us."

"I don't see how it's any good for me. I'm hurtin', baby!"

He was beginning to sound far too much like one of his Country-Western lyrics. To forestall any breakout into song, Callie asked, "Got any new gigs lined up?"

"One or two. Still waitin' to hear about the county fair, one."

"Hope it works out. Well, I've got to go, Hank. Take care."

"So you don't want the TV?" Hank hurriedly asked.

Callie hadn't even thought about the big screen TV she'd been talked into putting on her credit card some months ago, *until I get a little cash from my next gig.* She hadn't held her breath on that and had always considered the thing a tacky eyesore. Hank, however, loved watching his games on it.

"It's all yours, Hank. Enjoy," she said and hung up, fairly sure that holding on to his beloved TV would significantly soothe whatever "hurtin'" Hank might really be going through.

Callie spared perhaps twenty more seconds thinking about him before putting it behind her. With her personal items heading to Keepsake Cove soon, she knew she had some work to do. She'd been living out of her suitcase since taking over the cottage, treating the place as a museum of sorts for Aunt Melodie and not moving a thing. But it was time to be practical and start packing up her aunt's clothes.

The more Callie thought about it, though, the more daunting the project became. Aware that she needed a push, she picked up her phone.

"Delia, remember that offer to help if I needed it?" Callie barely spoke ten more words of explanation before Delia said she'd be right over.

When Callie welcomed her in, Delia had several cardboard boxes in tow. "Luckily I had a few deliveries to the shop today. I thought we could sort Mel's things into what you'd like to keep, what to donate or toss, and what to think about a little."

"How about a fourth category?" Callie suggested. "Things you might like to have."

"That's very sweet, Callie," Delia said. "We'll see."

They got busy in the upstairs bedroom, pulling out items from the closet and laying them on the bed. Aunt Mel had been taller than Callie and slimmer than Delia, so dresses and skirts went immediately into a donation box. Callie kept a few blouses that were particularly nice and could be tucked in or have their sleeves rolled to fit. Shoes went into the charity boxes.

When they came to purses and scarves, the sorting slowed.

"I remember Mel buying this at a craft fair in Baltimore," Delia said, holding up a colorfully embroidered bag.

From the look on her face, Callie could see that it brought fond memories. "Please keep it," she said. She did the same with several scarves that were definitely Delia's color, and her neighbor accepted them with minimal protest. They attacked the dresser drawers, then the closet in the second bedroom, and within an amazingly short amount of time—at least to Callie, who'd feared a days-long project—all had been cleared.

"Well!" Callie said, standing up and rubbing her hands after closing the flaps on the last box. "We've accomplished a lot! There's some very nice items to be donated and not all that much to be tossed. Aunt Mel must have been really organized, never letting things pile up."

"'Something in, something out' was her motto," Delia said. "It helped that the closet space in these cottages is so limited."

"I hope it'll help me," Callie said, knowing she'd have to pare down her own wardrobe to essentials unless she wanted to rent storage space somewhere.

Delia helped her lug the boxes meant for charity downstairs and recommended places in the area that Callie might consider. She declined an offer of coffee, saying it was getting late, and headed to the door.

"Thanks for these, Callie," she said, holding up the items she was taking with her, obviously touched. "It's nice to have something of Mel's, something tangible."

"I'm sure she'd want you to have them," Callie said, holding the door for her. She heard a muffled trill come from inside the roll-top desk where Grandpa Reed's music box was still locked up. Delia heard it too, and she glanced around the room, looking for the source.

To head off questions she couldn't answer, Callie quickly thanked Delia for her help. "I couldn't have done it without you," she insisted, to which Delia laughingly answered, "Pshaw!" and wished Callie a good night.

As Callie closed the door, she turned in the direction of the corner desk. "That does it. You're going to the shop, which is apparently your proper place. At least if you start playing there, you'll be simply one of dozens of other music boxes, and it won't be so unnerving." She unlocked the desk, pulled out the square wooden box, and marched it across the way to *House of Melody*. There, she set the music box on its shelf behind the counter, stepped back, and waited. Hearing nothing beyond her own breathing, she turned and went back to her cottage.

Later that night, wrapped cozily in her terry-cloth robe after a relaxing shower, Callie fixed a mug of cocoa and plopped on the sofa. Jagger immediately jumped onto her lap, and she stroked him idly as she sipped, enjoying the quiet time. As she stared absently toward the small coat closet, she said aloud, "We forgot about that one." Jagger's ear twitched.

"I'll ask Delia for another box in the morning. It shouldn't take me long to fold up the things in there." She imagined herself doing so during her lunch break, and tried to remember exactly what was stored inside. She'd glanced into the closet only once, not having needed a jacket on the warm days she'd been in Keepsake Cove.

Curious, she set down her mug, eased a reluctant Jagger onto the adjacent cushion, and went over to open the closet door. Two coats— a black wool and a tan, lightweight trench—along with jackets for winter and spring hung there, nearly filling the narrow space. A couple of empty hangers waited for visitors' coats. The shelf above held a tidy assortment of knit hats, scarves, and gloves.

Callie stooped down to see a pair of snow boots on the floor beside slip-on rubber gardening shoes. She'd pulled herself halfway up before she stopped and knelt back down on the floor. She'd spied a box at the back, behind the long winter coat and nearly hidden in the shadows. Curious, Callie reached in and pulled it out.

It was gray metal, about twelve inches by twelve, and, as she soon discovered, locked. She shook it lightly, half fearing she'd hear the sound of disposable cell phones rattling inside. Instead, she heard the soft swish of paper.

She went to get the ring of keys, which she'd left on the kitchen counter, and searched through it for one to fit the small lock. The only small key was the one she already knew was for the roll-top desk. All others were for doors.

She and Delia had gone through all of the drawers in Aunt Mel's bedroom and hadn't come across any loose keys. There was the small desk in the guest bedroom, but Callie didn't feel up to searching through it right then. Instead, she set the metal box beside the small coffee table and sat back down on the sofa to finish her cocoa. Jagger instantly reclaimed his spot on her lap.

"What do you know about that thing?" Callie asked the cat as she scratched his head. "Hmm? Something I need to know about, inside? Or just a collection of old Christmas cards?" As she asked it, Callie knew that what was in the metal box was more important than old cards—at least to Aunt Mel, who'd taken the trouble to lock it.

Jagger, however, simply tucked his nose into the folds of her robe and exhaled. Whatever he knew, he wasn't sharing.

Seven

While Tabitha watched over *House of Melody*, Callie took off on what she decided would be a regular lunchtime excursion through Keepsake Cove, which she'd barely seen so far. With its brick walkways, ornamental street lights, hanging flower baskets, and Dickensian shop fronts, it was an experience in itself. But her goal was to get to know the shopkeepers, many of whom had been Mel's friends, and who, she hoped, might eventually be hers.

She passed by the window of *Shake It Up!* and waved to Delia, who was seated behind her counter. Callie paused to glance at the several salt and pepper shakers that graced Delia's window display that day. A pair of ceramic black and white cows sat next to two brown owls. The owl shakers perched above boy and girl figures dressed like cooks in white aprons and caps. Miniature Coke bottle shakers stood next to kittens with tiny holes at the tops of their glazed ceramic heads. There seemed no limit to the variety, and Callie could imagine spending an entire day browsing through Delia's shelves to see them all. How many salt and pepper shakers did a person need? That, of course, was beside the point. Collecting was the point, which you did because you enjoyed having them. Callie supposed collectors actually did use their special shakers as the occasion arose, but very carefully.

The shop next to Delia's carried costume jewelry. The sign said *Pearl's Bangles and Beads*, and Callie's first thought was that the apostrophe in *Pearl's* was a mistake. Then she caught a glimpse of the shop's proprietor through the window, a stout, sixty-ish woman, and remembered her from Aunt Mel's funeral. Gradually the woman's name came to her and Callie smiled. *Pearl*. The Bangles and Beads were Pearl's.

She wondered if Pearl's wares might compete with Tabitha's handmade jewelry, which Tabitha said she constructed from all kinds of beads. But the window in front of Callie displayed vintage jewelry, representing the styles of many decades and crafted from a wide range of materials. Though she hadn't yet seen Tabitha's creations, from her assistant's quirky sense of fashion Callie guessed they would appeal to a very different clientele than Pearl's. She entered the shop, ready to introduce herself, but quickly found there was no need.

"How are you, my dear," the woman with the close-cut cap of white hair said as she hurried forward to take Callie's hands in both of hers. "Pearl Poepelman, in case you don't remember, and I'm sure you don't. That's very much okay, dear," Pearl said, patting Callie's hands and looking solicitously into her face from several inches below. Her navy blue dress flowed over an ample, motherly bosom, its severity lightened considerably by a multitude of turquoise and silver necklaces, all vintage, Callie was sure. "You've had plenty to deal with over the last several days. Trying to keep all of us straight is the least of your concerns."

Callie smiled and thought she picked up a faint New York accent. "I do remember you, Ms. Poepelman—"

"Mrs., dear, but call me Pearl, please."

"Pearl, then. I remember how kind you were at my aunt's funeral."

"Don't even mention it," Pearl said, shaking her head firmly as she stepped back. "We look after each other here at Keepsake Cove." She paused and gave a sniff. "Well, most of us do."

Callie guessed who Pearl might be thinking of as less charitably minded, and her lips curled in a strained smile. "I did meet my *Carlectibles* neighbor," she said. "He wasn't particularly welcoming."

Pearl rolled her eyes. "Karl's probably the biggest fly in our collectible ointment. Anytime the association puts up a proposal for the betterment of the Cove, Karl is totally against it, no matter how sensible it is. I'm sorry you got stuck next to him."

"The privacy fence between us should make it manageable," Callie said. "Does everyone in the Cove live in cottages behind their shops?"

"Oh, no, dear. I don't, for one. I need more space. Can't imagine trying to cook a big dinner in that tiny kitchen," she said with a laugh. "Or serving it. Where would everyone sit? And those miniscule closets!" As she spoke, her phone rang, and Pearl rounded a glass-topped counter filled with sparkling silver, gold, and crystal jewelry to get to it. "I use mine for storage, only" she added before picking up the phone. "Pearl's Bangles and Beads. What can I do for you?"

Callie waited a moment, and when it was clear the call would go on a while, she waved and pointed to the door. Pearl held up her hand in a "hold on" gesture, then scribbled something on a scrap of paper, which she thrust toward Callie as she continued to respond in monosyllables to her caller. It was the website address of the Keepsake Cove Shop Owners' Association. A direct invitation for Callie to check it out and join. Callie made an OK sign and headed on out.

Outside, she glanced around and wondered where to go next. The sign on the shop across the street called to her: *Kids at Heart*.

She crossed over and grinned as she spotted familiar, memory-invoking toys: aging (but forever young) Barbie dolls, Lego sets, and Lincoln logs. Surrounding those were toys from older generations: porcelain dolls, cast-iron trucks, and slightly scratched wooden pull-toys. She walked in to see a slim man with thinning hair dealing with a customer. His unbuttoned sweater vest partially covered a loosely tucked plaid shirt that drooped over faded brown trousers. He looked over at Callie and called genially, "Be with you in a moment."

Callie set about browsing through the shop's intriguing wares, resisting the urge to wind up jack-in-the-boxes or tip over baby dolls dressed in organdy to hear them cry "ma-ma." Her temptations must have been evident, for when the shopkeeper joined her after his customer left, the first thing out of his mouth was, "Go ahead, play with them. Everyone does. I'm sure your customers lift the lids of your music boxes all the time."

"They do. It seems to be irresistible. I guess you remember me from the funeral, huh?"

He nodded and held out his hand. "Bill Hart. That's H-a-r-t."

Callie shook it and glanced back at the shop name, *Kids at Heart*.

"Right. Heart, Hart," he said, rocking his hand with a laugh. "I, ahem, *toyed* with the idea of using our actual name, similar to what your aunt did, but decided to go with what was understandable."

"There's so many clever names, and such a variety of shops here at Keepsake Cove. I'm trying to get to know them all, but it'll take time. Right now, just getting settled in and learning my way around my own place requires so much of it."

"Come to the next association meeting," Hart said, sliding his hands into his trouser pockets and rolling back comfortably on his heels. "Besides putting names to faces, you can learn a lot about people when they start arguing with one another." He grinned as he said it, and Callie guessed that he wasn't one of the arguers, though she thought Pearl Poepelman would likely dig in and hold her ground when she wanted.

"Was my aunt active in the group?"

"She was. Mostly pitching in on committee stuff. But she spoke up once in a while about things she felt strongly about."

"Like what?"

Hart, hands still in pockets, looked ceiling-ward as he considered that. "Like ... oh! Like those flower baskets hanging from the street lamps?"

Callie nodded. "Love them."

"Mel's idea. Of course, not everyone was convinced that the expense was worth it. But Mel won us over." He laughed. "I was one of the not-so-sure ones. But now I get lots of positive feedback on the baskets from customers. And during the holidays, when the greens and the sparkly stuff goes in? Wow! Keepsake Cove looks great. People show up by the dozens just to pose for Christmas card photos."

Callie smiled. She liked knowing that Aunt Mel had played a key role in what had grown into an important part of Keepsake Cove.

"But then there was that other thing ... " He paused, frowning.

Callie prompted. "Yes?"

Hart shook his head. "Never mind. It was nothing. I shouldn't have mentioned it."

"Yes you should, Bill!" A woman suddenly popped out of the *Kids at Heart* back room, holding a silver-painted toy airplane that she'd apparently been working on. She held out her hand to Callie. "Hi, I'm Laurie Hart, Bill's wife." Laurie was dressed in an oversized Orioles T-shirt and jeans, her long blondish hair half in and half out of a ponytail, which led

Callie to wonder if she was always the "back room" person of their business. Then again, Bill's attire wasn't exactly *GQ*. But it was a toy store, so why should it be? Pearl Poepelman dressed up for her jewelry customers, and the Harts dressed appropriately for theirs.

"I would have come out sooner to say hi," Laurie said, "but I was in the middle of gluing the propeller back on this thing. Bill, I think we should clue in Callie about the situation."

"But it's a big nothing, honeybun."

"Maybe, maybe not."

Callie waited, her curiosity growing as the two debated until Bill finally shrugged and turned to her. "Your aunt proposed something to the association that stirred up a little controversy."

Aunt Mel? Controversy? Those were words Callie never expected to hear together.

Laurie nodded firmly "She suggested that the association put a limit on the term of treasurer."

Okay. Not exactly a bombshell. "There hadn't been one?" Callie asked.

"Uh-uh. Duane Fletcher has been treasurer since the association formed, at least twenty years ago. Other officers in the group changed, but Duane stayed put."

"But he's the only one of us with professional-level money handling experience," Bill explained. "Duane worked several years as bookkeeper for a small firm in DC before buying his shop, so his handling the association books makes perfect sense. Plus, over the years, as our funds grew, he had to set up a complicated system of records and banking. Someone new could totally mess it up."

"As *he* said," Laurie added.

"There's been no oversight of the treasurer all this time?" Callie asked.

"Krystal Cobb, our current president, says she looks over the books from time to time," Bill said. "She said everything seems fine."

"So where's the controversy?" Callie asked.

Bill tilted his head toward Laurie to explain.

"The problem," she said, "is that Duane is pretty popular in the Cove. Some of his friends took Mel's proposal as a personal attack on Duane, an implication of incompetence or worse. I don't think she meant that at all, and was just proposing something that most organizations consider to be sensible practice."

"Yes, I'm sure that's how it was meant," Bill said. "It's just ... to kick Duane out after all the work he's done? I mean, how could he not be offended."

"I know, sweetie, I know." Laurie reached over to give her husband a one-armed squeeze. "Nobody wants to hurt anybody."

She turned to Callie. "You see the problem? Even Bill and I can't agree. But forewarned is forearmed, Callie. At least you'll know what the glares and snide remarks might be about when you come to a meeting." She grinned. "You don't happen to be a CPA by any chance, do you?"

Callie laughed. "Afraid not."

"Well, it'll all work out in time." Laurie looked down at the wooden airplane in her hand. "For now, I'd better get back to my work."

"Of course." Callie made her farewells to the couple and left, glad to have met the likeable pair but wondering about the controversy they'd brought up, especially since it involved Aunt Mel.

She was heading back to *House of Melody* when she decided to stop at the Keepsake Café. Hunger was her motivating force, but not only for food. Callie also craved more input on the Duane Fletcher situation.

$\mathcal{E}ight$

$\mathcal{C}$allie pushed open the door of the Keepsake Café and glanced around, expecting to see Brian Greer. Instead, a pretty, thirty-something woman stood behind the counter chatting with a customer, her dark hair pulled back in a ponytail. She looked over as Callie stepped in.

"Hi! Welcome to Keepsake Café." She polished the already-sparkling countertop as Callie headed toward a stool, then slid a laminated menu in front of her. "First timer?"

"Second, actually. I'm from *House of Melody* across the street. Callie Reed."

The woman's face lit up. "Oh! *You're* Callie! Hi! I'm Brian's sister, Annie. Annie Barbario."

Annie's *"You're* Callie!" exclamation made for a moment's pause, but Callie let it slide. "Nice to meet you, Annie."

"I help Brian out every so often," Annie explained as Callie glanced over the menu. "My husband Mike and I live about twenty minutes away. I'm mostly looking after our two kids, so this gets me out with the grown-ups once in a while. What can I get you?"

The delightful memory of her last order along with her admitted tendency to stick to favorites made for an easy decision. Callie set the menu down. "Ham and Swiss on rye."

"Coming right up." Annie called out the order in a voice that Pearl Poepelman, several doors down, might have heard. Brian's muffled voice responded from the kitchen.

Annie stayed where she was, looking ready to chat, so Callie asked, "If you're helping out, does that mean Brian's taking off soon?"

Annie laughed. "You think Brian would leave this place in anyone else's hands? You don't know him very well, do you?"

"Well, no, I don't," Callie agreed with a smile. "A bit possessive, is he?"

"Put it this way. If you look up 'control freak' online, Brian's picture will pop up front and center."

"Hey," Brian's voice called. "I can hear you, you know."

"Oh, admit it, Brian! You wouldn't leave Emeril Lagasse in charge if he offered."

"Have you seen how that guy works? He'd wreck the place!"

Annie leaned toward Callie and whispered, "He's also a neat freak."

Callie grinned, though that didn't sound like a totally negative thing to her as she thought of Hank's habits of total disarray—much like his life, actually.

Within minutes the control-slash-neat freak stepped out of the kitchen with Callie's ham and Swiss on rye, with its side of chips, coleslaw, and pickle. Annie took the plate from him, but he continued on toward Callie's spot.

"How're things going?" he asked.

"Pretty well." Callie took a hungry bite from her sandwich and wiggled her eyebrows appreciatively. When she could speak again, she told of her start at getting to know the Keepsake Cove shopkeepers. "Bill Hart invited me to the next association meeting."

"Good idea," Annie said. "Save you a lot of walking around. When's the next one, Brian?"

Brian leaned over to check the wall calendar. "Tomorrow night."

"Perfect. You two should go together. That way Brian can introduce you to everyone."

"Excuse my sister," Brian said. "She thinks I'm the control freak in the family? At least I confine it to my kitchen. She tries to handle people's lives."

Callie laughed. "I'm game if you are. Where is it?"

"The library meeting room, over in the main section of Mapleton. It's walkable, but driving gets you there and back faster. Which one works for you? The meeting starts at seven."

Callie thought a moment. She'd intended to ask Brian about Duane Fletcher but changed her mind, now that she was there. Too many listening ears around for an honest discussion.

"How long of a walk?"

"Ten, maybe fifteen minutes."

"That's fine. Meet you outside at a quarter of?"

"Sounds good." New customers came in, sending both Annie and Brian back to work. Callie quietly worked at her lunch as she listened to the light chatter around her, feeling more and more at home in Keepsake Cove. Soon, though, the responsibilities of *House of Melody*—and maybe a psychic call for help from Tabitha?—beckoned her, and she finished up, paid, and waved goodbye. As she crossed the street, she averted her gaze from Karl Eggers's shop. No sense starting her afternoon on a downer.

There was no sign of Tabitha when Callie opened the shop's door, but her voice called out from the office. "Be with you in a minute!"

"It's just me."

"Great! Come on back. I just unpacked an order, and we have a problem."

Uh-oh. Callie headed to the office to find Tabitha holding a square, dark-stained wooden music box with a delicate design of inlaid wood on its lid. It looked beautiful and in good shape as far as Callie could see. "What's the problem?"

"This." Tabitha opened the lid and a familiar tune began to play, smoothly and clearly. Callie shrugged and raised her brows questioningly.

"It's *Ode to Joy*," Tabitha said. "Jonathan Harman wanted *The Blue Danube*."

"Oh. That's not good."

"Uh-uh," Tabitha agreed. "He's been waiting for this, like, forever. He's going to be ticked."

"I wonder why he didn't mention his order when he was here?"

"Probably just forgot about it, at least for the moment." Tabitha grinned. "Maybe he was dazzled by your beauty. But I remember him checking on it with Mel several times. It's a special order and came all the way from Switzerland."

"Switzerland! Yikes! Whose fault is it? Ours or theirs? I'm thinking of the shipping costs to return it."

"Right. We can check, but I'd be more worried about Jonathan's reaction. He's our best customer, and he can be a bit prickly if things don't go just right. You don't want him to start buying elsewhere."

Callie frowned. "Well, first things first. Let's look up the original order." She woke up the shop's laptop sitting on the secretary desk and did the search with a little help from Tabitha. The first thing she found out about the music box was its cost, which made her gulp. It was significant, as was the shipping fee. She scrolled until she found what she needed. "Aha! It wasn't our fault. We clearly asked for *The Blue Danube.*"

"That's good. But I don't know if that will make Jonathan feel better." Callie drew in a deep breath. "One way to find out."

She pulled up the contacts list she now had on her phone and pressed the number for Harman. Her call went to voicemail, and she left her message. "Mr. Harman, uh, Jonathan, it's Callie Reed. The music box we ordered for you from Switzerland arrived. There's something we need to discuss." She left the shop's number and hung up. "Well," she said, shrugging. "We'll see what happens."

By late afternoon, things had been quiet for some time, and Callie, alone in the shop, glanced at the wall clock to confirm that it was near closing time. She hadn't heard back from Jonathan Harman and was wondering what that might mean when she suddenly caught sight of him climbing out of a dark sedan at the curb.

Uh-oh. She'd soon learn how "prickly" the man could be. Harman was dressed more formally than when they'd first met, in a dark suit and tie, and she watched as he took a leather briefcase out from the passenger seat and locked it in his trunk. *Lawyer?* she wondered briefly, then remembered Tabitha mentioning something financial. Whatever that involved.

"I got your message," Harman said as he walked in. "Spent the afternoon in Baltimore, so this was the earliest I could stop by. Hope I'm not holding you up?" He shot a glance at Callie's clock.

"No, it's fine. I said there was something to discuss, so I'm glad you came."

"Let me guess: the price on my music box went up since I ordered it."

"No, the price is the same. But it arrived with the wrong music." Harman frowned, and Callie plowed on. "Instead of *The Blue Danube*, it plays *Ode to Joy*."

"Hmm." He was silent for several moments. "That's it? I mean, that's the only problem? The box is in good shape?"

"Oh, yes. It's perfect. And beautiful. See for yourself." Callie reached down to a lower shelf, where she'd set the item, and placed it on the counter in front of him.

Harman reached for it, turning the box every which way, then set it down carefully to lift the lid. The notes of *Ode to Joy* chimed out. Callie waited quietly. He let it play to the end, then closed the lid. "Well!" He looked at Callie. "It's certainly not *The Blue Danube*."

"No, and I'm very sorry. We checked, and it was their mistake, so there'll be no problem returning it. But it'll probably mean another long wait to get the right one."

Harman stared silently at the music box. Then, to Callie's surprise, he smiled. "Don't bother."

"Really?"

"Really. I can't say I'm not disappointed. I have a thing for Strauss and Austrian music. But hey," he said, grinning, "Beethoven was German. Close enough, so why should I quibble? He was a pretty decent composer, right?"

Callie grinned back. "That's what I hear. So you're okay with the music?"

"I love the box. It's absolutely beautiful. And the music, though not my first choice, is beautiful, too. I'll keep it."

"Great!"

"On one condition."

Callie, who'd begun reaching for the packing box, stopped.

"That you'll join me for dinner." Harman followed this with a disarming laugh. "Just kidding. That's not really a condition. But I would love it if you did. You see, I passed up dinner in Baltimore with some friends so I could get here before you closed up. I was that excited to see my new music box. But now I'm starved, and I hate dining alone. No strings attached, honest. Just a pleasant way to enjoy a meal. I intend to discuss music boxes the entire time."

Callie laughed. "How can I pass that up?"

She was about to say more when Karl Eggers suddenly burst into the shop. He flapped a large manila envelope.

"This is yours. It came to my shop." He thrust it at her.

Callie took the envelope. It was addressed to her but one number of the address was off, which had sent it to Eggers's place. She started to thank him but he brusquely overrode her. "Last time. Tell your people to get it right or it goes in my trash."

Oh.

"Another thing. Your customers can't park in front of my shop. That space is for my customers only."

"Mr. Eggers, I ... " Callie began, but Eggers had already spun around and was striding out.

Callie looked at Jonathan Harman, dumbfounded. To add to her consternation, she realized that Grandpa Reed's music box, sitting high on its shelf behind her, had begun to play.

Nine

Callie sat across from Jonathan in a booth at the Mapleton Grill, which, she realized, was only a block away from George Blake's law office. She'd ridden over in Jonathan's car, during which time she'd worked on regaining her composure after Eggers's disturbance.

"He can't claim parking spots on the street," Jonathan had said, which Callie was glad to have confirmed. But she didn't doubt Eggers would come up with some other form of harassment if that one didn't work, and it only fueled her agitation. And why had Grandpa Reed's music box played? She'd only heard the music before when positive things had happened. There was nothing positive about the scene back at the shop. But, she asked herself, why should she think the music's playing had to mean anything? She needed to get a grip.

Their orders came swiftly, and Jonathan started on his steak sandwich while Callie turned to her simple but tasty platter of tilapia with grilled veggies, finding it a nice change from the quick-and-easy meals she'd been eating at the cottage. Her mood improved.

"So, was your day in Baltimore work-related?" she asked before taking a sip of her water.

Jonathan nodded and swiped his mouth with the napkin. "I can do most of my work from home. I do financial planning. But once in a while I have to venture out to meet with clients face-to-face."

"That sounds interesting," Callie said, but apparently in a tone doubtful enough to make Jonathan laugh.

"It is to me. But I don't expect everyone to be into it, so I won't bore you with details. The gist of it is that I help people plan for their future, mostly for their retirement, through investments."

"I see. And at the end of the day, to unwind from that, you, ah, wind up music boxes?"

Jonathan grinned. "To a degree. I also admire their beauty, craftsmanship, and, if any, their history."

"So I guess you don't go for the quirky ones."

"Not usually. But I have added a tchotchke or two to my collection, just for fun. Remember, I said it was my grandparents who got me into it all, and they had all kinds in their collection."

"It was a shame they couldn't have passed them on."

Jonathan nodded, his expression regretful. "Their music boxes held a lot of memories."

Callie poked at her fish. "I feel the same way about my grandfather's music box."

"I noticed you had it back on the shelf, where Mel always kept it. I was glad to see it again." Callie waited to hear if he'd also noticed the music box suddenly playing, but he only picked up one of the French fries that had come along with his sandwich and bit off the end.

Callie steered the conversation back to Jonathan's collection, which he seemed more than happy to talk about. She listened to enthusiastic and detailed descriptions of his favorites along with tales of minor treasures discovered in unexpected places, marveling the whole time at his fervor and extensive knowledge of the subject.

When he paused to get back to his meal, she told him so. "You've just made clear how much I still have to learn in order to run *House of Melody* competently."

Jonathan laughed. "Sorry. I tend to get carried away. It just happens to be one of my favorite subjects. Other than handling people's money. But don't worry, you'll catch up in time. You have the interest and drive, and that's what matters."

"I hope so. Aunt Mel gifted me with a wonderful opportunity. I want to make the most of it and not ruin what she worked so hard to build. But this is my first venture into retail. It's a bit of a struggle."

Jonathan looked at Callie speculatively. "A client of mine gives seminars on retail business management. I have a couple of his published books on the subject. Would you like to look them over?"

"I'd love to!"

"I'll drop them off tomorrow. And if you need help managing all the money that will start pouring in, give me a call."

Jonathan said it with a twinkle and Callie laughed, sure that level of success lay a long way off, if ever. What a luxury it would be, though, to have a little money to spare. An image of Hank knocking at her door quickly came to mind and she swiftly banished it. That door had been closed and firmly locked.

Jonathan dropped her off in front of her shop after their dinner, offering, as he pulled up, to walk her back to the cottage door.

"No need," Callie said. Keepsake Cove seemed so benign compared to Morgantown, at least the section where she'd lived. She thanked him for the dinner treat and climbed out. As she watched him drive off, Callie caught sight of Brian, strolling toward his own place on the opposite side of the street. She waved, and he waved back but maintained his slow pace.

Callie turned onto the narrow path that ran between her shop and Karl Eggers's, aware but not bothered that it became quite dim where the buildings blocked the light from the street. She hadn't thought to turn on her cottage's outside lights before leaving during the daylight, which would have been a help now that darkness had fallen. But again, it wasn't a worry. She'd gone only a few feet, though, when a dark shape suddenly loomed at the far end of the path. Callie froze, more in surprise than fear, until the figure lurched toward her. That's when she screamed.

Callie ran blindly back toward the street, her feet slipping briefly on the damp ground, only to slam right into another dark form as she exited the path. She struggled as her arms were grabbed until a familiar voice said, "It's me!" Brian Greer held Callie to steady her. "What's wrong!"

"I, there's ... " Callie stammered, pointing behind her.

A deep but non-threatening voice sounded from the shadows. "I didn't mean any harm."

"Elvin, is that you?" Brian asked.

A tall hulk of a man, with a scruffy beard and dressed in grubby denims, stepped out hesitantly.

"Elvin, you can't go into other people's yards like that, especially at night. It scares them."

"I'm sorry." He glanced at Callie when he said it but quickly looked down. "I saw headlights coming. I don't like bright lights shining at me. Miss Reed isn't there anymore. I thought it was okay."

"Callie lives there now, Elvin. She's Miss Reed's niece. Callie, this is Elvin Wilcox. He's a big guy but don't let him worry you. You wouldn't hurt anyone, would you, Elvin?"

Callie's heart had slowed back to normal by then, and she relaxed as she saw the large man looking abashed.

"I didn't mean to scare you," he said.

"I'm glad to hear that, Elvin."

"Elvin," Brian said, "did you have anything to eat today?"

Elvin nodded. "I cut up a dead branch for Mrs. Dixon. She gave me a nice dinner for that. Chicken. And dumplings."

"Would you like a sandwich to take home for tomorrow? I had some leftovers today."

Elvin nodded, and Brian turned to Callie. "Will you be all right?"

"I'll be fine. Thanks, Brian."

As she headed on back to her cottage, Callie could hear Brian talking to Elvin. When she unlocked her door and stepped inside, she flicked her outside lights on and off to signal all was well. Then she scooped up Jagger, who'd hurried over, apparently in need of a little comfort himself. *Must look into motion sensor lights*, she told herself and nuzzled her face against the cat's warm, furry body, aware that her heart was still beating a little faster than usual.

❧

The next day, Tabitha arrived dressed non-startlingly as *Elementary's* Joan Watson, though Callie didn't identify the TV character immediately. "Everything she wears on the show is a statement," Tabitha claimed, and Callie nodded, not remembering enough about the character's wardrobe to get into a discussion. What she most wanted to talk about was Elvin Wilcox.

"Poor Elvin," Tabitha said when Callie asked about him. "Might be some kind of PTSD going on with him, mixed in with who-knows-what."

"From a war experience?" Callie found Elvin's age hard to judge, unsure if the man was too young for Vietnam or a little too old for Iraq.

"Could be, or maybe from something else. I never asked. Elvin doesn't chat much."

"Does he live on his own? I didn't get the impression anyone was looking after him."

"Keepsake Cove pretty much looks after him. I think he took over an old place that was sitting empty, not too far out of town. Apparently nobody's complained. I see him wandering around town sometimes."

"That's sad." Callie told Tabitha about their encounter the night before.

"Wow, that'd scare the bejeezus out of me if I didn't know Elvin. But I'll bet he was just as shaken up. Lucky for both of you that Brian was around."

Callie agreed. Two customers appeared at the shop door, which put a hold on the conversation. As the woman, dressed in touristy beach clothes complete with golf visor and rhinestone-studded flip-flops, began to wander among the music boxes, her husband hung back, his low interest and impatience apparent from the steady jingling of the change in his pockets.

Tabitha stepped forward with an offer of help, but the woman smiled sweetly. "I don't really know what I'm looking for. But I'll know it when I find it."

"Can you find it a little faster," her husband grumbled. "This is the fifth store we've stopped in."

"Oh, Donald," his wife said. She turned her back to him and continued her browsing.

Focused on her customer, Callie was a bit startled when Jonathan Harman hurried in. "Just wanted to drop off the books I mentioned," he said, reaching into a bulky-looking canvas bag. He pulled out two thick paperbacks and one slipped out of his hand, landing at the feet of the impatient husband.

The *Maryland is for Crabs* T-shirted man bent over to retrieve it for Jonathan, reading the title aloud as he held it up. "*Retail Management: How to Best Serve Your Customers.* Ha! The guy next door could sure use a copy."

His wife repeated her by then rote-sounding "Oh, Donald," but the man went on. "We asked for suggestions for our grandson. The kid's third birthday is coming up, and it's a toy car store, right? You know what he told us? 'Come back in ten years when he's old enough to appreciate fine collectibles.' You call that any kind of customer service? 'Come back in ten years'?"

His wife rolled her eyes but Jonathan smiled, taking the book and placing it on the counter along with the second one. Callie opened her mouth to speak, but Donald suddenly barked, "There's that vagrant again. Someone should do something about him!"

All turned toward where he was pointing and saw Elvin Wilcox lumbering across the street opposite *House of Melody.*

"He's harmless, Donald!" his wife said, but the man shook his head.

"Didn't seem that way to me. And the guy next door sure didn't think so. He chased him off. Called him a panhandler."

"Elvin's not a panhandler," Tabitha said, jumping to his defense, and four people began talking at once—everyone, that is, besides Callie. She'd been distracted by the sound of *The Skaters' Waltz* coming from Grandpa Reed's music box.

Ten

Jonathan had hurried off, and the husband and wife tourists were finally moving on after taking at least thirty minutes to choose an inexpensive, wind-up musical snow globe for their granddaughter. Callie had seen the surprised look on her assistant's face when the notes of *The Skaters' Waltz* rolled out, though Tabitha hadn't said anything at the time. Callie, however, felt it coming, so when the shop door closed behind Donald and his wife, she wasn't surprised when Tabitha turned to her and asked, "What made Mel's music box play?"

"I don't know," Callie answered truthfully.

"You didn't lift the lid or anything?"

Callie shook her head. When the silence lingered, she admitted, "It's been doing that once in a while. Just playing on its own for no reason that I can come up with."

"Really?" Tabitha's eyes widened as she stared at the music box in question, reminding Callie of the look Jagger assumed when a squirrel or bird paused outside a window he'd been monitoring.

Callie told her about the first time it had happened, which was shortly after she'd broken up with Hank over the phone. "The box was locked inside the roll top desk, then."

Tabitha digested that for a few moments. "When else?"

"When I came across an email that Aunt Mel had started to write to me but hadn't finished."

"What did it say?"

Callie took a deep breath. "It said there was something she wanted to tell me. But the email ended there. She'd apparently begun it just before I called her about coming to visit. She might have decided to tell me in person."

"And did she?"

Callie shook her head sadly, thinking of the things left unsaid between them because of her aunt's death.

"The next time I heard it play was as Delia was leaving the cottage. I'd given her a few of Aunt Mel's scarves. That's when I decided to bring the music box back here. It was starting to unnerve me. I thought if it played here, it would just blend in with all the others."

"It didn't blend in for me."

"I know." Callie paused, thinking *in for a penny*. "There was one other time it played. Last night. I was packing up Jonathan's new Swiss music box when Karl Eggers stormed in, upset over having to deal with misdirected mail and about my customers parking in front of his shop."

"Oh, Karl," Tabitha said, flapping a hand dismissively, but she stared thoughtfully at Callie. "You're getting messages. From Mel."

"No, it can't be," Callie said, though she'd wondered the exact same thing.

"Think about it. The unfinished email? There was something important she didn't get a chance to say. She's trying to say it now, maybe in the only way she can."

"But how—assuming you're right—am I supposed to understand what the message is? It's musical notes, not words!"

"Yes, but that music box meant the world to Mel, you know that. It makes sense that she'd gravitate to it. Oh! This is so exciting! Messages from the other side, and happening right here in Keepsake Cove!"

"Hold on, Tabitha. That's quite a theory, and I'm not at all sure I go along with it. For all we know, it's just the mechanism of an old music box slipping."

Tabitha shook her head decisively, so Callie begged, "Until we figure this out, one way or another, please let's just keep it between you and me, okay?"

"Oh, absolutely. Mum's the word. But will you let me know if it happens again when I'm not around?"

Callie promised, glad when a customer's appearance brought the subject to a close. Had she done the right thing by sharing what she did with Tabitha? She'd come to like and respect her helper on all things shop-related, despite the psychic claims and talk of Tarot cards. Which, of course, should have predicted the response she'd gotten. Still, Callie found it a great relief just to talk about the strange happenings of the music box. Bringing it out into the open made it feel much less mysterious. Perhaps she'd soon be able to laugh the whole thing off.

With that vague hope, she tried to keep busy for the rest of the day and her mind off the music box. It helped that she had the Keepsake Cove Association meeting to look forward to that night.

❦

Callie had expected that the walk to the meeting would give her time to discuss things with Brian, like the controversial association treasurer. But the dark clouds that gathered during the late afternoon threw a wrench into her plans by dropping a deluge minutes before it was time to leave.

Her phone rang as she stared dismally out the cottage window. "How about I pick you up out front in my car in ten minutes?" Brian asked.

Callie agreed and looked around for an umbrella. Her own things still hadn't arrived from Morgantown, but she discovered a folding umbrella of Aunt Mel's on the closet shelf. Soon she was holding it opened over her head just outside *House of Melody*, realizing that she didn't know what kind of car to look for. Not that she'd be capable of picking out a Ford or a Buick, but if Brian had said black SUV, she'd recognize that. On the other hand, a van made more sense for a café owner, so she watched for that.

To her surprise, the toot of a horn alerted her to a two-toned vehicle making a left turn onto her street. The long red car with a dark convertible top pulled up next to the street light, with Brian behind the wheel. Callie collapsed her umbrella and scooted in, sliding onto the black leather bench seat.

"Quite a car," she said.

"Like it? I got it for a steal." Brian watched Callie buckle herself in, then shifted into drive.

"How old is it?"

"1967. A genuine antique! But in great running condition. All I had to do to it was … " and Brian began ticking off the various repairs and replacements he'd done to the car, most of which flew over Callie's head. She did pick up that what she was riding in was a Chevy Impala that had been in someone's relative's garage for years before being hauled out and offered for sale. Brian, it seemed, had only recently discovered a passion for refurbishing ancient—make that *classic*—cars, which was what he talked about the entire drive to the library.

Callie couldn't fault the guy, since he had no idea she had another topic in mind to bring up. Plus the ride was short. So she simply nodded and offered positive-sounding murmurs when they seemed appropriate, then climbed out once he parked in the library's lot.

They trotted together under Callie's umbrella to the front door, then headed to the meeting room. Callie picked up sounds of a gathering crowd.

"Oh, good, you made it!" Delia cried from the coat rack where she was hanging up a dripping rain slicker. "It totally slipped my mind to mention tonight's meeting to you. I needed a last-minute appointment with the dentist." She rubbed her jaw. "Cracked molar. If I talk funny, it's the novocaine. I promise, I haven't been tippling."

Callie grinned. "You sound fine. Sorry about the molar. I actually learned about the meeting from several people and hitched a ride with Brian in his amazing car."

"Oh, so you got the top fixed?" Delia asked Brian, straight-faced.

"Yup! It closes all the way now. Good thing on a night like this, wouldn't you say?"

"Absolutely. Of course, you did have an umbrella with you, Callie, right?"

Callie shook her head, smiling, then watched as the two continued in the same vein, Delia teasing Brian over the climbing costs of refurbishing his "bargain" car, and Brian predicting he'd make a million from it some day.

"As if you'd ever part with it," Delia said.

"People, let's get settled," a woman's voice sounded through a microphone. "We have a lot to cover tonight."

The three headed toward the lined-up metal chairs, Callie leading the way to a back row where she could get an overview of the group.

The woman waiting at the podium looked to be around fifty, with the overhead light picking up strands of silver in her otherwise dark bob. Bill Hart had mentioned the association president's name as Krystal Cobb, and from the name as well as her sparkling jewelry and even the bright dots on her jacket lapels, Callie pictured her managing a glass collectibles shop. Then Delia whispered that Krystal sold collectible dolls.

After her mild surprise, Callie's first thought was that competition existed with *Kids at Heart,* which she remembered also carried dolls among their toys. But she supposed that some overlap might appear in several shops, and expected she'd come across musical items as she wandered about Keepsake Cove.

Krystal Cobb asked the association secretary to read the minutes of the last meeting, and a tiny, elderly woman stood up in the front row to do so in a querulous voice, the top of her gray head barely visible to Callie. After the long, barely understandable report, Krystal then called on the treasurer, and Callie perked up. A heavyset man in his mid-forties rose from the end of the same first row.

"Well," he said, "we placed ads in the *Eastern Shore Gazette* to the tune of ... " He listed the amounts and ticked off other expenses that came out of the association's checking account, which totaled up to significant numbers. He mentioned membership fees paid, investment dividends, savings account dividends, and more, talking rapidly as though he realized his report was tedious and uninteresting to most. Callie, in fact, found her attention wandering, until when he came to the end Laurie Hart called out from her seat a couple of rows back from Duane, "Will there be a link to that report on the website?"

"Of course," Duane answered. "In the Members Only section."

"Along with receipts for the expenditures?"

Murmurs sounded among the group, and Callie caught a quick stiffening of Duane's spine before he smiled genially. "I have the receipts, of course. I could scan them, but it will take a while."

"Waste of your time, Duane," a male voice called out. "You're doing enough as it is. A great job."

"I'm just saying …" Laurie began, but Duane interrupted.

"As I said, I have the receipts for everything, absolutely everything, which I've kept for years. Anyone is welcome to stop by and look them over. I'll warn you, though," he chuckled, "it's a lot. Load up on caffeine and clear your calendars for the following week."

Many laughed, but Callie saw Laurie and a few others frown. What would Aunt Mel's reaction have been, she wondered. Mumbles among the members followed until Krystal Cobb rapped her gavel to quiet things down. Callie thought Krystal would comment on the point, but she simply moved on, asking for ideas on a proposed Keepsake Cove collectibles festival.

Thoughts were offered, seconded, or rejected as Callie listened. At one point, Brian objected politely but firmly to the idea of bringing in outside food vendors, for obvious reasons, and he got many nods of agreement on that point, especially when he pointed out the number of locals he and other restaurateurs of the area would hire as temporary help. Delia suggested adding fun things for families, such as face painting and games, and volunteered to look into the possibilities.

Finally, the discussion, having gone as far as it could go at that early stage, started to repeat itself, and Krystal called the meeting to an end. "Patty and Jack handled our refreshments tonight, and they'll be highly offended if you don't finish them up," she said with a smile, and chairs scraped as members rose without further urging to head toward the food table.

Brian and Delia made sure to introduce Callie to several shopkeepers as she sipped lemonade from a paper cup and nibbled at cookies. Pearl Poepelman breezed by to squeeze her arm and say she was glad to see here there. Callie was chatting at one point with Dorothy Ashby, who owned a vintage sewing shop, when Duane Fletcher wandered over.

"Duane," Dorothy asked, "have you met our association newcomer, Callie Reed?"

Fletcher was only two or three inches taller than Callie, though his heavily padded frame might have made him more than twice her weight. He smiled genially and held out his hand.

"Welcome! What kind of collectibles are you offering?"

"Music boxes. Melodie Reed was my aunt."

"Reed!" He slapped his forehead. "Of course. I'm an idiot. Forgive me. I did hear that a relative had taken over *House of Melody*. We're delighted to have you. Though," he said, "we all miss Mel terribly."

"Thank you." Callie looked for any sign of insincerity, but Duane Fletcher's statement appeared genuine, from his furrowed brow to the slight catch in his voice. Perhaps he'd never taken Aunt Mel's move to replace him as treasurer personally?

Dorothy excused herself and Duane launched the usual getting-to-know-you questions, asking Callie where she'd moved from and what sort of work she'd done previously. She was used to getting polite nods to her mostly brief replies, but her answers to Duane were met with surprising interest. His follow-up questions and knowledgeable comments invited her to elaborate as his eyes rarely left her face. She found herself feeling like the most fascinating person this man had encountered in quite a while, which, of course, she rather enjoyed, especially after being around Hank for so long. When Krystal Cobb joined them, Callie experienced a spurt of annoyance that shook her out of the pleasant cloud that had begun to envelop her.

Krystal chatted only a minute before apologizing to Callie for needing to draw Duane away for something. Callie saw Krystal take his arm and continue to hold on tightly as they walked away, her head tilting toward his. The man, despite his lesser physical attributes, had a definite magnetism, and it seemed not only with women. As Callie watched the two wind their way through the crowd, a few men turned to speak to Duane, slapping his shoulder amiably. The feeling, though, clearly wasn't universal. Laurie Hart was unaffected, and apparently others who'd agreed with Aunt Mel about regularly refreshing the office of treasurer.

The lights of the room suddenly blinked. "The library closes in fifteen minutes," a stout woman at the door warned, her hand at the light switch.

Refreshments were quickly gathered up and chairs folded and stacked against the wall. Callie met up with Brian at the coat rack and the two walked through the parking lot at an easier pace, the rain having slowed to a light drizzle.

"Meet enough people tonight?" Brian asked as he turned the ignition and nudged his car toward the growing exit line.

"Quite a few, thanks to you and Delia. I got to talk to Duane Fletcher near the end."

"Ah, Duane. What did you think of him?"

Callie turned in surprise, hearing the precise question she'd been planning to ask Brian. "He's very personable," she said cautiously.

"And?"

"And I don't know. We only spoke a few minutes."

"You didn't fall under his spell?"

Callie laughed. "I admit he has great charisma. You've noticed it too?"

"Me?" Brian paused to check traffic before making a turn onto the street. "Not so much," he said, "though I admit the guy has a way with people. He's probably the most successful shop owner in the Cove, so his customers obviously love him."

"What does he sell?"

"Glass thingamajigs. You know, old perfume bottles, glass animals, things like that."

"Which is what I first thought Krystal Cobb sold. I wouldn't have guessed Duane for that kind of shop. How do you know he's so successful?"

"From his spending. He recently did a major remodel of his cottage, I mean, top to bottom from what I hear. He must have a dozen cell phones by now, since he always has the latest model in his hand. He took a nice trip to Hawaii last winter. And he ... " Brian stopped, staring at the hood. "Hear that?"

Callie shook her head. All she heard was the usual running motor sounds.

"Hmm. I thought I heard the carburetor ... " Duane Fletcher's personal luxuries were dropped as Brian's interest and speculation turned to his car and its possible problems.

Thankfully for Callie, they'd neared *House of Melody*. As he pulled to a stop, Brian made a move to get out but Callie held him back.

"Don't bother. I'll go through the shop and out the back to my cottage."

"You're sure? There's no danger of another Elvin scare. But Elvin isn't any danger at all, you know."

"That's what I've come to realize. Poor guy. Well, thanks again!" Callie climbed out, her shop key in hand. Once inside, she waved one hand out the door to Brian before closing and locking it.

As she wound her way through the shop by the light from the street, she paused a moment in front of Grandpa Reed's music box.

All remained silent, and Callie continued on.

Eleven

"Cream and sugar?" Delia called from her kitchen. She'd invited Callie to her cottage for late-morning coffee, since Keepsake Cove shops didn't open until noon on Sundays. It was Callie's first visit to Delia's cottage, and she was fascinated with the different look it had from her own, despite the similar construction. Delia favored a Victorian style, which she'd expressed through things like camel-back loveseats, fringe-trimmed lampshades, and curio cabinets filled with many kinds of collectibles, including, of course, salt and pepper shakers. She also had a Victorian-style bird cage, inside of which hopped her parakeet, Pete.

"Just cream, thanks. Or milk. Whatever you have," Callie said. She stood next to the ornate, white-wire cage, where she'd been addressing soft greetings to Pete.

"He doesn't talk much," Delia said as she carried a tray into the living room and set it on a mahogany drop-leaf table. "Yet," she added as she raised one leaf of the table. "We're working on it." She handed

Callie her coffee in a delicate china cup on its saucer, saying, "I know. It's small. But I brought the pot along for refills."

"It's lovely," Callie said, meaning it, as she sat on one of the love-seats to take a sip. "And the coffee's great."

Delia held out a plate of cookies and tarts, leftovers, she explained, from the association meeting, and then settled on the opposite love-seat. "My cups may be fragile, but my coffee's always strong. What did you think of the meeting last night?" She took a swallow from her own cup that drained half of it before looking over for Callie's answer.

"Interesting. A great introduction to Keepsake Cove in general." Callie paused. "And Duane Fletcher in particular."

"Oh?"

Callie smiled and shook her head. "Not in that way."

"He does have a way about him, though, doesn't he?"

"He does. I understand Aunt Mel stirred up a bit of controversy over him."

Delia sighed. "It was so silly. All she suggested was what made total common sense for any group. But people rushed to Duane's defense as if she'd accused him of something."

Callie took a bite of her cookie. "Do you think she actually was? I mean, did she have her suspicions but then couch them in that general proposal?"

"Suspicions that Duane might be pilfering?" Delia shook her head firmly. "She never said anything at all to that effect, at least not that I ever heard."

"Brian said that Duane seems to be quite a bit more successful with his shop than anyone else in the Cove."

"Yes, and that might make a few people jealous. Not Mel, though, of course. She never thought that way. Duane is actually just a darned good salesperson."

Callie paused. Delia had a much more positive opinion of Duane than Brian or Laurie Hart. Who was right, and what was anyone's opinion actually based on? Had Delia simply succumbed to Duane's "spell"? She was a good friend of Aunt Mel's, and she'd been wonderful to Callie. But that didn't mean she was automatically right about everything. Or wrong, either.

"How did Duane and Aunt Mel get along after she spoke up?"

Delia hesitated, then grimaced. "It was tense."

So, Callie thought, he did take it personally, and his seeming sadness over Aunt Mel's death may have been an act. Had his offer to throw open his treasury records for examination been bogus? An offer he was sure nobody would take him up on?

Delia refilled Callie's coffee cup and her own. Pete, the parakeet, then drew her attention with sudden activity and chirping. She went over to talk fondly to the bird. "He's telling me he wants his cage moved outside—I think. I've started doing that, and he seems to really like it. Ever had a parakeet?" she asked Callie, who admitted she had not.

Sensing that Delia had had enough talk about Duane, Callie let the subject drop and chatted about birds and pets. As it drew close to time for both of them to get to their shops, she grabbed one more cookie, then helped Delia carry cups and plates to the kitchen.

"By the way," Callie said as Delia began rinsing their cups, "I came across a second cell phone of Aunt Mel's in one of the drawers. It appears to have been kept in use, but there was nothing on it. No contacts, no messages, nothing. Do you have any idea why she would have had it?"

Delia continued rinsing her cup, then set it very carefully on a kitchen towel. She stared at the cup for a few moments before answering. "I don't know, Callie. But I had my suspicions."

"Oh?"

Delia turned to look at her. "Mel and I were good friends. But that didn't mean we knew everything there was to know about each other. Mel had her secrets, as most of us do, and if she chose not to share them with me I didn't pry. But now that she's gone ... "

Delia sighed, and Callie wasn't sure if it was from grief over her lost friend or for what she was about to say. Finally the older woman spoke.

"I think there was someone in her life, someone she couldn't tell anyone about."

"By someone, you mean ... ?"

"A romantic relationship."

"Oh. And if she couldn't tell anyone ... ?"

"He might have been married. Mind you, I'm just guessing," Delia said. "But it's an educated guess. A few times I popped into *House of Melody* when things were slow and caught Mel on her phone. She always ended her call immediately and slipped the phone into a pocket with no explanation. Not that I demanded one, but friends usually offer it, don't they, even if it's just a 'had to check with a customer' or something like that? But who hangs up on a customer in such a hurry? Then there were overnight trips when she'd ask me to look after Jagger but gave me a very vague story for where she'd be. Mel didn't lie. But when she didn't talk much about her activities, it kind of waved a red flag for me."

"I see." Callie frowned, taking that all in. Aunt Mel had never so much as hinted at having someone special in her life. "I had wondered a little why she'd remained single. It's sad, isn't it, and frankly surprising if she was in a relationship she had to hide."

"As I said, I don't exactly know. But that might be the reason for the second cell phone."

"Yes," Callie said, but also thinking *maybe*. Then she remembered the locked metal box, which she'd put back in the hall closet. What did it contain?

Time for talk was over, as they both needed to open their shops. Callie looked forward to the half-day, to be followed by a full day off on Monday. Her things were scheduled to arrive from Morgantown then, and after a full week of stepping into Aunt Mel's life, it would be great to reclaim some of her own.

Sunday afternoon brought loads of vacation shoppers to Keepsake Cove, many heading to or from Ocean City and other Eastern Shore spots. In chatting with her customers, Callie learned more about her surroundings, including the quaint waterfront village of Oxford, whose bookstore, *Mystery Loves Company*, occupied a building that had once been a bank. She determined to make time soon for a visit. But how far was Oxford? Brian's earlier suggestion of a bike excursion came to mind, but she stuck with her decision to put that kind of thing off for the time being. A solo drive would do.

Tabitha wasn't scheduled to come in that day, but Callie was pleased to see how comfortable she felt handling the shop on her own. Most of the music boxes she sold were bought as gifts, but she pulled up Aunt Mel's notes for one customer who introduced herself as a regular and was able to guide her toward items that were to her taste—music boxes with a *Wizard of Oz* theme that had been newly stocked. She enjoyed seeing the excitement on the woman's face and was even happier to make the sale.

When things grew quiet, Callie stepped out the shop's front door to breathe in a little fresh air and feel the sun on her face. It was a beautiful day, the slight breeze and strong sun having dried up all the previous day's rain, and Callie savored it. She thought of installing a small bench in front of her window, for herself as well as a convenience for customers, and wondered if there was any town regulation against it. If there wasn't, though, Karl Eggers was sure to complain. But that would be his problem.

She caught sight of a familiar figure walking toward her—Elvin Wilcox. He looked much less forbidding in bright daylight than in the shadows, especially as he spotted her looking at him and quickly ducked his head. But he continued to approach, and nodded politely when Callie said hello.

"I'm looking for work," he said, coming right to the point. "Miss Reed always hired me to cut her grass."

"Oh!" Callie's grass between the cottage and the shop actually did need cutting. She was sure it hadn't been touched since before her first visit, but she hadn't had the time to even think about it.

"I'd be happy to have you cut it, Elvin," Callie said, "but what about a lawn mower?" Elvin obviously hadn't brought one with him.

"I use Miss Reed's. It's in the back shed."

"Ah." Callie had meant to investigate the shed tucked in the shady area behind the cottage. Now, she supposed, was a good time. She checked up and down the street and saw no customers heading her way, so she beckoned Elvin to follow her around to the back. The door to the shed was unlocked, which might have surprised her except that the contents were unlikely to tempt any burglar. Aunt Mel's simple push mower sat among a few basic gardening tools and a half empty bag of mulch. Callie knew she could probably handle cutting the grass of the small yard herself, but with her day off to be filled with unpacking and Elvin standing expectantly beside her, she was fine with handing the job over.

She asked Elvin what he charged, then waved toward the mower. "Let me know when you've finished," she said. "I'll be in the shop."

With no chug of a gas-powered mower to remind her, Callie soon forgot about Elvin as she became once again occupied with customers. So she was surprised when he eventually walked in, grass clipping clinging to his now-sweaty denims.

"All done?"

He nodded, and Callie opened her cash register to pay him.

"Miss Reed had me come once a week in the summer," he said as he pocketed his money.

"I'm not sure I'll need that as often. Can I just call you?" As soon as she said it, Callie bit her tongue. Someone in Elvin's circumstances wouldn't have a phone, would he? But he surprised her by reciting a number, and she made a note of it.

Elvin left without further comment, and Callie walked to the back office to make a quick check of her yard. All looked fine. It was later, after she'd closed up and gone outside, that she winced, spotting a few flowers that had been mowed down. Easily replaceable, she assured herself. She continued on to the shed and found her mower back inside but the blades clogged with cut grass. Plus the door had been left swinging open.

Not the greatest job performance, but Callie supposed allowances needed to be made. She sighed, decided to clean up the mower later, and went inside to deal with dinner as well as get ready for tomorrow's delivery.

Twelve

Callie's small living room was filling rapidly as the men from the moving truck steadily carried in her things. She had grossly underestimated the size and amount of her belongings, which seemed to be expanding like a sea of giant Chia pets in the room.

"Where do you want this?" one stocky man with muscular arms asked, holding a large black hassock wrapped in clear plastic.

Why had that come along? Callie hadn't asked for furniture, and if she had, she wouldn't have wanted that ugly piece, which would be totally out of place in Aunt Mel's decor.

"Would you like it?" Callie asked.

The man studied it. "Sure."

"It's yours," Callie said, happy to sign whatever would take it from her sight.

When the crew finished, Callie gazed around with despair. The living room was piled high, and that was only what she could see.

More boxes and bags crowded the upstairs hallway and bedrooms. She closed her eyes and wished it would all just disappear.

Jagger, who'd dashed up the stairs and under a bed at the first tramp of strangers' feet, peeked through the railing from the top stair.

"All is clear," Callie assured him.

But then a voice called "knock-knock" at her front door, and Jagger pulled back and disappeared. Annie Barbario, Brian's sister, stuck her head in the doorway. "Can you use some help?"

"Could I! Are you really offering?"

"Sure!" Annie stepped in, looking very unlike a mother of two in her ponytail, shorts, and tee. "We watched them unload from the café. I was helping Brian clean up his shelves and figured you'd have a lot to deal with."

"But ... your own work?"

Annie shrugged. "Brian can finish it. I didn't think we'd need his help here. But he said to call if we did." Annie glanced around. "So, what do we have here? Mostly clothes?"

"Clothes, books, odds and ends. Far too much to keep. There's not much room." Callie was still stunned by Annie's generous offer. She barely responded when Delia peeked in as well.

"Come on in," Annie said, waving her inside. "Callie's stuff needs sorting, right, Callie?"

"Big time. I couldn't run up to Morgantown to do it, so everything other than what I turned over to Hank got packed and sent here. I have no idea where to start."

"How about ... " Annie covered her eyes and spun around twice, pointing at a big box when she stopped. "There!"

"Might as well," Callie agreed, laughing. She opened the box up to begin pulling shirts and pants from plastic wrappings.

"What do you think of separating like we did with Mel's clothes?" Delia asked as Callie's clothes began to scatter. "A pile for what you'll definitely keep, another for what you won't, and one to think about. We'll ask and you decide."

"Sounds good," Callie said. "After that, I think I'll need to separate out winter things to put into storage. There's just no way I can fit everything into these closets."

"That's what I do," Delia said. "I mean, keep things in storage." She opened a box near her and lifted out an armful of knit shirts. "Brian, too?" she asked Annie.

Callie had forgotten that Brian likely lived behind his café, and she glanced over at his sister.

"Brian probably owns exactly two of everything," Annie said. "Dress slacks, jeans, button shirts, and tees. No problem there, other than keeping up with laundry."

"Men have it so much easier," Delia said.

"Someone—one of his customers, I think—told me that Brian gave up a job in DC to open up his café," Callie said as she worked at emptying her box. "Is that right?"

"Yup." Annie held up a light cotton jacket, got a nod from Callie, and carried it over to the hall closet. "He was a government affairs representative at the Airport Authority. Hated it." Annie laughed. "As I said, he's a bit of a control freak. He likes to make his own decisions, not take orders from someone or to have to oversee others." She held up a trench coat. "Winter or summer?"

Callie considered. "Fall and spring, actually. Hall closet, I guess—until it gets too stuffed. How did Brian decide to run a café?"

"He used to come out to spend a day or a weekend with us and got to really like the area and the slower pace."

"I like that, too," Callie said, and Delia nodded vigorously.

"The café went up for sale," Annie continued, "and it was a snap decision. I couldn't believe it. My brother, who weighs pros and cons endlessly before making any decision, changed careers in a second."

"He must have been ready," Delia commented. "There's a box full of heavy sweaters here. How about I just mark it for storage?"

"Might as well." Callie said. "I've got another box here full of wool stuff. Let's put both outside for now to make some space."

The living room started reappearing as they carried items upstairs and broke down empty boxes. Callie made coffee and offered tuna salad sandwiches, which was all she had on hand. Delia pitched in, chopping celery and onion as Callie stirred together mayonnaise and tuna and Annie continued unpacking. Jagger, who clearly had supersonic ears, flew into the kitchen at the first hiss of the can opener into a tuna can, and within minutes all were contentedly refueling.

By the middle of the afternoon, Callie collapsed the final box and announced that they were done.

"Yay!" Annie cried, doing a little dance. She then pulled out her phone. "Brian, we need you for hauling." Callie began to protest, but Annie waved her down. "He'll love feeling useful," she said, pocketing the phone. "Any preference for the donations?"

Callie looked blank for a moment, and Delia reminded her of the charities she'd sent her aunt's things to. She also recommended her storage facility, which had smaller, climate-controlled units perfect for clothing. By the time Brian showed up, destinations had been decided, with Callie's discard bags and storage boxes ready to be divided up between Brian's car and her own.

"This is just what you're getting rid of?" Brian asked, looking as though he imagined Callie's upstairs to be packed floor-to-ceiling. Which wasn't so far from the truth, Callie admitted.

"Never mind," Annie said. "Just open your trunk."

Callie joined Delia in setting off to the storage facility, waving a grateful goodbye to Brian and Annie, who would head in another direction. With Delia's help, Callie arranged for and unloaded her winter clothes into the storage unit, knowing she would return in a few days with sturdier plastic containers to replace the cardboard ones. She then locked it, and they both dusted off their hands.

Delia brushed off Callie's effusive thanks, but as they returned to the car, Callie asked a question that had just occurred to her. "Did Aunt Mel have a storage unit?" She didn't remember any comment to that effect by her aunt's lawyer, George Blake.

Delia shook her head. "She claimed she didn't need one. Mel was a lot like Brian as far as keeping her things to the minimum. I don't know how she did it."

Callie wasn't sure if she was glad not to have one more thing of her aunt's to sift through or disappointed that there was no other source of answers to the mysteries that were gathering. Then she thought of the locked metal box on the floor of the hall closet. If she couldn't find the key, there was surely some way of getting into it.

But not right away.

First, she needed to catch her breath after the grueling hours she'd just spent. After that, her cupboards, which were exceedingly bare, had to be restocked.

∞

Callie had paid for her groceries and was pushing her cart toward the store's exit when she heard her name called. Turning, she saw Jonathan Harman picking up his own small bag at the end of the express check-out aisle.

"Hello again," he said, coming over. "I saw you earlier as I drove by your shop. The moving truck had just pulled up. Everything go all right?"

"It did, thanks to plenty of help from my wonderful neighbors. If they hadn't shown up—unexpected, mind you—I'd still be wallowing in unpacked boxes. As it was, it took three of us to handle it all."

"Sounds exhausting. I'm sorry I didn't think to stop. Let me make it up to you by taking you to dinner."

"But ... " Callie waved toward her cartful of food.

"It can all be stowed, right? Don't tell me you feel like cooking to-night?"

Callie grinned tiredly. "Not in the least. But I'm also a mess." She had showered but thrown on the first things she could dig out—rumpled shorts and a tee. Her hair, though freshly shampooed, had been simply tied back.

"Don't worry about it. The only dress code at Dino's Diner is shirt and shoes, and the menu is full of comfort food." Comfort food sounded great to Callie. Her weak protests having been swept away, she agreed.

Jonathan followed her to *House of Melody* and helped carry her bags into the cottage, where she quickly popped several items into the refrigerator and freezer. She left her car behind, then, to climb into his.

Callie felt a moment of awkwardness as Jonathan pulled away from the curb and passed Brian coming from the other direction, both cars moving slowly enough for Brian to spot her perched in the passenger seat. It would be the second time he'd seen her with Jonathan, and she hated to think he might misinterpret the situation, especially after she'd turned down his initial tentative overture. Jonathan had been very clear that these dinners were strictly platonic, which was perfect for her, but there was no way she knew of to explain that to Brian without embarrassing them both.

Thankfully, she was soon able to think of other things as they arrived at the diner and were quickly shown to an orange-seated booth. She accepted a huge laminated menu and began to study it.

"They're open till the wee hours," Jonathan said. "I sometimes stop in when I've been working late."

"Do you cook much for yourself?"

"I do when I feel like it and have the time, which doesn't come up that often."

Callie knew the feeling, though she'd stocked up that evening on ingredients for actual cooking at the cottage. No more opening cans of soup. Well, at least less of it. She should probably fix a nice dinner for Jonathan sometime soon, to thank him for his thoughtfulness. But perhaps invite Delia or Tabitha, too, just to avoid sending the wrong message.

She decided on macaroni and cheese, which brought back cozy childhood memories, and asked their waitress to add a salad to it. Jonathan chose beef stroganoff.

"They have really fast service," he said, "which probably means very little is fresh. But I figured you'd want to turn in early and not dawdle."

"You were right. This is so nice of you."

Jonathan shrugged. "Everyone in Keepsake Cove is nice," he said with a grin.

Callie nodded, her thoughts flying to the three helpful people of that afternoon. But then she remembered Karl Eggers. And Duane Fletcher had come across as nice, but at least some people had reservations about that.

"Do you happen to know Duane Fletcher?" she asked.

"The glass-collectibles guy? I've met him."

"But don't really know him?"

"No, other than that he clearly likes his luxuries."

"I've heard comments on that. Would you say his shop does well enough to support them?'

"Hard to say. The couple of times I was in the shop, it was quiet, but it could have been just an off-time. He also might draw income from other sources, such as investments."

Yes, that could be it, Callie thought, glad to have a reasonable explanation.

"However," Jonathan went on, "when I threw out a few investment terms, he didn't seem familiar with them." He shrugged. "Who knows."

Yes, who really knew? But Callie found herself wondering, along with Laurie Hart and possibly Aunt Mel, if the association should be checking up more on its treasurer.

Their food arrived, and Jonathan asked if Callie found the books he'd given her at all helpful. She admitted she'd only had a chance to skim a few chapters but that they looked quite interesting.

"I'm feeling less overwhelmed now," she said, "and should be able to really study them. It's amazing what having your own things around you again can do to one's frame of mind."

"You must feel less like a visitor and more like a real resident."

"Exactly. I've finally started to put down roots. I like it."

"Well, here's to the future success of *House of Melody* under the management of Callie Reed!" Jonathan lifted his water glass as a toast and Callie tapped hers against it, smiling but also ruefully thinking that, wonderful as it was, she'd still willingly give it all up to have Aunt Mel back, alive and well.

Deep down, Callie knew that her aunt would have helped her improve her life in other ways by giving her the needed advice and encouragement. They had just started to move in that direction when Aunt Mel died. It shouldn't have happened. Something was so wrong with the way her aunt died, though Callie didn't know what. The best way to thank Aunt Mel for all she'd received from her would be to find out the truth, whatever it turned out to be.

The macaroni and cheese worked its magic, and when Jonathan suggested dessert, Callie had to fight off a yawn while she shook her head. She passed on coffee, too, feeling more than ready to head on home, though she tried to cover it and urged Jonathan to order coffee for himself.

Jonathan claimed to have a busy day ahead, probably picking up on Callie's weariness, and asked for the bill. Within minutes they were heading back to her place. As they rode, Callie mentioned her encounter with Elvin Wilcox after he'd dropped her off the last time.

"He was in your yard?" Jonathan asked, shocked.

"He was hiding from your headlights, which apparently bothered him. I got the impression he felt comfortable at my aunt's place. She must have been good to him."

"But at night? That sounds like lurking to me."

"Brian Greer talked to him about it. I don't think it'll continue. And I plan to get motion-sensor lights."

"Good idea."

Jonathan pulled up in front of her shop, and, after turning off his ignition, reached for his seat belt. "I'll walk you back," he said.

"No, please, that's not necessary," Callie insisted, regretting that she'd brought up the incident, which Jonathan probably took as a plea for protection. "I'll be fine. I'll flick my outside lights to confirm that, once I'm inside. Okay?"

"Well …"

Before he could say more, Callie jumped out, thanking him, and hurried to the path along the privacy fence. Once in her cottage, she clicked her lights as promised, then heard the sound of Jonathan's car restart and drive away. She glanced into her kitchen, which still had unpacked bags of cereal and canned goods and considered putting everything neatly away. But she veered toward the stairs instead, picturing the soft bed waiting for her.

Jagger apparently thought that was a fine decision, as he followed along closely at her heels.

The woman behind Callie in the check-out line kept poking her. Stop that, Callie wanted to say, but she couldn't get the words out. Poke, poke, poke; the sharp finger jabbed against Callie's shoulder, even though it was clear there was no way Callie could move forward. How could she, when she was blocked in front by a huge ... bear! The bear turned and said ...

Callie woke with a start. What was that? She sat up, blinking. What had wakened her? As her eyes adjusted to the faint light seeping through her sheer curtains, she realized Jagger stood at the end of her bed, his back arched. A deep, warning growl rumbled from his throat as he stared at the window.

"What is it?" Callie whispered. Was it Jagger's movement that had wakened her? She threw back the covers and eased out of the bed, noting that the cat didn't turn his head her way. His posture and stare remained frozen, pointing toward the window.

Fully awake by then, Callie crept toward the dormer window, every nerve on edge. She leaned on the small window seat and pulled back the curtain, at first seeing very little. Her yard and the back of her shop were dark, cast in shadows as the light from a partially covered moon angled over her shop toward the cottage. Then movement caught her eye. Jagger's, too, as he instantly leaped from the bed toward the glass.

The sound of the large cat bumping against the window with a piercing yowl caused whoever was at the shop's back door to whirl, swinging a hand-held light toward Callie, who instinctively jumped back. But she caught herself quickly and lunged for the sash, unlocking and throwing it up.

"Who are you? What are you doing there?" she shouted.

The flashlight went dark, as did the yard. Callie could barely see the dark figure anymore, but she heard footsteps running.

"Stop!" she cried, but the steps pounded faster.

Thirteen

allie ran downstairs and hit the switch to her outside lights. Adrenaline on high, she yanked her front door open. The shock of chilly night air against her skin stopped her. Was she crazy? She closed the door and called the police.

The siren and flashing lights had barely reached *House of Melody* when her phone rang.

"Callie, it's Delia! Are you okay? What's going on?"

"A burglar. Trying to get into my shop, I think. The police are here. I'll call you back."

Callie had no sooner pressed *end* than her phone rang again. It was Brian.

"Do you need help?" he asked, adding he could be there in seconds.

She repeated what she'd told Delia. "Gotta go," she said. Wrapped in her trench coat, her feet jammed hurriedly into clogs, Callie opened the door to the two approaching patrolmen and described what she'd seen. Though she assured them all was well in the cottage, they insisted on checking that for themselves before moving on to the shop. She watched through the cottage window as they did so, having been told that others were combing the surrounding area for a fleeing suspect.

After what seemed like hours, a young patrolman reported back. "No sign of anyone, ma'am. The back door to your shop, however, was slightly ajar. You said you'd left it closed and locked. Are you sure about that?"

"Yes, absolutely!"

"Because sometimes people forget," he said. "It happens. They have other things on their mind, or they get distracted."

"No, I'm sure I locked it."

He looked annoyingly unconvinced but asked her to come with him into the shop and check for any signs of disturbance. She did so, going over every inch of the shop, and saw nothing missing or out of place.

"Which probably means I stopped him before he got inside," she said, still assuring the officer that the door had been locked.

"Yes, ma'am. We'll send someone to dust for fingerprints," the patrolman said. He looked young enough to have been in elementary school when Callie finished high school, but he still managed to project a superior air of authority. She also detected in his tone an implication that further investigation would, of course, be a waste of time, but that they'd go through the motions. Had he been one of the responders after she'd found Aunt Mel dead? She didn't like to think so but couldn't really say.

She thanked the man, then watched as he returned with his partner to their patrol car. Delia hurried over within seconds from her side of the shrubs, a long jacket thrown over her nightgown and her hair, free of its pins, hanging below her shoulders. She'd obviously been watching and waiting until all was clear. Brian arrived as well, and Callie told them everything in detail, gratified to see no signs of skepticism in either face.

"The guy—I'm assuming it was a man, though I can't be sure—somehow got my shop's back door open, though nothing on the door or its window was broken."

"Better get your locks changed," Brian said. "Maybe your burglar was an expert lock-picker, but I'd guess someone with that kind of skill generally heads for more lucrative prey."

"Brian's right," Delia said. "You'd better change them. Mel might not have been super careful with her keys. I've had one to her cottage for looking after Jagger when she was away, but not to her shop. Maybe Tabitha does, I don't know, and I wouldn't suspect her for a moment of anything shady. But who knows where it might have been mislaid for someone else to get their hands on it?"

"I can give you the name of someone in town who replaces locks fast and reasonably," Brian said.

"And I'll return the cottage key," Delia said.

"Don't be silly," Callie said. "You're probably the person I trust most in this whole town. And you're a very close second," she said to Brian. Then she looked over at Karl Eggers's house, which had remained dark and silent during the entire episode. She didn't say it out loud, but she couldn't help thinking that her neighbor on that side would have to be a very sound sleeper to have missed all the commotion. Delia and Brian gazed in that direction as well but kept their thoughts to themselves.

"Would you like to stay at my place for the rest of the night?" Delia offered, pulling her jacket tighter as a chilly breeze stirred her hair. "My spare bed is always made up."

"Thanks, but I'll be fine. No one's likely to try anything again tonight." Callie had a sudden thought that gave her a shiver. "But first

I'm moving something." She hurried back into the shop and carefully lifted Grandpa Reed's music box off of its shelf. When she carried it outside, Brian and Delia were still waiting.

"Just to be on the safe side," she said, patting the music box.

She sent them both off, apologizing for the disturbance that cost them a good night's sleep. Both Delia and Brian waved that off, as if responding to a neighbor's screams in the middle of the night was as normal as, well, helping her unpack and handle her copious belongings. Callie realized how extremely fortunate she was to have them in her life.

She closed and locked her cottage door, then returned her treasured music box to the roll-top desk, carefully locking that up, too. Instead of heading back to bed, she found the box of chamomile tea that she'd opened for her first morning in the shop, wanting its calming actions once again. Though she'd managed to hold it together well enough in front of the others, the truth was the entire incident had shaken her thoroughly. Now that she was alone, she knew there was no way she was going to simply fall back to sleep.

Callie carried her steaming mug to the living room, wrapped a cozy throw around herself, and settled onto the blue and white sofa. She curled her feet under the throw just as Jagger jumped up. He offered his head for scratching, and Callie was glad to oblige.

"If it weren't for you," she said, "I might never have awakened, and that burglar would have gotten away with whatever." As she said it, though, she remembered the dream that she'd had. Someone was poking her. It had felt so real.

"Was it you?" she asked the cat, but she couldn't picture that. Jagger had been poised stiffly at the end of her bed when she woke, not by her side. She took a long sip of her tea. She knew what Tabitha would say. That it was Aunt Mel. Callie shook her head, but there, in the pre-dawn hours of her dim living room, the idea didn't seem that fantastic.

"Miss Reed! I heard about what happened last night. Is everything okay?" The thin, older man, not much taller than herself, popped into *House of Melody* within minutes of Callie opening her shop. His appearance struck her as quite mouse-like, with a near-total grayness that began at his sparse hair, continued through a colorless shirt and slacks, and ended in somewhat-scuffed Hush Puppies. His agitated manner accentuated the image. He thrust out his hand. "Howard Graham. Owner and operator of *Christmas Collectibles*. We're across the street from *Shake It Up*."

Callie shook his hand, addressing him as Mr. Graham.

"Howard," he corrected quickly. "I would have dropped by when you first moved in, but my wife had surgery—knee replacement—and I haven't been in all week."

"I'm sorry. I hope she's recovering well?"

"Yes, thank you. Painful, but she'll be fine soon." His glance bounced around the shop as he spoke. "Our niece was able to keep the shop running for us for a few days. We don't live here in the Cove, so I didn't hear about your break-in until this morning."

"An attempted break-in," Callie said.

"So nothing was taken? And no damage? That's been our fear, ever since we opened. Our collectibles are so fragile. Glass ornaments, you know, and such. If vandals broke in, it would be a disaster!" He fairly shook at the thought.

"I imagine several shops are in the same boat." Callie thought of Delia's salt and pepper shakers and, of course, Duane Fletcher's glass collectibles. Her music boxes might not be as delicate, but they would certainly suffer. She had to admit she'd been thinking of her burglar mostly as a thief, not a vandal, and glanced at the shelf that had held

Grandpa Reed's music box. She doubted any thief would consider it valuable enough to steal, but how awful would it be to find it smashed!

"We thought of installing an alarm system," Howard said. "It's expensive, so we've put it off. But now ... " He looked at Callie rather accusingly, and she wondered if he held her responsible somehow for that added cost. But then he shrugged. "Well, that's the way it goes." He stepped toward the door. "I'd better get back. I just wanted to say I'm sorry about your scare. Let's hope the police catch the culprit and that'll be that."

By the time Tabitha arrived, the locksmith Brian recommended was already at work. "What's up?" Tabitha asked, looking puzzled as she eased by the man and his tools. She was dressed that day in flowing chiffon, and she clutched the edges of the material carefully to herself. The locksmith looked just as perplexed at the sight of her as she was with him but said nothing.

"Replacing the locks," Callie explained, then examined Tabitha's costume. "Ophelia?" she ventured, flashing on a familiar film version of *Hamlet*.

"Galadriel," Tabitha corrected. "From *The Lord of the Rings*?" she added at Callie's blank look. "One of the royal elves."

Callie nodded then. "Right."

"Of course, I don't have Cate Blanchett's fabulous hair. But I do what I can. So why are you changing the locks?"

Callie told about the almost-break-in of the previous night—or early morning—leaving out her strange dream. The locksmith, she figured, had enough oddities to deal with for the moment.

"Ohmygosh!" Tabitha cried. "Did they catch him?"

Callie shook her head. "He ran off as soon as he realized he was spotted. The police told me they put out an APB on him, but no success."

"Yeah, I guess it would be easy to disappear in this town at night. Was he all in black?"

"Dark clothes, hiding in dark shadows. I can't even say for sure that it was a *he*."

"Bummer." Tabitha scowled, her hands on her hips, looking much less ethereal and fairy-like than on her arrival. "Why here?" Her gaze roamed the shelves. "Is there a black market for music boxes somewhere?"

Callie shrugged. "The police thought he might be hoping to grab some quick cash—which I don't keep around—or maybe the office laptop. Who knows? The puzzling part, and the reason I'm replacing the locks, is that the lock didn't appear forced."

"Really! Wow."

"And before you ask—"

Tabitha held up her hand. "Wouldn't even think it. I've seen how careful you are. You wouldn't forget anything like that."

"Thank you. I'm not sure the responding officers were convinced. For all I know, they suspect that what I saw was just shadows from swaying trees. They sent someone to dust for prints on the door and also took mine. But I washed down the outside of the door just the other day. Elvin had left dark smudges on the white paint."

"Elvin?"

"He cut my grass on Sunday afternoon. When he was done, he must have tried to come in through the back door to let me know. But I'd left it locked, as usual." Callie sighed. "So anyway, since the door was just washed, the only prints they'll likely find are mine."

"Because your burglar wore gloves."

"Probably."

The middle-aged locksmith packed up his tools and stood with a slight wince. "All done, ma'am. Front and back." He locked and un-locked her door twice before handing over the new keys. "If you need more of those, I can duplicate them easily at my shop."

Callie took them, along with his bill, and set about writing out a check. "Do you get a lot of people bringing in keys to get copied?" she asked.

"Oh, sure. All the time."

"And you'd have no idea … never mind." She'd wanted to ask if the key someone brought in could be verified as belonging to that person but realized that sounded pretty ridiculous. She handed over the check and thanked the man for his prompt service.

When he was gone, Tabitha wandered between the shelves of music boxes, her gown flowing lightly. "I don't understand, Callie. There's no good reason for someone to try to break in here."

"What you said about a black market for music boxes made me wonder. Maybe I should be looking into those high-end ones in the glass cases? Could they be particularly rare?"

"I doubt it. Mel ordered almost all of her stock through the usual companies. You could check, though. What woke you?" she asked, getting back to the burglar. "Did he make some kind of noise?"

"No." Callie grimaced, then told her about her vivid dream.

"Ahhh."

"I know what you're thinking. But it was just a dream."

"Callie, I believe there's no such thing as *just* a dream. You were getting a message. A warning." Tabitha's gaze rose over Callie's shoulder. "Where's Mel's music box?"

"I took it back to the cottage, to be safe."

"Well, there you go. That's probably what Mel was worried about. That her family's music box was in danger."

"Or maybe that her entire shop was in danger. Assuming it was Mel waking me up, that is. Which we don't know."

Tabitha's lips curled wryly. "Oh, we know."

Callie smiled. No use arguing. If Aunt Mel really was looking out for her, why not just take it as a good thing? And if it was all simply coincidence and in Tabitha's imagination, well, who did it hurt? Might as well just roll with it.

Movement at the door caught her eye. "Looks like we have a customer," she said.

Time to move on to more worldly things.

Fourteen

By that evening, the stress of the previous night's burglar, dealing with the police, and the subsequent loss of sleep caught up with Callie, and she thought longingly of her soft bed as she returned to her cottage. But the living room and much of the upstairs was still a cluttered mess, and bags from her grocery shopping sat on the counter, unpacked. She groaned and muttered "important things first" as she quickly fed her hungry cat. Then she dropped onto the blue sofa and kicked off her shoes, leaned her head onto the back cushion, and closed her eyes.

That's when the phone rang.

It was Aunt Mel's landline, the handset sitting on the end table near the door. Callie seriously considered letting it go but wondered if it might be the police, who had taken both her cell and the cottage's numbers. She dragged herself up to answer.

"Hey, babe!" that too-familiar voice greeted her, prompting a second groan.

"How did you get this number, Hank?"

"It's listed, babe," he said, his tone strongly implying *duh*. "You haven't been picking up on your cell. What's she got there? One of those black rotary dials? Or is it hanging on her wall with a crank on the side?"

Callie ignored the question. How old did he think Aunt Mel had been? Ninety? "What do you want, Hank?"

"Just want to hear your voice again," he said, and Callie's eyes rolled. "Get your stuff okay?"

"Everything came yesterday." It felt like weeks ago rather than a day. "You have the TV, right?"

"Yup. But I'd rather have you here."

Somehow, Callie doubted that. "Look, Hank, I've had an awfully busy couple of days—"

"Thought I'd come down to see you."

"No! You can't."

"Why not?"

"Because I said so," Callie said, knowing she sounded just like her mother. But wasn't that what her relationship to Hank had become, parent and child? He, of course, being the child.

"Listen, Hank. No visits. It's over. We're done. Please, just let it go and move on."

"But babe—"

"Goodbye, Hank. Enjoy your TV," Callie said and hung up. As she stood by the phone, a short trill sounded from inside the roll-top desk, and Callie didn't even flinch, having almost expected it. Had Tabitha's convictions gotten to her? Callie shook her head. More likely exhaustion had hit her.

With hopes that dinner would perk her up, she headed into the kitchen. Her grand plans of actual cooking had flown, and she opened

115

her freezer to pull out one of the heat-and-eat dinners she'd bought for emergencies. To her mind, this qualified. She peeled off the plastic and popped it into the microwave. Instant fuel, if not flavor, was on its way.

By the time she progressed to a healthy dessert of fresh cherries, Callie felt energized enough to put away the rest of her groceries. That done, she brewed a small pot of coffee and carried a mugful into the living room, thinking she might work at one of the boxes of books that awaited her. But first she'd enjoy her coffee.

As she relaxed on the sofa, sipping, her gaze wandered about before landing on the closet door, and she thought of the locked metal box inside. Organizing her books became much less important.

What might be in that box? How would she get into it to find out? Those questions and more ran through her mind as she stared at the door. She set down the coffee mug and went to retrieve the box, now pushed behind her own winter boots and partially covered by a long winter coat. She pulled it out and set it on the coffee table. She'd already checked all of the keys from the ring George Blake had given her with no success. Aunt Mel must have had a key to the box, but it hadn't been on the key ring, nor had Callie come across any stray keys when sorting through her aunt's things.

She thought of the locksmith who'd just changed the shop locks. Could he pick this one for her? She supposed he could, but did she want him to? She didn't know what they'd find inside. How many sets of eyes would Aunt Mel have wanted to see it? The locksmith was out. Callie would break into the box herself.

She went into the kitchen, to the drawer that contained Aunt Mel's small collection of tools. Pawing through them, she selected a screwdriver and a hammer and carried both back to the living room. She set the metal box on the floor, then knelt down and pried the screwdriver into the slit between the lid and the bottom half, just over the lock.

She hammered at it, once, twice, several times, over and over. She was just about to give up when it broke.

Callie set down her tools and stared at the box for a few moments. Then she tried to lift the lid. The resulting dents from her hammering made it difficult, and she had to pry and jiggle. Finally it lifted, and she looked inside.

What she first saw were envelopes and loose papers, exactly what she'd heard when she first gently shook the box. She pulled them out and laid them on the floor next to her. At the bottom of the box was a clear plastic container with a corsage inside, the flowers long-dried and the pink ribbons holding them together faded. She lifted the corsage box out to examine. No label or note identified it, but she saw a pink plastic band attached to the flowers, making it a wrist corsage. It had to have been from a prom. She couldn't imagine wearing a corsage of that type anywhere else.

Setting it aside, she picked up the largest envelope. It had her aunt's name, *Melodie*, scrawled on it, and inside was a Valentine card covered with red hearts, lace, cupids, and bows. Inside, on a slightly yellowed page, a neatly rhyming verse offered sentimental thoughts, finishing with "I Love You." That line was underlined three times with exclamation points added. It was signed, *Tom*.

Who was Tom?

The signature was only three letters, but the handwriting, with its carefully rounded letters, looked young, possibly teenaged. That fit with the corsage, to Callie's mind, though there was no indication that they'd come from the same person. The verse, though, was simplistic enough to appeal more to a young person, along with the elaborate decoration. She opened a second envelope and found a birthday card, just as ornate as the Valentine card, with professions of love. It, too, was signed *Tom*.

From the yellowed condition of the paper and the similarity of the signature, Callie put the two cards into the same time frame. Possibly Aunt Mel's high school years? It was a guess, but along with the corsage, she thought it was likely. Since they'd apparently been hand delivered and were undated, those small clues were all she had to go on.

The loose papers, with their ragged edges, looked torn from a large notebook and folded several times. Scribbled notes, possibly passed during class? These were unsigned, but had messages like *Late practice today—will miss you!* or *Movie Sat. nite with Jake and Tina?* There were dozens of these, and Aunt Mel had cared enough about them to save them. Callie smiled to herself as she realized that now these messages would be sent by text. Her aunt was fortunate to have the paper versions to collect and savor.

Callie had sorted through most of the notes before coming across one of a very different kind. This one was on actual stationary but still undated. It looked like something that would have been mailed, but its envelope was missing. The writing was more mature, but to Callie's inexpert eyes, there were similarities to the teenaged scribbles. The note referred to a meeting with Melodie after so long and the happiness it had brought. It was brief and signed only with *T*. Tom, of course. It had to be.

Callie leaned back on her heels, absorbing what she'd just found. Was this the person that Delia suspected was secretly in Aunt Mel's life? A high school romance revitalized years later? If so, why the secrecy? Because Tom was married seemed the most likely explanation, but that didn't fit with the Aunt Mel that Callie knew or that all her friends knew. Callie just couldn't see her aunt acting selfishly, in a way that would hurt someone—Tom's wife. But Callie could vouch for the fact that love sometimes had a way of overriding a person's better side. Still . . .

She wished she knew more about Tom. The notes told her nothing other than that her aunt had cherished them. Had love blinded her, though? Had Tom possibly used Melodie, convinced her that their relationship couldn't be out in the open when in fact this was convenient only for him?

If Tom had a wife, had she been oblivious to the affair? Aunt Mel had obviously been cautious, but had Tom? If his wife had found out, what would she have done? Had there been a strong reason that convinced Aunt Mel to agree to the secrecy? Perhaps Tom's wife was unstable enough to hurt him. That fit better with Callie's knowledge of her aunt's character—that she would want to safeguard him. But then why conduct the affair at all?

Or would Tom's wife have come after Mel? Callie flashed on the vision of her aunt's body, lying on the floor of the shop in a pool of blood, and her stomach clenched. Could a vengeful woman have caused that?

She glanced toward the roll-top desk. The music box inside was silent. What that meant, if anything, Callie didn't know. Maybe, she thought, it simply meant that its playing at odd times was total coincidence.

She looked back at the array of papers. Was she making too much of them, or could she truly connect them to her aunt's death? The secrecy troubled her. People sometimes killed to keep secrets from coming out. Might Tom, the person Aunt Mel seemed to have sacrificed so much of her life for, have decided he couldn't afford the risk anymore? That struck Callie as a more horrible scenario than a vengeful wife. But in one way it was more credible. Tom could have asked Aunt Mel to meet him in the dead of night for whatever concocted reason, and she would have trusted him enough to do so. Callie pictured her aunt stealing silently down the cottage steps that night while her niece slept, then letting Tom into the shop for the supposed urgent meeting. When she happened to turn her back to him, he could have struck in a way that made Mel's injuries appear accidental.

Callie hated the image she'd conjured but admitted its possibility. At this point, though, she was aware it was all imagination without a shred of proof. She suddenly flashed to her almost-burglary. Was there a connection? If Aunt Mel's death was, in fact, murder, might her burglar have been the murderer, returning for some reason?

The thought was one that she knew had been lurking, deep down, but that she'd only now allowed to come forward. But was it true? It was one thing to conjure up speculations. What she needed was more information. That included finding Tom.

Fifteen

Callie spent the remainder of her evening searching through Aunt's Mel's bookshelves, which she and Delia had left intact in the guest bedroom. Though the room was small, the shelves covered much of the wall space and held an extensive collection. The search for a high school yearbook, which might have identified Tom, proved fruitless and gobbled up hours, some of that coming from being side-tracked too often by other books.

As she slipped wearily into bed, Callie considered the fate of her own yearbooks. She'd left them at her childhood home, assuming somewhere in the back of her mind that her room and its contents would be preserved museum-like, waiting for her to take the notion of reclaiming them. In fact, items deemed worthy of saving had been gradually packed up by her mother and moved to the attic. Would that have been the same for Aunt Mel's high school memorabilia?

Her aunt had inherited Grandpa Reed's music box collection. She'd probably handled his estate, including contents of the house she'd grown up in. But if she'd left behind some of her own things years before, would they have survived? Only Aunt Mel and Grandpa Reed could answer that. If anything of Callie's father's had been sent to him at that time, Callie wasn't aware of it, and his too-early death meant she couldn't ask him.

She turned off her light and willed herself to turn off her overly active thoughts. They'd kept her going through her exhaustion for several hours, but she needed to rest. She was sure they'd be waiting for her in the morning, hopefully with fresh ideas.

❧

Callie was right. Within seconds of opening her eyes the next day, she knew what to do: contact her mother. Easier said than done, though, because her mom was off on another trip. Where was it this time? Callie grabbed her phone to search through emails for recent ones from Elizabeth Reed Jablonski, her mom's name since remarrying. She found one and was reminded that her mother and stepfather had flown off to Tahiti on their latest excursion.

Could she reach them? She had no idea where the pair might exactly be at the moment. Traveling through a mountain area with sketchy cell phone service? Nor did she know if either of them had adapted their phones to that location. Neither Elizabeth nor Frank worried much about keeping in touch when they were away, preferring to "immerse themselves in the experience" as they put it. All Callie could do was try.

She typed an email—her mother's preferred form of messaging—and asked where her father had gone to high school, figuring Aunt Mel would have attended the same one. She added hopes that her mom and

Frank were having a wonderful time and hit *send*. Then she headed for the shower. Time to get ready for a new day at *House of Melody*.

∾

Tabitha arrived that morning dressed quite normally, something nearly as startling to Callie as her assistant's first "Joan Crawford" appearance had been.

"The cards advised it," Tabitha explained, looking just a bit uncomfortable in a plain white cotton blouse paired with black slacks. Her thick, chestnut-colored hair hung simply, one side pinned away from her face with a plain barrette. "I think of it as a kind of creative cleansing," she added. "A way of clearing the path to new possibilities. I hope your customers will understand."

"I'm sure they will," Callie said, intrigued to see the real Tabitha for the first time.

"They had advice for you, too," Tabitha added.

"They?"

"The cards. I did a reading on you—you know, because of your burglar."

"Okay ... " Callie said, not sure how she felt about that but willing to listen. "What kind of advice?"

Tabitha's face turned solemn. "They warn that you should be very cautious about any new friends right now."

Callie digested that for a moment. "The only problem is that everyone here in Keepsake Cove is new to me."

Tabitha dismissed that difficulty with a head shake. "It might not be clear right now, but in my experience what the cards tell me is usually spot-on. I'd take it very seriously."

123

Callie could see that Tabitha certainly did. "Then I will, Tabitha. It would help if a name were given, or even an initial."

"It doesn't work that way. Just think hard about any new friends you've made or might soon make."

Callie didn't have to think too hard about Delia, Brian, or Annie. She was sure they'd pass the "card" test. Tabitha, too, of course. Was Jonathan Harman becoming a friend? More of an acquaintance, she felt, or friendly customer, though he'd shown himself to be very thoughtful. Did the cards think she needed to be cautious of him? Hard to imagine.

Karl Eggers certainly wasn't on the friends list, and Callie had no idea what that meant as far as the cards were concerned. Were they saying she needn't be cautious with him? Then there was Elvin Wilcox, who was in another category altogether. She'd met several of the Keepsake Cove shopkeepers, who couldn't be called friends yet but might eventually be. Callie thought she'd always been reasonably careful with new people, though admittedly under simpler circumstances in the past. Now she was very much on her own, stepping into Aunt Mel's life, in effect. And Aunt Mel's sudden and mysterious death, along with other events, had put her pretty much on edge. Being cautious, therefore, was a given.

Tabitha had gone back to the office to unpack a new order of music boxes when a large, dark-skinned woman dressed in a flowing red dress came into the shop.

"What's this I hear about a burglary? Are you all right?" A multicolored scarf, wrapped once around her neck, hung gracefully below her hips. She looked Callie over from head to toe before circling rapidly through the shop and answering her own question. "Everything looks in good shape. Excellent!"

"Um, have we met?"

The intense expression left the woman's round face as she laughed heartily. "I forgot! We almost met that day you came to visit Mel. It was all she talked about, and when I saw your car with those West Virginia plates parked out front, I almost stopped in. But then my husband texted me to hurry back, that we had a flood of customers. So what could I do?" She laughed heartily but then grew solemn. "I was at the funeral. But I know how that goes. Am I right?" she asked kindly, and Callie nodded silently.

"Orlena Martin," the woman said, first holding out a hand but then engulfing Callie in a great hug instead. When she released her, she pointed down the street from the Keepsake Café, in the direction Callie hadn't visited yet. *Treasured Boxes*. You have boxes with music. I have boxes to fill with treasures. But they're wonderful treasures in themselves. Come see them. You will be amazed."

"You will, Callie!" Tabitha called out from the office. "Hi, Orlena."

"There you are!" Orlena cried. "I wondered. And what are you today?"

Tabitha stepped into the office doorway, her box cutter in hand. "Today's a rest day. The cards called for it."

"Aha. Rest is good." Orlena's smile was understanding, and Callie liked this new acquaintance, pretty sure that Tabitha's cards would approve, too. "I didn't hear about your burglar until this morning at the café," Orlena said to Callie. "My husband and I were off all day yesterday searching for new treasure boxes, or I would have been here first thing."

"So you don't live behind your shop?"

Orlena grinned. "That little dollhouse? You haven't seen my husband or you wouldn't ask. No, we need space. So, what was your burglar after?"

"That's a good question. Since he never made it in, I can only guess," Callie said, not anywhere near ready to share her wild guess of a murderer returning to the scene. "Howard Graham of *Christmas*

Collectibles suggested vandals, but I don't know. There was only one person. I had the idea that vandals worked in groups."

Orlena frowned. "Sometimes yes, sometimes no. But vandals like to cause destruction for their own idea of fun. That means noise. Lots of noise. If they have half a brain—and who knows if they do?—they would know they'd wake the town."

"This person was definitely being quiet."

"So what told you he was there?"

Callie hesitated, aware of Tabitha listening for the answer. "I'm a light sleeper, and so is Aunt Mel's cat," she answered.

"Oh, Jagger! I'm so glad you kept him, and it sounds like he has repaid you for your kindness. Well, happily there was no harm done then, right?"

"Right."

Orlena gave Callie a second great hug and turned to leave. "I will post on the Keepsake Cove website that we should all be extra alert."

"Has this kind of thing happened much in the Cove?" Callie asked, following Orlena to the door.

"Not at all. Our little community has been very peaceful and crime-free. Perhaps because we're tucked away here on the Eastern Shore, which is not so highly populated, you know? The people who are here have been around for generations—the watermen, the farmers—and by and large they are good people. Or it's people who have retired here from the cities across the bridge and tend to behave themselves. Of course, we draw vacationers on their way to and from the beaches. But they're looking for fun and relaxation, aren't they?" Orlena frowned. "That's why what happened is so shocking. We're just not used to this kind of thing."

Me neither, Callie thought.

"Were you at the association meeting?" she asked aloud, not remembering having seen Orlena there.

"No," Orlena said. "I keep in touch with what I need to through the website. I don't enjoy squabbles."

"Do you mean over the long-term treasurer?"

"Exactly."

"Does that mean you're okay with Duane Fletcher's handling of the group's finances?"

"No, my dear, it does not. But sometimes," she said, "it is wiser to be silent." With that enigmatic comment, Orlena swept out the door, leaving behind a puzzled Callie, who turned to Tabitha for help.

"That's just Orlena," Tabitha said with a shrug. "She likes drama. She might say more on the subject in time, but it'll take work."

Callie thought that Orlena's sudden reticence seemed a sharp contrast to the outgoing liveliness she'd first demonstrated. Was she hiding something? If it had anything to do with Duane and Aunt Mel's conflict, Callie wanted to know about it. But how would she go about prying it out?

At lunchtime, Callie left Tabitha at the shop and headed over to *Kids at Heart*. She'd decided to talk to Bill and Laurie about Duane Fletcher, since it was Laurie who'd first brought up the controversy over him. She hoped Laurie might have more to share.

The day had grown quite warm, with the humidity inching the air toward stifling, and Callie was glad she'd put on a sleeveless cotton dress that morning. Hank had once described its color as "Pepto Bismol pink," and this snide remark had kept her from wearing it much back in Morgantown. She smiled, thinking that choosing the dress that day without a second thought was a very positive sign.

She passed by several shoppers fanning themselves, sipping giant iced drinks, or dealing with dripping ice cream cones, and when she stepped into *Kids at Heart,* the rush of air conditioned air, even after her short walk, was a wonderful relief. Bill and Laurie were talking with a man near the back of the shop, who Callie assumed was a customer until she recognized Howard Graham, the shopkeeper from the day before who'd been upset over her almost-burglary. He looked a little less colorless this time, wearing a printed shirt tucked into his gray slacks. But the blue in the print was pale and barely stood out over a dingy white background. Howard, himself, seemed as agitated as he'd been when she'd met him.

Laurie waved her over, ready to start introductions until she saw that Callie and Howard knew each other. "We were just counting up the members who would support us in getting an audit," she said. "Are you in?"

"An audit on the association's books?"

"It's the only way," Laurie said. "Duane has years' worth of record books. None of us has the time or expertise to examine all of them, and he knows that."

"Hiring someone would be expensive," Bill said.

"But it could put a plug on future loss," Howard piped up. "Who knows how much might have already gone missing?"

"*Might* is the operative word," Bill said.

"Oh, Bill," his wife said, rubbing his shoulder. "Can you really overlook his lavish lifestyle and—"

"Lavish lifestyle?" Bill laughed. "I haven't noticed any diamond pinky rings or champagne-filled Jacuzzis on his premises."

Laurie bit back a smile. "That's not what I mean and you know it. We can estimate pretty closely what all our shops here in Keepsake Cove bring in—some a little more, some a little less. We're all making a living, but nobody, other than Duane, is taking round-the-world vacations or buying new cars every year."

"He's single, Laurie. Fewer expenses," Bill argued, though somewhat weakly.

"We should get an audit," Howard said. "That way we'll know for sure."

"Is it the expense that's stopping you?" Callie asked.

Laurie nodded. "It will have to be voted on. Duane has plenty of friends who'll vote against it. The same ones who want him to remain as treasurer. We'll need votes for our side. Can we count on you, Callie?"

Callie hesitated. "I'm a newcomer to this, Laurie. I know my aunt started the whole thing, but from what I understand, she only proposed limiting the treasurer's term."

"Which was obviously because she thought Duane should be removed."

"Not so obviously, honey," Bill said. "It was just a proposal for the association's rules."

"I'm wondering if Duane's having such supportive friends says a lot about him? I mean, as far as his trustworthiness?" Callie asked.

Laurie shook her head firmly. "The man's a world-class schmoozer. You met him. Didn't he come across as your new best friend?"

"Well ... "

"Right. It works on a lot of people. It's how con men work."

"That's exactly right," Howard said. "And I don't want a con man handling my money!"

Bill sighed but appeared to give up. Laurie and Howard looked at Callie expectantly.

"Let me think on it a bit," she said, and saw their disappointment.

"Don't take too long," Howard said. "We need to plug this hole! I don't intend to finance another trip to Tahiti unless it's my own!"

Bill groaned, and Callie figured it was time to take off. She promised to get back to them soon. Once out the door, she pulled out her cell phone. The mention of Tahiti had reminded her to check for an answering email from her mother. But all she found were spam emails about online dating and digestive aids. Since she was interested in neither, she tucked the phone away, looked around, and thought about what to do next.

Sixteen

After wandering up and down the street in the hot sun, grow-ing warmer but not in regards to finding what she was searching for, Callie finally stopped a cheerful-looking woman with a Keepsake Cove shopping bag over her arm and asked if she knew where the glass collectibles shop was.

"You mean *Glorious Glass?*" The woman set down her bag, handed a large drink cup to Callie to hold, and rummaged through her large purse, finally pulling out a wrinkled Keepsake Cove brochure that located all the shops on a map. "Here's where we are," she said, pointing with a sparkly painted nail, "and here's where you want to go." She traced a dark line until it turned right, off the main street. "You can't miss it."

Callie thanked her and took off, finding the shop easily with the map she now had in her head. The window of *Glorious Glass* glittered with all things imaginable made of glass, in every shape, size, and color. Callie gazed, her head spinning as she thought of needing to keep track of such a vast inventory. Her music boxes were hard enough, but their size kept their numbers far lower than Duane Fletcher's.

She saw Duane through the window, sitting alone behind his counter, and hesitated, unsure exactly what she hoped to accomplish by being there. Then he looked up and spotted her and waved for her to come in. She headed for the door.

"Welcome, welcome to my little shop," Duane said as he bounced up. "Nothing so grand as yours, of course, but I'm proud of it."

"It's beautiful," Callie said, blinking as the overhead lights reflected off the countless glass figurines, candy dishes, perfume bottles, and vases. "Glorious indeed!"

Duane beamed. "The name comes from my mother, Gloria. It was her love of all things glass that started it all. She amassed a wonderful collection. When she died, it just made sense to bring it all here and carry on in her memory."

"That's similar to the beginnings of *House of Melody*."

"Mel and I talked about that. And we're not the only ones. Most of the shopkeepers here in the Cove have turned their personal collections into a business. It's wonderful to get paid for working at something you love."

"It is, as long as it can support you."

"Of course. And I've been very fortunate in that. Very fortunate. But," he said, lowering his voice although there was no one around to hear, "it's also drawn a bit of envy, I'm afraid."

"Really?"

He nodded. "It's to be expected, I suppose, though it hurts. I've worked hard at my business and reaped the rewards. I've also tried to do my bit by pitching in with the Keepsake Cove Association, and believe me, the treasurer's job is time-consuming, tedious work. But I've been happy to do it, to help out, you know? But doing for others,

I've found, can turn around and bite you." He brightened. "But never mind! You're not here to listen to my little problems. Tell me, how are you settling in?"

Since Duane didn't ask about her burglary attempt, Callie assumed he hadn't heard about it yet, and she decided not to mention it. Instead, she talked about the customers and inventory she was getting to know. It was nothing terribly fascinating, but she saw—and enjoyed—the same intense interest from Duane that she'd experienced at the association meeting. But his bringing up the controversy over his treasurer-ship surprised her, vague though it had been. Duane had seemed genuinely hurt by it, but she couldn't help wondering if that was one of the ways he'd gained sympathetic supporters. Had he been enticing her to join that group, or was he truly a wronged innocent?

The shop phone rang, and Duane excused himself to answer it. Callie turned to browse through his collectibles as he did so, only half-overhearing until she caught the words "cruise" and "Mediterranean." At that point Duane said "hold on" and punched a button on his phone before setting the receiver back in its cradle. He then hurried to a back room, and Callie heard only murmurs as he apparently continued the conversation on another extension. If he was planning a nice trip, as it had sounded, Callie could well imagine how Howard Graham would react to that.

Duane returned in a couple of minutes without explanation, and his eyes went to the butterfly paperweight that Callie had picked up to admire.

"Lovely, isn't it? You have excellent taste," he said. "It comes from Greece. I love the colored glass of the wings and the tiny bubbles in the globe it's resting on. Would you like it?"

"Um ... " Callie hesitated, appreciating the piece but not having thought in that direction.

"I don't mean to buy. I meant as my gift."

"Oh, I couldn't possibly—"

Duane raised a hand to stop her. "I'd love for you to have it. It'll be my 'welcome to the Cove' gift. A sadly belated one." He took the delicate piece from her and carried it to his counter, where he quickly slid out a box and packing materials.

Callie followed, surprised but also pleased. Though the paperweight wasn't outrageously expensive, it was an unexpected and thoughtful gesture.

"Thank you," she said when he handed the box to her. She lingered a few more minutes to chat before taking off, smiling and cradling her new treasure. It wasn't until she got back to *House of Melody* and saw Tabitha dealing with one customer while two others browsed through the shop that Callie realized no one else had entered *Glorious Glass* the entire time she was there.

⚒

Once things quieted in the shop, Callie unpacked her glass butterfly to show Tabitha, who oohed and ahhed but then said, "I hope you're paying attention to the warning about making new friends."

"No worries. I'm still in the getting-to-know-you mode."

"Okay then." Tabitha turned the paperweight over carefully in her hands for one last examination, then set it back on the counter. "Nice of Duane," she said. "Mel had one, you know. A paperweight, I mean. Not of glass, and not a butterfly. It looked like a souvenir from someplace. Some kind of historic building or house."

"I don't think I've come across that."

"I remember her using it to hold down all the paperwork that was piling up from the committee she was heading."

"For the association?"

"Right. It was for Memorial Day weekend, to, you know, draw the crowds. Mel arranged for all the outdoor decorations like flags and flowers, an artist to do charcoal sketches, strolling musicians, and advertising, of course. And she had to keep track of the bills to hand over to Duane."

"Uh-huh." Callie was glancing around for a safe place to keep her new paperweight for the time being. It wasn't going to be put to work anchoring papers, that she knew.

"But you know how organized she was," Tabitha said. "She scanned them, too."

"The bills? Did Duane ask her to do that?" Callie settled on the empty spot where Grandpa Reed's music box had been.

Tabitha shook her head. "She did it for herself. She said she didn't want to take a chance that any of it got lost. Which, frankly, I considered a waste of effort, because, you know, if someone didn't get paid, they're going to be sure to send a second bill, right?"

"Right." But Callie had formed another interpretation of what her aunt did. A customer walked in, and she let Tabitha take care of it as she followed her train of thought. By "got lost," was Aunt Mel concerned about something else once the bills were in Duane's hands?

When Tabitha was free again, Callie asked, "Did Duane know that my aunt had scanned all the committee's bills before she turned them over to him?"

"Duane? I don't know. She never said."

Callie strolled over to straighten a music box that had been shifted out of place. Then she asked, "So Mel volunteered for a lot of committees?"

"Lots, mostly for holidays. She headed one around Easter, and another for Small Business Saturday right after Thanksgiving. For, you know, Christmas sales."

"And scanned the bills?"

Tabitha shrugged. "Don't know. I only remember that last one, Memorial Day."

They both grew busy then as a group of women, apparently all friends, flooded in, resulting in much chatter and several satisfying sales.

❧

Later on, after Tabitha had left and things had grown quiet, Callie went to the back office to do a search through the laptop there. It didn't take her long to find what she was looking for. Mel's photo files for May of that year held several scans of committee expense reports, saved as jpegs. Callie studied them briefly, then looked for scans around Easter but found none. She then checked each month's photo files, going back to December, but there were no other scans.

Aunt Mel had apparently started the practice only on her last committee job. Why? Had she begun to notice a discrepancy between what she thought had been spent on behalf of the association and what Duane claimed to have paid out? Delia had told her that things had become tense between Mel and Duane. Might that have been due to more than just her aunt's proposal to set term limits for the treasurer? If so, what had it led to? Violence?

A vision of her aunt being struck and killed in the middle of the night came to her. Callie found it far easier to picture a faceless Tom in that position than someone with whom she'd just had a pleasant face-to-face encounter. But if in fact it was Duane who'd struck, his purpose for being in the shop could have been to destroy Aunt Mel's saved scans, couldn't it?

The laptop, though, had been locked up in the secretary desk. Callie had watched her aunt do it that evening as she'd closed up the shop. Duane, if it had been him, might not have expected that and might have been unprepared to break into the desk. That would then have provided a reason to try to break into *House of Melody* a second time, but with more tools. Could Duane Fletcher have been the burglar? Callie tried to think whether the shadowy figure she saw from her window had Duane's rounded shape, but she couldn't say for sure.

She shook her head, knowing that, as with Tom, this was all conjecture. She was able to come up with motive but no actual evidence for either of the men, which meant there was nothing she could do beyond carefully filing it all away.

Her concentration was suddenly broken by shouts out front. Recognizing Karl Eggers's voice, Callie hurried to her front window to see Elvin cowering under a barrage of threats, and she grabbed for the door. As soon as she stepped out, Eggers turned his wrath on her.

"You! You're part of the reason this bum hangs around here. The other part is Greer over there, handing out free food." Eggers glared across the street toward the Keepsake Café.

"Don't call Elvin a bum," Callie said. "He's a hard worker and earns his money."

"At what? Jobs a ten-year-old could do in half the time? You hire him for things like that and he's always around, scaring away my customers. I won't have it!"

"You have nothing to say about it, Mr. Eggers. I'll hire exactly who I want. If you're losing customers, it's more likely because of you causing a scene like this."

Eggers glared at her. "You're no better than your aunt. Trouble-makers, both of you."

Callie felt steam rise at that comment, but before she exploded, Jonathan pulled up and jumped out of his car, asking Callie, "What's the problem here?"

"This—" Eggers began, but Jonathan cut him off.

"I asked *her*."

"My neighbor doesn't approve of my choice of handymen," Callie said, still struggling to control herself. "Or my genes either, it appears."

"Your ge—?"

"I won't have derelicts loitering around my place," Eggers said, shaking a fist. "I'll get the police to take him off if he comes around again."

"No police!" Elvin cried, suddenly backing away.

"There won't be any police," Brian called as he burst out of his café and strode across the street, a white apron tied at his waist. "Eggers, leave this guy alone. He's not hurting anyone's business by being here." He put a calming arm around Elvin's shoulder.

"Then take him into your café," Eggers challenged gruffly, "and see what happens."

"No problem." Brian turned to Elvin. "Want a chicken pot pie? I've got plenty."

Elvin looked back and forth uncertainly between Karl Eggers and Brian and finally nodded. Eggers spun around without further comment and stomped back into *Car-lectibles*.

"Thank you, Brian," Callie said.

"Good going," Jonathan added, and Brian's gaze shifted from Callie's face to his in surprise, as if he'd only just realized Jonathan was there.

"Don't let Eggers scare you," Brian said to Callie. "He can be loud, but it's a lot of bluff and bluster." He gave Jonathan a single nod before turning Elvin toward his café. "C'mon. Let's go get that pot pie."

Jonathan watched for a moment, then said to Callie, "Glad I happened by."

Callie smiled, though aware that Brian was who'd gotten the situation under control.

"Was he right, though?" Jonathan asked. "I mean, does this guy Elvin hang around a lot? He was skulking in your back yard the other night."

"Just that once. He does come around looking for work, but not just here. For other shops, too."

Jonathan looked uncertain. "I heard about the incident you had here the other night. The break-in?"

"No actual break-in. Just someone attempting it, I think."

"Yes, well, could it have been Elvin? I mean, I see he's got problems, but ... "

Callie shook her head. "No, it wouldn't have been Elvin. Why would he ... " She stopped herself. Why wouldn't it have been him? She had no real basis for ruling the man out.

"Did you see anything to help identify the person?"

"No, it was way too dark. But Elvin would have no reason to break into my shop."

"None that you know of," Jonathan pointed out gently. "I'm just saying maybe you should be careful. Just because Eggers is a jerk doesn't automatically mean you can totally go the other way with trusting this guy."

Callie wanted to say *But Brian likes him,* yet she didn't. She knew that Jonathan—and Tabitha's Tarot cards—each had a point: *Be cautious.* That meant no picking and choosing.

Seventeen

*T*hat evening, Callie got the email she was waiting for from her mother. Although understandably puzzled over why Callie would be asking about her father's high school, she produced the name of it: Warfield.

Can't tell you how I happen to remember that, she wrote. *Robert B. Warfield High, to be precise. The older I get, the more I find I'm able to pull up odd things from the past but can't for the life of me remember where I put something important the day before.* She went on to report on her trip experiences and the beautiful scenery, of which she intended to send photos later.

Callie shot off a thank you along with a promise to explain all, soon, and immediately began an online search for the high school. With the full name, the school's website popped up quickly, and she was excited to see a link there to past yearbooks. She'd calculated that her aunt would have graduated thirty-five years ago, so she pulled that year up first. To her dismay, the graduating class was a large one—

over 300 members. Approximately half were male. After sifting through nearly 150 names, Callie had found 38 boys named Tom. She looked at her list, leaned back in her chair, and groaned, especially when she realized Tom might be a year or two older, or even younger, and in another class.

Callie wished mightily that Grandma and Grandpa Reed had been able to afford a small exclusive school to send their children to, or that Tom's parents had been vastly more imaginative when naming their son.

What to do? Callie then remembered that one of the notes from Tom had mentioned late practice, but was it football, baseball, or something else? He hadn't specified, because of course Mel would have known. Scouring through multiple team photos, therefore, wouldn't be of help.

Then Callie saw a link to the person who had organized the class's twenty-fifth reunion: Patty Wilkens. The link was at least ten years old, but it was something. Callie clicked on it and typed out a message explaining that she was the niece of Melodie Reed, who had recently passed away. She hoped Patty Wilkens remembered Melodie from their high school days, since Callie was trying to get in touch with Melodie's good friend, Tom. If Patty could help, would she please respond?

She sent the email off with crossed fingers, hoping first that it was a working address, and next that she would hear back. Emails from strangers, even one containing the name of a former classmate, were too easy to be suspicious of and deleted. After browsing a few more minutes through the yearbook site, Callie checked her email to see if her message had bounced back. It hadn't. Good. Now she could only wait and hope for a response.

The next morning, while opening her shop, Callie saw Brian outside his café, lowering the awning against the morning sun. She stepped out and crossed the street, calling out a greeting as she approached. He turned and looked pleased to see her.

"Might have to replace this thing pretty soon," he said as she drew near, pointing to a worn area above him that looked ready to tear.

Callie looked at the spot and nodded solemnly. "Appears so."

"Sun damage," Brian explained. "That and wind."

"A deadly combination," Callie agreed, which produced a smile from Brian.

"Come in for coffee?" he asked.

Callie shook her head. "I just wanted to say that I thought it was very nice of you to come to Elvin's rescue the way you did yesterday."

Brian shrugged. "I wouldn't call it a rescue. Elvin probably would have been okay with you there, and that guy with you, uh..."

"Jonathan," Callie supplied. "Jonathan Harman. He's a music box collector. And he wasn't actually with me."

"No?"

"He just happened by and stopped when he saw the commotion. But I thought you calmed things down beautifully. I liked that you stood up to Karl's challenge and took Elvin into your café."

Brian grinned. "Karl didn't like it much, did he?"

Callie glanced over at *Car-lectibles*, half expecting to see Karl Eggers's bearded face at the window, glowering at them. "I don't understand why he gets so vehement over Elvin. Yes, Elvin is scruffy. But I don't see anything threatening about him."

"Well..."

"What?"

"There was an incident, once. But it was some time ago." Callie waited as Brian hesitated. "I guess you'll hear about it eventually," he said, "so better from me than Karl."

"What happened?"

Brian checked for anyone possibly heading their way, then said, "Elvin was walking down the street after he'd finished trimming Mel's backyard bushes. It was a hot day, and I'm sure he was tired. A couple of kids, twelve-year-olds on bikes, thought it was a great idea to harass him, zipping around too close, popping wheelies and grabbing at twigs that were stuck in his hair. Elvin doesn't handle being startled well. I'm sure it was that, plus being tired to begin with, that brought it on."

"Brought what on?"

"He went ballistic. Started whirling around and shouting. Scared the kids half to death, not that they didn't deserve it, but also scared several strolling shoppers. Somebody called the police, which only made things worse. I was back in my kitchen and didn't know what was happening until it was too late, or I would have run out to help."

Where did it happen?"

"In front of *Christmas Collectibles*."

Callie pictured Howard Graham quaking at his shop window filled with breakables. He would have been one of the first to press 911 on his phone.

"The police did a good job of calming Elvin down. I'll give them credit for that. But they handcuffed him and took him off, which I was extremely sorry to see."

"Was he charged?"

Brian shook his head. "No, thank God. No one had been hurt, only shaken up. They did see that Elvin got a medical evaluation, and I believe he's continued with some sort of outpatient care—meds, perhaps.

Most people who know him understand that Elvin wasn't to blame for the incident, and that he was acting defensively, not offensively."

"But not Karl."

"Apparently not. But Karl's not exactly a broad-minded person."

"I got that impression, too."

Callie and Brian silently contemplated that for a moment before realizing that Keepsake Cove traffic was picking up and they needed to tend to their businesses. Callie thanked Brian for telling her, then trotted back to *House of Melody* without throwing a glance toward *Carlectibles*, whose proprietor she wasn't in a particular mood to see.

But once back in her shop, she mulled over Brian's story. She felt sorry for Elvin, of course. But it had shown a side of the man that she might need to be wary of. Tabitha's Tarot card warning came to mind, and, much as she privately scoffed at such things, the warning had stuck with her. Brian had stressed that it was an isolated incident and that Elvin, with treatment, was now beyond that kind of behavior. But how could he be sure?

Jonathan's suggestion that Elvin might have been her intruder had also stuck with her, little as she liked it. Though she couldn't think why Elvin would want to break into her shop, she also couldn't totally dismiss the idea. Did someone with Elvin's difficulties act with the same reasoning as everybody else? Could he, for instance, have decided he wanted a special music box and thought that was the only way it could be his? Had he done it once before and in the stress of the situation become violent with the person who tried to stop him?

As she had previously with both Tom and Duane, Callie pictured Aunt Mel coming across an intruder in her shop that night, but this time the face on the intruder was Elvin's. Possible? She had to admit it was, but *probable* was something else.

A customer approached her door, and Callie pushed the thought to the back of her mind to deal with later.

Tabitha had returned to her preferred style of unusual dress, though less startlingly, wearing a 1980s-style shoulder-padded top and tapered pants that Callie thought might still linger in many closets. It was the poufy hair that made the look, and that hairstyle could still be seen around as well. She and Tabitha were chatting about whether the shop should carry musical dolls, as a customer had suggested, when Jonathan walked in.

"What do you think, Mr. Harman?" Tabitha asked. "Would you buy a musical doll if Callie carried them?"

Jonathan, dressed casually in polo shirt and jeans, which signaled he was working from home that day, looked puzzled. "Musical dolls? Uh, no. I didn't know there was such a thing."

Tabitha whipped open a catalogue to show him several pages of mostly porcelain dolls, dressed in elaborate gowns or ethnic costumes. There were a few baby dolls, which apparently played lullabies.

"I'll pass," he said with a grin. "But I guess they'd appeal to plenty of others."

"I'm just not sure I want to go in that direction," Callie said. "I'll think about it."

"I stopped in today on behalf of a client of mine." Jonathan pulled out a clipping of a music box that had two galloping horses pictured on its lid. "She asked for my help finding this for a niece who's crazy about horses. Think you can get it?"

"No problem." Tabitha reached for another catalogue and began paging through it.

As he waited, Jonathan noticed the butterfly paperweight on the shelf behind the counter. "Pretty," he said. "You moved Mel's music box?"

"Back to the cottage," Callie said. "Just for now, to be safe. The paperweight is from *Glorious Glass*, Duane Fletcher's shop."

Jonathan nodded. "So you went over there. What did you think?"

"He has an amazing array of glass items. Not so much with customers, at least while I was there."

"Here it is," Tabitha said. She laid the opened catalogue in front of Jonathan to show him the photo of a horse-topped music box.

"Yes, that's it, and the price looks right. How soon do you think you can get it? My client needs it by Thursday."

"Let me give them a call. Maybe they can put a rush on it."

Callie watched her assistant, impressed once again with her efficiency. As Tabitha got on the phone, Jonathan turned back to Callie.

"Any fallout from last night's episode?"

"No, everything's been quiet. I'm assuming Elvin's fine, especially after being treated to dinner by Brian."

"I may have been out of line suggesting that Elvin could have been your burglar. I was just concerned for your safety. I really don't know the man, other than that he obviously has some problems."

The episode that Brian had shared came to mind, and Callie said, "He does, but I understand he's been getting help. He's trying hard."

"Does he have a job?"

"He picks up odd jobs around Keepsake Cove. He did yard work for my aunt, and I hired him for that a few days ago. No real complaints, other than the loss of a few flowers, which are replaceable."

"Well, I could use some help right now. A small tree came down near my driveway, and I don't have the time or inclination to deal with it myself. I'd like it cleared away. Does he do things like that?"

"I think so. I can give you his number, if you like."

Jonathan nodded. "It's not a huge job, but besides saving me some trouble, it would give me a chance to know the man better. I'd like to be more comfortable with the idea of him hanging around here."

Callie wrote down Elvin's number, pleased that he'd get some work, though not sure how she felt about Jonathan feeling a need to look out for her. But it could be just a neighborly kind of concern, and getting to know and better understand Elvin had to be a good thing.

"They can get it here by Tuesday," Tabitha said, talking about the horse-themed music box. "That okay?"

Jonathan said it was perfect, and she put the order through.

After Jonathan had gone, Tabitha said, "Nice of him to bring you some business. And Elvin, too."

"So you heard that?"

"Some. I was on hold for a while."

"Think Jonathan passes the Tarot card test?" Callie asked, half-jokingly.

Tabitha frowned. "I don't know. I could try to do a reading on him. It's always harder, though, when the person's not right there."

"I wasn't there for the one you did on me."

"Yeah, well ... "

Tabitha hesitated, prompting Callie to ask, "What?"

"It's just ... you're pretty transparent, Callie. Not necessarily to everyone. It might be just to me."

"Transparent?"

"Uh-huh. It's why I came right back here to work for you. I knew right away we'd get along. Our energy clicked."

"Energy?"

"Right. But Jonathan Harman isn't the same. I wouldn't be able to do a decent reading without him being right there, helping."

"He's not transparent?"

"Oh, no," Tabitha said, looking in the direction that Harman had gone. "Great customer and all that, but transparent? Uh-uh."

Callie considered asking Tabitha about other Keepsake Cove folks' energy and transparency but decided to let it go. Tabitha looked at people one way, Callie another. It was probably best to keep them separate.

Eighteen

On her way to grab lunch at the Keepsake Café, Callie ran into Delia coming out of the café carrying a wrapped sandwich and drink. "Thursday special," she told Callie. "Veggie sandwich on nut bread. My favorite."

"Sounds good," Callie said. She realized that Delia, who ran her shop on her own, couldn't leave it for any length of time and therefore ate her lunches alone. "I'm just heading in to pick up something. Would you like company?"

"I'd love it."

"See you in a minute." Callie jogged across the street and was glad to see Annie at the counter when she entered.

"Hey there, music box maven," Annie greeted her. "Great to see you. What can I get you?"

Callie ordered the Thursday special to go, then took a seat as Annie passed the order on to Brian in the kitchen.

"Ready in a minute," Annie said. "Got your stuff all organized and put away?"

Callie laughed at the idea. "Not even close. But I'm working at it when I can."

"Yeah, I heard about the trouble you had that night. Sorry about it."

"Thanks. It could have been worse." Sure that Annie knew the details through Brian, Callie moved on to ask about Annie's family. "Kids still in school?"

"One week to go. With this warm weather they've been champing at the bit, probably driving their teachers insane. We're taking them on a bike ride tomorrow to work off some of that energy. Hey, why don't you come with us?"

Brian appeared then, with Callie's sandwich wrapped neatly in foil. "Come where?" he asked.

"The bike ride. Brian's coming and bringing all the food, right, Brian? We're going after the shops are closed, when it'll be cooler. Come along. It'll be fun!"

"Um ... " Callie said, feeling a bit blindsided though she did like the idea of going with a group. Brian's reaction seemed encouraging. "I'd have to get a bike," she said.

"No problem," Annie said. "We'll scrounge one up for you. Great! Brian will pick you up right after closing and bring you over to our place, right, Brian?"

"Nice of you to let me get a word in, sis. Are you sure you want to go, Callie? Love to have you, but don't let Annie here bulldoze you."

"No, it really does sound like fun. I could use some exercise, and I'd love to meet your family, Annie."

That settled, Callie paid for her sandwich and an iced tea and headed over to *Shake It Up!*, a smile on her face as she anticipated the excursion.

Delia was just finishing with a customer as Callie arrived. She pulled up an extra chair behind her counter for Callie.

"Business always seems to pick up when I'm ready for a break," she said, spreading out her brightly colored maxi skirt as she sat. "Let's hope we'll have a few minutes to ourselves."

"Have you always run the place on your own?" Callie asked, opening up her sandwich packet. Annie had added paper napkins to her bag, and she spread one out on her lap.

"Pretty much. I've hired an occasional helper—college kids on summer breaks, mostly. But there was a definite lack of enthusiasm, other than for their paycheck, and by the time they learned enough to be a real help they were heading back to school."

"Tabitha's been a Godsend for me." Callie bit into her veggie sandwich, her eyes lighting up as she chewed. "This is great," she said after a few moments.

"I knew you'd like it." Delia took a sip of her drink, then said, "Tabitha's a gem. If she had a clone, I'd hire her in a flash."

"She thinks I'm transparent."

Delia smiled. "That's probably Tabitha-speak for she likes you."

"I met Orlena Martin yesterday. Nice lady."

Delia, her mouth full, nodded.

"She got a little mysterious at one point, though."

"Mysterious?"

"She was lively and outgoing until the subject of Duane Fletcher came up. Then she suddenly clammed up. It was like she knew something but wasn't willing to talk about it."

"I don't know what in the world she would know that she couldn't say out loud," Delia said. "I wouldn't take it seriously. There's been too much innuendo going around about Duane, in my opinion."

"I stopped in his shop yesterday," Callie said, wiping her mouth with one of her paper napkins.

"Oh?"

"Just trying to get to know as much of Keepsake Cove as I can. While I was there, Duane was on the phone. He seemed to be making plans for a cruise."

"He loves to travel."

"I didn't remember him being at Aunt Mel's funeral. Was he away then?"

"Not on the day of the funeral. But he'd been gone for a few days and came back with a bad cold. He told me he didn't want to spread it around, so he stayed home."

"'Gone'? Like, on another cruise?"

"No, this was work-related. A glass arts show in Baltimore. He took a booth. It's good advertising for his shop."

"When I was at *Glorious Glass*, I didn't see any help. Does Duane close up when he's away?"

"He does," Delia said. "It's one reason I don't do collectible shows. Or take many vacations, either. When I do take one, it's during our slow period in January. I guess Duane can afford to close up shop more than I can."

Callie nodded noncommittally but wondered about the "affording" part. Delia didn't seem to question it, unlike Laurie Hart or Howard Graham, who were quick to consider pilfering. But Callie thought she'd picked up a look on Delia's face and a tone in her voice when she talked about Duane that hinted at feelings beyond neighborly ones for a fellow shopkeeper. She also remembered Delia's response the morning after the association meeting, when Callie had unintentionally implied romantic interest in Duane. Delia had seemed worried, and then relieved when Callie corrected that. Callie could understand the attraction, but she hoped Delia wasn't mistaking Duane's charm for reciprocal interest on his part. Duane, she suspected, turned on his charisma to one and all, and if it turned out that he misled or hurt the dear, sweet woman next door by doing that, Callie would be very upset with him.

A customer came in, and Delia got up to wait on her. As she did, Callie considered what she'd learned: that most likely, Duane had been away on the night of Aunt Mel's death. Did that eliminate him from suspicion? Not necessarily, but she'd see what she could find online about the glass show.

⚬⚬⚬

Her first chance to do so came that evening. With her after-dinner coffee in hand, Callie started a search on her laptop for the show Duane claimed to have participated in. She found *Glass Arts, Baltimore*, an annual event that had taken place the day of and the day after Aunt Mel's death. She clicked on the exhibitors list, which was extensive since the show had taken place at the huge Baltimore Convention Center, and found *Glorious Glass* listed. So Duane had apparently been there.

However, the show's hours were 10:00 a.m. to 9:00 p.m. The medical examiner had given the time of Aunt Mel's death as between 2:00 and 4:00 a.m. Callie wasn't that familiar with Maryland roads, but she quickly learned through the online maps that there was more than enough time for Duane to have driven from Baltimore to Keepsake Cove to be at the shop during that time frame.

That didn't prove that he'd done so, of course. But it didn't eliminate him, either. Callie tucked that information away for the time being, to be called up if needed.

At midday the next day, Callie had left *House of Melody* in Tabitha's capable hands to explore Keepsake Cove a little more when she spotted Elvin in the distance. She skipped several shops she'd intended to visit in order to catch up with him. As she approached, she saw he'd been unloading boxes from a van parked in front of *Stitches Thru Time*, the vintage sewing shop whose owner, the older woman named Dorothy Ashby, she'd talked with at the association meeting.

"Thank you, Elvin," Dorothy said as she handed him what Callie assumed was payment along with a tall glass of ice water. Seeing Callie, Dorothy greeted her but then hurried back into her shop to answer a ringing phone.

Elvin pulled out a raggedy handkerchief to wipe his face before taking a thirsty swallow of his water.

"Hot day for this kind of work," Callie said.

He nodded, holding the cold glass against his reddened face. "Hot yesterday, too, for cutting up a tree."

"At Jonathan Harman's?"

Elvin nodded. "But he called me into his house to cool off a couple of times."

"That's good," Callie said, glad to hear Jonathan had given Elvin the job. She wondered what Jonathan's house was like and was only able to imagine a vague structure surrounded by greenery.

"He has a lot of music boxes," Elvin said, which made Callie smile, knowing she should have automatically put that into her picture. She thought of her speculations about Elvin after Brian told her about the harassing incident. Though she still wasn't comfortable with the idea of this man as a thief or worse, she couldn't let herself totally dismiss it.

"I know Jonathan collects music boxes. Do you like ... ?" she started to ask, but Elvin interrupted her.

"He talks a lot. I have to go back again to finish the job. I could have finished it yesterday if he'd let me."

Callie knew Jonathan wanted to get to know Elvin and wondered how much success he'd had. She could picture Elvin scowling, as he was now, struggling to be polite but unhappy with the loss of time.

"Will that be a problem?" she asked. "Did you have another job lined up?"

Elvin shook his head. "I can do it. It's just ... " He stopped, looking puzzled, then shook his head again. He lifted his glass and drained the last of his water as Dorothy came back outside. As he handed the empty tumbler to her, he suddenly turned to Callie and asked, "Why?"

Surprised, Callie hesitated, unsure exactly what he was asking. She was saved from answering as Dorothy chatted about more deliveries expected and her plan to call Elvin back to help. She also remembered she'd wanted his help reaching something for her and pulled him into the shop. Callie moved on, still wondering what Elvin had wanted to know. Something to do with Jonathan and their conversation? But she thought she'd seen a fleeting look of anxiety in Elvin's eyes, which brought up her own question: *Why?*

Nineteen

*C*allie closed up *House of Melody* a few minutes early that evening, less worried about missing one last sale than she was about the upcoming excursion with Brian, Annie, and Annie's family. She'd realized—too late—that she'd never ridden a bicycle any farther than around her old neighborhood and was having second thoughts about what she'd gotten herself into. Annie's enthusiasm had been infectious, pulling Callie into believing she'd love the outing. But now she pictured herself sweating and panting as she struggled to keep up with a group of experienced riders, all throwing pitying glances her way as Annie shushed her boys' plaintive questions about why they'd brought along this straggler.

At the cottage, she hurriedly fed Jagger, then changed out of her skirt and blouse into shorts and a tee. Sturdy footwear, she realized, would be a good idea, and she dug around her still-disorganized closet until she found the matching left and right shoes of a pair of Reeboks. Sunlight streaming brightly through her window reminded her about sunscreen, and she slathered some on, then found an old baseball cap to plop on her head. Just in time, it turned out, as her doorbell rang. She trotted down the stairs.

As she opened the door, she saw to her relief that Brian was dressed as casually as she was—no serious-looking compression shorts, goggles, or padding. Maybe she'd be able to keep up after all. "Should I bring a water bottle?" she asked, having just thought of it.

"If you want, but we'll have plenty of water with us," he said. "Annie will have an extra bike helmet, too," he said, "so you might want to ditch the cap. Especially," he added, "since it's a Pirates hat. You'll be riding with a bunch of Orioles fans."

"Good point," Callie said, grinning as she snatched it off. She couldn't even remember how she'd acquired the hat. Possibly Hank had gotten it for her—a good enough reason to ditch it for good.

The top of Brian's antique red Impala was down, and as they climbed in he mentioned that Annie's place was just a short drive out of town. Callie saw a large cooler in the back and asked how they were going to manage to carry the food.

"We'll divide it up with everyone. No problem," he said, and Callie leaned back in her seat and buckled up, feeling more and more comfortable about the excursion ahead.

"How old are Annie's boys, by the way?"

"Justin's ten and Ben just turned eight. We'll probably be taking it easy so he can keep up," he said, which Callie thought was excellent news. "We're going to bike over to the cove. There's an area with picnic tables where we can stop to eat. Have you been to the cove?"

"I've hardly been anywhere yet," Callie said. "I'll love seeing the spot that Keepsake Cove is named after."

"Keepsake Cove named itself as the shops appeared. The cove itself is just the cove," he said, raising his voice as the car picked up speed and air whooshed around them. "The Eastern Shore is riddled with them. It's a wonder that it manages to hold together with all the coves, creeks, and rivers that wind through it."

"I remember you said the whole Eastern Shore was pretty flat. No hills to pedal up."

Brian glanced over, seeming surprised that his comment had stayed with her. "No hills to coast down, either," he warned.

"That's okay," Callie said. She was enjoying the feel of the wind blowing her hair. "Ben and I will be just as happy to poke along." She lifted her face to the sun. It felt wonderful to be out.

～

Annie and Mike's house was easy to pick out with two young boys on bikes, obviously eager to get going, circling the driveway. The modest two-story sat on a large lot, its neighbors on each side barely within shouting distance and dense trees at its back. As they pulled up, Callie spotted a vegetable garden on one side, several of its plants already tall enough to be staked. The boys called out greetings, and Annie came out on the porch to wave them all inside.

Brian grabbed the cooler and Callie followed, tramping across the wide porch past white-painted rocking chairs and into the welcoming, comfortable-looking living room. Annie's husband, Mike—a friendly grin splitting his five o'clock shadow—rose from the sofa and was quickly introduced to Callie. Then everyone started talking at once as Annie gave directions for filling bike bags, grabbing helmets, using the bathroom one last time, and heading out the door.

"Your bike is the green one," Mike told Callie as they gathered back outside.

"It's Jenny's," Ben informed her. "She lives over there." He pointed to the brick house down the road.

"I'll try to get it back to Jenny in one piece," Callie said, testing the height of the seat and finding it good.

"We'll go easy on you," Ben said, pulling his helmet over hair as dark as his dad's. "Mom said you're probably not as tough as us."

"Ben!" Annie cried. "That's not exactly what I said."

"That's okay," Callie said, laughing. "I'm sure it's true."

"We won't be going very far," Mike said. "And we stop when anyone calls out that they need a break."

They lined up, Mike in the lead, followed by Justin and Ben, then Annie, Callie, and Brian. Mike reminded the boys of the rules and then they kicked off, the six of them pedaling on the wide shoulder with little traffic to worry about in either direction.

The temperature had dropped from steamy to just warm, and Callie enjoyed the comfortable pace, which allowed her to take in the scenery with minimal pedaling effort. Justin and Ben chattered the entire time, pointing out friends' houses, sharing tales of past rides, or trading jokes. An occasional car horn tooted as it passed by, giving the group a wide berth, and Callie joined in with the Barbario family's waves and calls.

After a good half hour, or so, Mike turned into the picnic area of the cove. Callie pulled even with the others on the lightly graveled ground and braked. "It's beautiful," she said as she gazed around her. The water was clear and calm except for ripples from several paddling ducks. Tall trees shaded the picnic area on each side, and the only sound was the occasional chirp or quack.

"Mom! We forgot bread for the ducks," Justin cried.

"No we didn't." Annie opened one of her bags and pulled out two Ziplocs filled with bread chunks. She handed them to her sons, who quickly ran to the water's edge. "Don't get your shoes wet!" she called. The adults then got busy brushing off one of the picnic tables and laying out the food and drinks.

Once they all settled down and dug in, Callie thought she'd never enjoyed a meal so much, and she said so.

"You worked up an appetite," Annie explained. "Everything tastes great when you're hungry and outdoors."

"Hey," Brian protested. "I put some effort into these sandwiches, you know. No baloney and Wonder Bread here."

Annie laughed. "I know. Just pulling your chain. You did a great job, bro."

"So great," Mike said, "that I'll have another ham and Swiss, if someone will please pass one over."

"That used to be my favorite," Callie said, handing it to him. "Until I tried the veggie." She crunched down on a crisp pickle spear.

"Business doing okay?" Mike asked Brian amiably.

"It's picked up since a certain shopkeeper moved in across the street," he said, grinning.

"Oh, come on," Callie said. "I don't eat that much. And when I do stop in, your place is usually hopping."

"This is Keepsake Cove prime time. Everyone's busy this time of year."

And yet, Callie mused, Duane Fletcher closed his shop two weeks ago to go to Baltimore.

"We're finished," Justin announced, jumping up. "Can we wade in the water?"

"If you stay close to the edge. You know the cove drops off suddenly."

"We know." Justin and Ben had their shoes and socks off in a flash and raced each other to the narrow strip of sand.

"Is swimming allowed?" Callie asked.

"It is, but not for these two," Mike said. "Not until they're older and we're confident about their abilities. For now they swim in our neighbor's pool."

Callie checked the curved shoreline, seeing only dense trees. "I don't see any Keepsake Cove shops. How close are they?"

"They're over to the left," Brian said, pointing across the water to the other side. "See that small clearing? That's another picnic area, just off Keepsake Drive, which bends toward it. Probably a half mile from your shop."

"Really! I'll have to walk over sometime."

Justin and Ben, having had enough of kicking through the water, begged Mike and Brian to play catch, which they willingly agreed to, moving away from the table to an open area. Annie turned to watch her family, a fond smile spreading over her face, and Callie, watching, felt the close bond among the five.

It brought back a long-ago memory of a time she and her parents visited Grandpa and Grandma Reed. Aunt Mel was there, and they were in her grandparents' big yard—or at least it had seemed big to Callie at the time. It was a summer evening like this, and eight-year-old Callie kicked around a soccer ball with her father, who was still healthy and active. Aunt Mel had joined in, she remembered, and the others had looked on as fondly as Annie was now, calling out and cheering for any small successes on her part.

She'd felt happy and so well loved. But now four of those people were lost to her, and the fifth—her mother—was half a world away with a new husband. Not exactly lost, but not in her daughter's life very much, either. Callie knew that was okay. She was all grown up and couldn't expect to be cheered on anymore. She'd been handed an amazing parting gift from Aunt Mel, pointed in a new direction after a wrong turn, and she had her memories.

She watched Justin and Ben laugh as they tossed balls too wild for either Mike or Brian to reach or rushed to stop a missed catch before it rolled into the water. She knew they thought these times would last forever. But things happen. She could only hope for their sake that they happened much, much later.

The noise of a motorboat drew her attention to the cove. She watched as the boat roared closer, a single person, a man, handling it, and she frowned. The noise had destroyed their peace and sent the small family of ducks squawking and scrambling.

"That's Duane Fletcher," Brian said. He'd paused, ball in hand and shielding his eyes from the sun. "Looks like he's got a new toy."

"Another one?" Annie said, and Callie grimaced as she watched the *Glorious Glass* proprietor circle the cove, churning its previously glass-like surface with seeming abandon. Duane, it appeared, had many interests—and many sides to him. Callie wasn't finding this one all that likeable.

Twenty

The next afternoon, Callie went to see Orlena Martin at her shop, *Treasured Boxes*, crossing the street toward the Keepsake Café and then heading left. After his appearance in the cove the night before with his new boat, Duane Fletcher was on her mind, and Callie wanted to pry more information about him from Orlena if she could.

She didn't stop into the Café on the way, preferring to parcel out her time with Brian. She'd enjoyed the bike excursion thoroughly. Annie's family was a delight, and that included Brian. But it was important to her to keep things on a friends basis for the time being. As for later on, who knew? But she didn't want to falsely encourage him. He was much too nice for that.

She approached *Treasured Boxes* and peeked in the window, seeing an array of stunning boxes—large and small, wood, metal, square, heart-shaped, and more. One more example of the amazing variety of collectible merchandise that the Keepsake Cove shops offered.

When she walked in, a customer was just leaving, and Orlena greeted Callie like a long-lost relative, engulfing her once again in a great hug. She wore a different caftan-like dress this time, but it was just as brightly colored. Bracelets jangled on her wrists, and her fingers were loaded with sparkly rings. That, along with the woman's vivid personality, made her an official go-to person, Callie decided, for any perk-me-up days that might occur.

Orlena gave her a tour of the shop, clearly proud of it. She pointed out the uses for various boxes beyond the decorative. "These smaller ones are perfect for special jewelry pieces. Customers sometimes come to me straight from Pearl Poepelman's place, wanting a special gift box for a necklace or bracelet they just bought from her. These larger ones would hold an heirloom family Bible very well," she continued. "And I sold a few of these much bigger boxes to families who wanted to store their father's or grandfather's military memorabilia. I have something for everyone."

"It appears you do," Callie said, picking up an exquisite velvet-covered box topped with an ornate silver medallion.

"That could hold more jewelry," Orlena said. "Then there's these lovely tea boxes, antique salt boxes, and boxes that are simply beautiful to look at."

"They rival my music boxes," Callie said. "And some of those are very ornate."

"Everyone should own something beautiful, something that gives them pleasure just to behold. Don't you think?"

Callie smiled. "I do. Even if it's as simple as a lovely stone or a shell that they found on the beach."

"But much better if they come to my shop and buy." Orlena laughed heartily. "Or your shop, my dear. How can I help you, now that you have seen my wares? I have a feeling you didn't come only for that. Am I right?"

Callie looked over in surprise. Was she as transparent as Tabitha claimed?

"Don't worry," Orlena said. "I am good at reading people. Very helpful for a shop owner. I can usually tell what a customer really wants, even though they might tell me something different. Now, what can I do for you?"

"Well," Callie said, hesitating. "I'm trying to figure out a few things."

"Yes?"

Callie had intended to circle around the topic of Duane Fletcher. But now she was sure Orlena would see through that. She went, therefore, straight to the heart of the matter. "I think my aunt may have been murdered."

"Oh!" Orlena's large eyes seemed to double in size, but she quickly composed herself. "Have you talked to the police?"

"I have no proof. All I have is my own suspicion." And possible messages through Grandpa Reed's music box, though Callie wasn't ready to bring that up. "No one I've suggested it to so far seems to agree, but I just can't buy the idea that Aunt Mel slipped and fell. It doesn't work for me."

Orlena was quiet for a while, and Callie wondered if she'd made a mistake. After all, Orlena didn't really know her. She might think Callie was delusional, or a troublemaker, or worse. But then the older woman said quietly, "It never worked for me either."

Callie let out a sigh. Maybe she wasn't totally crazy after all.

"I never said anything," Orlena continued, "because what did I know about it? I wasn't there, looking over the scene, was I? But I never understood why Mel was in her shop in the middle of the night. Do you?"

"No. I admit I didn't know my aunt that well. We hadn't seen each other for years, though we did keep in touch. So I can't say for sure that this was an unusual thing for her to do. But I do know she was healthy and active. She told me how she walked regularly and enjoyed playing tennis. I know of no reason she would have lost her balance so fatally."

Orlena nodded. "She always struck me as strong and healthy. But if she did not fall on her own, then someone pushed her, or struck her. Who? And why?"

"That's what I'm trying to figure out. Do you have any thoughts on that?"

"I wish I did, my dear," Orlena said, shaking her head sadly. "But because I never truly convinced myself that it could have been murder, I also blocked considerations of who could have done it. We play little mind tricks with ourselves sometimes, don't we?"

"We do," Callie said, again thinking about Grandpa Reed's music box. Had she been doing the same? "Since I can't prove that someone was in the shop at the time of Aunt Mel's death, all I've been able to do is look for motives, and when I think I've found one, I look for opportunity."

"Opportunity? But, dear one, it happened in the middle of the night. Everyone can claim they were fast asleep in their beds."

"I know, and if they were alone, who can prove they were or weren't? So that hasn't eliminated anyone, so far. Next I've wondered who could have got into the shop. It was locked. Did someone have a key?"

"That is something I would not know."

"What about Karl Eggers?" Callie asked, and she saw Orlena's brows shoot up.

"You think Mel would have given Karl a spare key?"

"It's just a thought. I know they weren't on good terms at the end, but were things better in the beginning? Might she have given him a key in the past, so he could watch over her shop while she was gone?"

"Highly doubtful," Orlena said. "Highly. Things were better between them years ago, yes, but that only meant they were on speaking terms. Mel would not have gone to Karl for a favor of that kind. Delia would be much more likely."

"Delia had a key to Mel's cottage but not the shop. That's what she told me, and I believe her. I saw the grief on her face after my aunt died. It was real."

"I agree. They were close friends, plus Delia couldn't hurt a fly, literally. I have seen her carry insects out her door to set them down on the grass rather than squash them." She paused. "As I would. I don't like bugs." A deep chuckle rolled out. She shook her head firmly. "Delia could not by any means be a murderer."

Callie nodded. It was what she'd decided long ago. "Karl, then, wouldn't likely have had a key, but he did want my aunt's shop in order to expand his business. He's clearly an angry man who likes to get his own way and not the type to coddle bugs or anything else. Is he capable of committing murder to get what he wants?"

Orlena sank down on a nearby stool, seemingly unable to consider a question like that while on her feet. "How can one know that?" she asked. "Until it happens."

"From past actions." Callie pulled a second stool closer and sat down. "You feel Delia isn't capable of murder because she's demonstrated how much she values living things. Has Karl shown the opposite? Cruelty to animals, perhaps? You've known him much longer than I have."

Orlena's eyes turned upward as she searched her memory. "No," she said. "Karl is brusque and sharp-tongued, but I have never known him to be outright cruel."

"He doesn't treat Elvin very well."

"True. He doesn't like Elvin near his shop. He worries the poor man will scare away customers. And," she said, turning to look at

Callie directly, "I can't say I truly blame him." At Callie's wince, Orlena challenged her. "If you did not know Elvin and saw this big, bearded man in dirty denims, scowling and blocking your way to a shop, would you ask him to please move or would you turn on your heel and go somewhere else?"

Callie remembered how Elvin had frightened her that first evening she'd encountered him in the dark. "I see your point. But there are kinder ways of going about it."

"Of course. But there are worse ways, too. Karl can be harsh, but I'm not able to say more than that. I'm very good at reading people, yes, but there is no way to see what is far below the surface. The kind of evil that moves one to commit murder, I fear, will be buried very deeply."

"That's a frightening thought."

"But something you should not forget."

A customer walked in, and Orlena's grim look vanished with a blink. "Good afternoon!" she said, rising from her stool to welcome the woman with a broad smile.

Callie waited, mulling over Orlena's words as well as what to ask her next as the shopkeeper dealt with her customer, helping the woman choose the perfect box for a collection of photographs. After the woman left and Orlena returned to her seat, Callie decided to bring up Aunt Mel's mysterious Tom. Though it felt a little like a betrayal, she told herself Aunt Mel was past needing her secrets kept. It was important to see if Orlena could tell her anything useful.

"I discovered," she said, "that my aunt had a hidden romantic relationship. So far, I've been able to find out very little about it, but my guess is this man would be one person Mel would let into her shop at that time of night if he asked her to—especially since I was staying at the cottage at the time. Do you know anything about him?"

"Ah, so you found out about that. That was something I picked up on, but only that the situation existed. Nothing more. I could see that Mel wanted to keep it to herself, so I did not pry."

Callie was beginning to deplore the existence of conscientious people who respected others' privacy. If Aunt Mel had been surrounded by nosy busybodies, perhaps she'd still be here! "She never dropped a clue as to who he was or where she went to meet him?" she pressed, frustration slipping into her voice.

Orlena shook her head. "I imagine Delia has said the same, am I right? If her best friend and close neighbor did not know, there's little chance I would, is there?"

Callie sighed. "I'm sorry. I didn't mean to imply that you *should* know. I just wish you *did* know."

Orlena nodded understandingly.

"Then what about Duane Fletcher?" Callie asked, her disappointment causing her to bring his name up too abruptly.

"Duane?" Orlena stiffened slightly, but if it was from surprise, annoyance over the continuing questions, or something else, Callie couldn't say.

"There were problems between him and Aunt Mel," Callie explained. "I need to understand how serious they'd become."

"That was something between the two of them. It was not my business."

"This wasn't about my aunt's personal life. It had to do with the Keepsake Cove Shop Owners' Association."

"I have already told you that I've kept my distance from that group's squabbles." Orlena got up, sending a strong signal to Callie that she'd had enough of the discussion.

"I'm sorry, Orlena, if I'm treading on sensitive ground…"

"There is nothing sensitive about it," Orlena said, her eyes flashing briefly before she composed herself, bringing up a smile. "I've just grown very, very tired of all this talk about Duane Fletcher. Either keep him on as treasurer or replace him. I don't really care. But this endless insinuation! It needs to be over."

"It needs to be settled, I agree. And there's a push to have the association's books audited. The thing is, Aunt Mel was the one who brought up the whole debate. I've found evidence that she was suspicious of Duane's accounting. She began scanning her committee expenses before turning them over to Duane. If he realized that, and had been covertly inflating the expenses, that gives him a motive to break into her shop somehow to erase those scans."

"And then kill Mel?" Orlena's tone was skeptical.

"It might not have been in his plan. But if she caught him, he might have thought it was his only way out."

Orlena shook her head firmly. "I have never seen anything like that in the man," she insisted. "Duane gets along with everybody. Any disagreements usually end up with the other person apologizing. Duane would never need to resort to violence."

"What about that evil that could be buried too deeply to see?" Callie asked quietly. "Isn't it possible that we only see what Duane lets us?"

Orlena rubbed at her temples. "All this talk of murder is too distressing." She smiled at Callie. "I should stay happy for my customers, no?" She walked to her window and spotted an older couple heading toward the shop. "And there they are. Enough sad talk. I wish I could solve your problem, my dear, but I am only me. Orlena. Not a magician who can snap her fingers and pull answers out of the air."

The couple arrived, and Callie politely left, feeling that she'd handled things badly, particularly about Duane. If she'd been better, more subtle, cleverer, she was sure she would have learned something from

Orlena about the man, something the shopkeeper was clearly holding back. As she walked to her music box shop, she wondered if she would ever discover the truth about Aunt Mel's death. Or would she only continue to annoy and antagonize Keepsake Cove shopkeepers but with no results? Somebody must know what had really happened that night. Somebody other than the killer. But who?

Catching a glimpse of Tabitha through the window, Callie thought that her assistant's answer would be that Aunt Mel knew and was trying to tell them through Grandpa Reed's music box. Was she? Callie shrugged. If her aunt was, she'd chosen a very inefficient way of communicating.

She walked into her shop and was greeted in an intriguing way. "You'll never guess who just called," Tabitha said.

Twenty-One

allie had to wait for the follow-up to her assistant's statement as the phone rang and Tabitha reached to answer it, making a "hold on" gesture.

"*House of Melody*," Tabitha announced, and Callie, her curiosity piqued but necessarily suspended, continued on to the office to get back to work. She'd pulled up recent orders on the computer when Tabitha joined her.

"That was Mrs. Weaver, checking to see if her special-order anniversary music box came in yet, which it did. She'll come by tomorrow." Tabitha grinned. "Or maybe the next day, or the day after that. We'll see."

"So, who called while I was out?"

"Oh, right! You'll never guess. But I already said that, didn't I? Mark Eggers!"

"*Mark* Eggers?" Callie asked, puzzled.

"Karl's nephew. The one he wants to manage a collectible train shop for him."

"On the *House of Melody* premises."

"That's the one. He wants to talk to you."

"Why?"

"He didn't actually say, but we can guess, can't we? He left his number, and he asked very, very politely if you would please call him back."

"Hmmm." Callie twirled a lock of her blond hair with a finger. "Think I should?"

"A call couldn't hurt, I guess. You could always hang up."

Callie twirled a bit longer. "Why not? Where's his number?"

Tabitha ran back to the front counter and got it for her, then waited as Callie put it in.

"Mr. Eggers? It's Callie Reed. You called earlier?"

"Yes, Ms. Reed," a smooth male voice responded. "Thank you so much for calling back. I wondered if we could meet? There's something important I'd like to discuss with you."

"Does it have to do with my selling my shop?"

"I'd really rather wait until we can sit down together. Could we meet for drinks or coffee this evening?"

Callie thought about that. She was interested enough to want to meet the man and perhaps learn a little more about Karl. Meeting at a public spot seemed like a good idea, better than him coming to her shop. She could always leave if she didn't like how things were going. "Coffee would be good," she said. "After I close up. Six fifteen." She suggested the diner Jonathan had taken her to on the day her boxes had arrived from West Virginia, and Mark Eggers agreed.

"You're meeting him?" Tabitha asked, her eyebrows raised.

"He sounded reasonably normal."

"Want me to grab the booth behind you?"

Callie laughed. "It'll be fine. I'm curious to see what the man has to say."

"I am too, frankly. We know what he's got in mind. How he thinks he'll talk you into it will be interesting. Just," Tabitha added, looking serious, "be careful." The shop phone rang again, and as Tabitha went to get it, Callie mulled over what she might have gotten herself into.

❧

The hostess at the front of Dino's Diner greeted Callie as she walked in. "One?" she asked.

"Actually, I'm meeting someone," Callie said, realizing she didn't know what Mark Eggers looked like. As she glanced toward the seated diners, a man in his mid-thirties approached her from a bench where he'd been waiting.

"Ms. Reed?"

Callie smiled. "Mr. Eggers?"

They shook hands and followed the hostess to a table beside a window.

Eggers was about Callie's age and had his uncle's burly frame. Unlike his uncle, though, he was clean shaven, which gave him a much less fierce appearance. His manner, as it had been on the phone, was mild and polite—again, unlike his uncle. But Callie was reserving further judgment until they'd chatted a bit more.

They ordered coffee and made small talk about the current hot weather. Once they'd stirred in their sugar or cream and taken first sips, Eggers got down to business.

"Ms. Reed," he began, then asked, "Okay if I call you Callie?" Callie dipped her head in assent and he began again. "Callie, I know my uncle is not the easiest person to get along with."

"All he's done since I've arrived here is demonstrate how much he'd like me to leave."

Mark let out a rueful laugh. "If it helps, he's like that with nearly everyone."

"Then I can't help wondering how he manages to deal with customers. People on the verge of handing over their money generally prefer to be treated more pleasantly."

"My uncle knows collectible cars," Mark said. "He's amassed the best selection in the area. That's all that the most rabid collectors care about. It's what they'll travel miles to find. "

Rabid. That word seemed to fit Karl Eggers as well, to Callie's mind. "Has he always been so angry?"

"I don't know if I'd call it anger," Mark said. He took a swig of his coffee. "He's simply very sure about how things should be and has little patience for when they're not."

Simply? Callie thought, raising her eyebrows. She was aware of dictators who'd had the same attitude.

Mark shrugged. *What can you do?* was written on his face. "It's who he is. We're used to it—the family, I mean. And he has many good points."

"That's nice to know," Callie said. "He's apparently single. Has he ever been married?" She expected the answer to be no, or very briefly.

"He was," Mark said. "But it ended tragically when my aunt died."

"Oh, I'm sorry," Callie said, having a flash of sympathy. "Illness?"

"Accident. He doesn't like to talk about it much." Mark lifted his coffee cup to his lips, signaling that he wasn't going to either. "What I wanted to discuss with you tonight was your shop."

Callie nodded, not surprised.

"I'm sure you know my uncle would like to expand his business with a collectible trains shop, and that he needs to keep it close to his existing shop."

"I know that he'd *like* to keep it close to his shop."

Mark ignored her input and continued. "He's offered me the position of manager of that train shop. Callie," he said, looking earnestly at her, "I really need that job."

Uh-oh.

"I was downsized recently from my last position, just before my wife and I had a new baby." He reached into his pocket to show Callie a photo of a red-faced newborn, swaddled in a hospital blanket, eyes squinting with a "what just happened here?" look. "Mark, Jr."

"Congratulations."

"Thanks." He smiled as he looked at the photo again before pocketing it. "We're very proud of him. But, as I'm sure you can understand, it makes for a situation where bringing in a steady income is pretty urgent. That, combined with my uncle's need for expansion, has moved him to make you a very generous offer." Mark paused, and Callie could see from his excited smile that he expected her to be blown away by what he was about to say. "Uncle Karl is offering *ten percent* over his previous offer to your aunt—which was quite good to begin with—for an immediate buy-out of your shop and cottage." When Callie opened her mouth to answer, he raised his hand. "*And ...* he's willing to give you ample time to sell off your inventory or to relocate, whichever you prefer." He stopped and waited, possibly assuming she needed a moment to catch her breath.

Callie did take a moment, but it was to choose the right words, not to recover from heart-palpitating joy. "I'm sure," she said, "that's a very generous offer—if I were interested in selling. But I'm not. I'm sorry."

"Ten percent higher!" he repeated. "You'd never get an offer like that in today's market."

"Perhaps I wouldn't. But that doesn't matter, anyway, since I want to stay."

"You want to stay? I understood your sudden inheritance caused you to be abruptly uprooted. Wouldn't you want to return to the life you were forced to leave?"

Not hardly, Callie thought, trying not to smile. "I'm actually very happy with the change," she said.

Mark looked incredulous for a long while, then collected himself and moved on to what apparently was Plan B. "If that's the case, then my uncle has another offer. He will pay you a generous fee for the rental of half your shop."

"Half my shop?" Callie asked, not sure she'd heard right.

"Half the space, so that we could set up our collectible trains, and you would keep the other half for your music boxes."

Callie's face must have shown the shock she felt because he hurried on. "Think of it. With two shops in one, we'd double the foot traffic! Customers who came in for trains would move along to your side as well to browse and buy, and vice versa. It would be a win-win situation!"

"Mr. Egg—ah, Mark, I barely have enough space for my inventory as it is. Keepsake Cove shops are not large."

"No problem," he declared. "There's plenty of vertical space to be used. And we could think about an addition at the back later."

"Do you really believe our particular customers would be inclined to cross over? I mean, collectible trains and music boxes? They don't exactly appeal to the same collectors." Before Mark could jump in with another argument, she shook her head firmly. "No. That's not anything I would consider."

Mark Eggers was silent, his face taking on some color, and Callie was fairly sure he wanted to call her responses the stupidest things he'd ever heard. For her part, she would have loved to say that just because he and his uncle wanted her premises didn't mean she had to sell or share them. Much as Karl might love to be a dictator, it was still a free country, last she checked.

They sat, each fuming internally, until Mark jumped up, shaking the table enough to rattle the salt and pepper shakers at its side.

"Fine! I thought you would be more reasonable about this, but apparently there's no room for business sense in that blond head of yours. I should have expected that. Good luck trying to meet your mortgage payments by selling your little wind-up boxes. We'll probably get your shop anyway after the bank forecloses!"

His voice had risen with each word, drawing the astonished stares of half the diners, including Callie's. He threw a few bills down for the cost of the coffee and stomped off. A stunned silence lingered in the restaurant, much to Callie's embarrassment. She felt trapped, since she couldn't very well leave until she was sure Mark Eggers was totally gone, nor was she about to apologize to the room for her companion's bad behavior. That was his job. She lifted her cup stiffly and sipped, and waited for normal conversations to resume around her. Although normal was probably too much to hope for.

She was staring out the window—and away from nearby tables—when she heard the sound of a throat clearing. Duane Fletcher stood there, smiling apologetically.

"I couldn't help overhearing," he said. Then he started to grin.

The grin set Callie to giggling, and he joined her in a body-jiggling laugh until they both had tears in their eyes.

"May I sit?" he asked, wiping his eyes, and Callie swept a hand toward the opposite bench.

"Room for business sense in that blond head?" Duane quoted as he settled in. "My God, what era was the man teleported from? Who says things like that anymore?"

"He's Karl Eggers's nephew."

"Aha."

Callie nodded. "Certain genes apparently run strongly in that family's DNA."

"Well, I'm sorry you took the brunt of them. Looks like you've had only coffee. Would you be interested in staying for dinner? I planned to eat alone, but I'd love the company."

"I'd enjoy that," Callie said, grateful to him for erasing the embarrassment of Mark Eggers's dramatic exit, though the image of Duane buzzing the cove with his boat edged in. She pushed it back, at least for a while.

A waitress, who Callie suspected had purposely hung back, suddenly appeared to clear the cups, and Callie and Duane quickly chose and gave their orders. Then Duane turned to Callie. "Mind if I ask what encouraged you to share a table with Karl Eggers's nephew?"

"Curiosity," Callie said. "I was pretty sure what he wanted, which was my shop. Karl wants to expand, you know. I was interested to see how he might approach it. I also thought I might learn a little more about Karl."

"And did you?"

"His offers have escalated enough to tell me he's really desperate to grab *House of Melody*. And I did find out something I hadn't known, that Karl lost his wife through an accident." Duane nodded, so she asked, "Do you know what exactly happened?"

"It was before Karl moved to Keepsake Cove. He's never been exactly cozy with the rest of us, so that's all I know. I'm not even sure how I happened to hear that."

Their orders soon came, diner food which Callie assumed only needed to be nuked, though her chicken scampi smelled pretty good. She and Duane turned to their food—he got spaghetti and meatballs, with a side order of French fries—and they chatted intermittently about more innocuous things. Duane brought up his new boat.

"I saw you with it, actually," Callie admitted. "Last evening in the cove."

"You should have waved. I would have given you a ride!" Duane tore off a chunk of garlic bread and popped it in his mouth.

"I tend to get seasick," Callie said, closing that door.

"A shame," he said between chews. "By the way," he said, "I noticed you here once before with that financial planner guy, Jonathan Harman. Are you seeing him?"

Callie squirmed at the question, unsure where it was leading. If she said no, was Duane going to suggest a date? But she didn't want to pretend anything. "Just friends," she said. "Or a friendly customer. He had rescued me from having to cook after an exhausting day."

"I just thought I'd bring something up in case you were."

"Oh? Bring up what?"

Duane shrugged. "It's probably nothing. Just something that bothered me about him. You know, a word to the wise to avoid problems down the line? But if you're not dating or anything…"

"We're not dating, but I don't mind getting other people's opinions. I'll ultimately make up my own mind, of course, once I get to know folks better."

"Sure," Duane said. "And as I said, it's just a feeling I got. A not-so-great feeling when the guy came to the house one time to talk about financial planning. I know my way around finances pretty well, but I thought I'd at least listen to his pitch. See if he had any new ideas. The whole time he was there, though, I got the impression he was … oh, how do I put it? It felt like he was casing the joint."

"Casing the joint?"

Duane laughed. "I know. Sounds like something from a gangster movie. But that's exactly how it came across. As though Jonathan

Harman was putting mental price tags on everything I own. It was kinda creepy."

Callie didn't know what to make of that. "What are you saying? That he intended to break in and make off with your things?"

"No, nothing like that!"

"He is a financial planner. Perhaps he was just estimating your buying habits versus your income?"

"Buying habits, sure. If you're talking about big ticket items, that would make sense. But Harman seemed much too fascinated with every little thing around him. It felt, I don't know, opportunistic, like he'd misrepresented his reason for being there, and I didn't trust him because of it." Duane laughed ruefully. "Then again, it might have just been me."

Callie smiled politely, unsure how to take any of that. She'd never picked up any vibes of the kind from Jonathan, though, of course, he'd never been to her cottage other than to quickly carry groceries in. But she did remember that Jonathan had told her he'd been in Duane's shop yet hadn't said a word about being in Duane's home to discuss financial planning. Did that mean anything? Had he omitted that for some reason? Was Duane being truthful?

Movement in the aisle caught Callie's eye, and she saw someone being led in their direction by the hostess. It was Delia. Delia spotted her at the same time, and Callie watched her friend's face light up. But Delia then saw who was with Callie, and her face quickly fell.

"Delia," Callie called to her. "Come join us."

Duane, startled, looked up, and then he stood, seconding the invitation.

Color rose in Delia's face. She looked flustered. The hostess paused, waiting for her decision.

"No, no," Delia stammered. "Thank you, but no. I wouldn't dream … that is, I really can't stay. I should be getting take-out, as a matter of fact. Lots of work to do at home, you know." She backed away, then pivoted and hurried off. Callie considered running after her to explain why Duane was with her but feared she'd only embarrass Delia more with Duane looking on. She felt awful but helpless, which morphed into anger with Duane—who was, after all, the root of it all. Why didn't he see how Delia felt?

But Callie reminded herself of the suspicions she had of the man, which she'd conveniently put aside when he joined her. If those suspicions were ultimately proven to be true, she should instead be glad that Duane didn't encourage Delia. The problem was, Delia wasn't going to see it that way, at least for now.

Callie realized she was partly to blame and scolded herself. There she was, chatting and laughing with Duane, giving Delia a mistaken impression in the process, instead of peppering him with questions on important points as she should have.

"Getting dessert?" Duane asked, blithely unaware of Callie's dark musings regarding him.

"Hmm?" Callie blinked. "Oh, um, yes. Good idea." She nodded, then smiled. It was a very good idea. She'd have more time to actually do something productive.

Twenty-Two

$\mathcal{D}$uane hadn't needed urging to order dessert for himself, and he dug into his chocolate pie à la mode with relish. Callie had ordered a small dish of ice cream, which, after finishing only half of her mega-sized dinner, she was only able to pick at.

"So," she said, tasting a dab of ice cream, "I was wondering about taking a booth at a festival. They sent me—my aunt, actually—an application. I'd have to transport a lot of my stock and spend two days there, and I'm not sure it's a good idea. Have you done things like that? Is it worth it?"

Duane nodded, having just scooped up a generous forkful of pie. "Several times," he said when he could talk. "But never too far from home. I'm trying to build clientele at those events, not necessarily make sales on the premises, although that's always nice."

"I'd have to close my shop at least part of the time. Tabitha wouldn't be able to take over full time. But then, so do you, I suppose. Or do you get someone to run your shop while you're gone?"

"No, I close up."

"And you don't mind losing the business?"

"It generally balances out," he said. "Plus," he added with a small grin, "I look at it as a small vacation. A couple nights in a nice hotel, great restaurants, a lot of it tax deductible as business expenses. And both Baltimore and the DC area have casinos, now."

Callie smiled back, though the thought of tossing away her money at a roulette wheel or slot machine didn't appeal to her. Apparently it did to Duane, unless he'd come up with a magical method that guaranteed winning.

"The festival I'm talking about," she said, "is in a small town in Pennsylvania, just north of the Maryland line."

Duane shook his head. "Too far. Waste of effort. Stick to the cities." He worked on another forkful of pie. "The bigger shows also give you a chance to see what's available. Scores of wholesalers come by with special offers. You get to know a lot of people. The last one I went to was at the Baltimore Convention Center. Huge."

That must have been the one happening when Aunt Mel was killed, Callie thought. "Frankly, it sounds exhausting," she said. "Noise, crowds of people constantly coming and going. I'm probably not as much of a people person as you and wouldn't do as well with that kind of thing. Plus, I seem to catch whatever bug happens to be going around."

"Not much danger of that during warm weather. Fall and winter are the flu and cold seasons."

"Oh, right," Callie said. But Duane had told Delia he'd stayed home from Aunt Mel's funeral because of a bad cold he'd caught at the glass show. She pressed a little more. "So that show at the Baltimore arena was recent?"

He held up two fingers. "Couple of weeks ago," he said when he could.

"And you always stay in town instead of commuting back and forth?"

"Always." Duane scraped at his plate for the few remaining crumbs. "Except once."

Callie lifted her eyebrows questioningly.

"The time that handyman was doing some work for me."

"Elvin?"

"That's him. I had him fixing the roof on my shed after doing the same on the sun room I added at the back of my house. Heavy rain was predicted, so I didn't want to put it off. But I didn't like the thought of him being around without me there, at least overnight. So I drove back and forth, and even dropped by in the middle of one of the days, just to let him know it could happen."

"But that wasn't during the latest show?"

"Last fall. Wore me out, all that driving, but it had to be done. Cost me plenty in gas, but I still made out. The guy works cheap," he said with a grin. "Well, this was great!" he said, wiping his hands with a paper napkin. He'd nearly licked his platter clean. "We should do it again sometime."

"Yes," Callie agreed weakly, wishing she'd come up with better questions to ferret out more from him. Besides the fact that Duane must have lied about having caught a bad cold at the last glass show, all Callie had learned was that, although willing to hire Elvin at a bargain price, Duane had a low opinion of his trustworthiness. Not exactly helpful as far as Aunt Mel's death was concerned, but it told her something about the man himself.

She picked up her box of leftovers—Duane had none—and led the way out. At least she'd come away with another night's dinner.

When Callie got home, she looked toward Delia's cottage and saw only a single light on in an upstairs room. A clear signal that her neighbor didn't want visitors. She sighed and let herself into her own cottage. She welcomed Jagger's excited greeting, even knowing it was based more on "Callie, Food Source" than on herself as a person. She'd take what she could get. After filling Jagger's bowl and leaving him to it, she tried calling Delia but got only her voicemail. She sighed again and went upstairs to change into comfy pajamas. She was in for the night.

Gathering up a basketful of dirty laundry, Callie carried it down to start a load, feeling low as she thought of Delia possibly sitting unhappily in her room and unsure if things could be fixed between them. If she had come away from the diner with the conviction that Duane was either guilty or innocent of killing Aunt Mel, it would have been worth it. But she didn't feel any closer to that verdict than she'd been before. Plus, she still had the unpleasant memory of how the meeting with Mark Eggers had ended.

Gloom threatened to descend, and Callie fought against it by keeping busy—folding laundry, listening to music, clearing away more of the boxes from West Virginia, until fatigue finally sent her to her bed. Before turning off the light, though, she checked through the emails on her phone. Maybe by some miracle she'd find one from Aunt Mel's reunion organizer with information about Tom.

The miracle didn't appear, but as she continued scrolling and deleting spam, her phone rang. It was Hank. Any other time she would have let it go, but at the moment, answering the call seemed preferable to being left alone to sink further into her dark mood.

"Hey, babe, you picked up!"

"Hi Hank. What's up?"

"Nothing. That's the problem. Our gig tonight got canceled. Outdoors and bad weather."

"I'm sorry. Will they make it up?"

"I don't know. Maybe not."

"Why aren't you out with the gang?" she asked.

"Just didn't feel like it, you know? I mean, I was all hyped up for the gig, and then it's like, nothing else is good enough. Except talking to you. Thanks for picking up."

"You're welcome," Callie answered, still surprised, actually, that she'd done so and that she didn't feel like hanging up.

"Everything okay with you down there?" he asked.

"Uh-huh," she said, thinking she at least had a roof over her head and a source of income, so no justifiable complaints.

"You don't sound all that sure about it."

"Everything's fine." She wasn't about to go into what was really weighing on her, or Hank would be on the road in a flash to try to fix things. Not that he had a prayer of actually accomplishing it. But sometimes he could be sweet in that way. "It's just one of those days," she assured him.

"Know what you mean. Used to be a lot better, though, remember?"

She did. There had been plenty of good times.

"Remember that time … " He launched into describing a night that Callie remembered well, when they both had been so young and everything was new and exciting. Hank's band had been playing to a good crowd. His solo got a standing ovation, and he'd pulled her up on the stage to share his moment. Okay, it wasn't Nashville, but it felt as good as, at the time. And Nashville was just a step or two away, or so they'd convinced themselves. It was a thrilling night.

But there were good times away from the spotlight as well. Great friends, unexpected fun events along the way. Callie enjoyed thinking back on it and laughed along with Hank as he reminisced. She allowed herself to feel nostalgic, partly because she'd been feeling so down, and maybe also being half asleep. But she snapped back to reality when Hank coaxed, "How about you come up for a few days?"

"No, Hank."

"C'mon. We could—"

"No, Hank. Sorry."

"I could come down there."

"Don't even think of it, Hank."

"But I thought—"

"You were mistaken." Why had she opened that door even a little bit? Didn't she know how quickly he could wriggle that pointy-toed boot of his into the smallest crack to worm his way in? "Hank," she said. "It was good talking to you, but that's it. I'm going to say good night and that'll be the end of it. Okay?"

"But—"

"Good night, Hank."

She hung up and stared at the phone, waiting for it to ring. When, after a full minute, it didn't, she exhaled and set it down. She turned off her light, chastising herself for her moment of weakness and sure she'd toss and turn half the night as punishment. But when she was eventually awakened by her phone's ring, a glance at the clock told her several hours had gone by and it was nearly six. She grabbed the phone, sure it was Hank and furious that he would call again. Then she read the caller ID: *Brian Greer*.

"Brian?" she said, shaking the fuzziness from her head.

"Callie, sorry if I woke you. I just learned that Elvin is in the hospital. It sounds serious. I'm heading over there and wondered if you'd come? I could use a little help."

"I'll be ready in five." She didn't waste time asking what had happened but swung her legs over the edge of the bed and jumped up to grab some clothes.

She'd get the details on the way over.

Twenty-Three

*B*rian's classic red Chevy was waiting at the curb as expected when she hurried out in cropped pants, a freshly laundered shirt, and sneakers, her hair hastily tied back. She slid into the passenger seat and buckled up, then gratefully accepted the personal-sized thermos of coffee he held out to her.

"It's last night's, reheated," he said. "But I figured it'd still be better than anything from the hospital vending machine." He waited for her to take a drink before pulling away from the curb, then told her what he knew.

"Elvin crashed an ATV into a tree sometime around two this morning. He wasn't wearing a helmet, so I'm guessing head injury. At the least."

"How awful!" Callie cried. "Where did it happen? Whose ATV? His?"

"Somewhere in the woods behind the cove. And no, it couldn't have been his, that's for sure. But I don't know whose it was."

She mulled over the information for a moment as he negotiated a left turn on the way to the highway. "Who called you?"

"The hospital. Elvin had a card in his wallet with my name and number listed as his emergency contact. Apparently I'm the closest thing he has to family."

"How sad," she said, and saw Brian glance at her with amusement. "I mean, of course, sad that he has no family, not that you—"

"I know. But," he said, "stand-in family that I am, I want to chew him out for doing such a stupid thing." His tone turned solemn. "I hope I get the chance."

Callie reached over to squeeze his arm. She barely knew Elvin and felt pretty bad. She could only imagine how awful Brian must feel.

❧

The early Sunday morning traffic was light, and they made good time to the medical center. The trip, Brian told her, would normally have taken forty minutes. They made it in twenty-five. Negotiating the huge campus, parking, and locating the area where Elvin would be took another frustrating fifteen. But once they finally spoke to someone who could update them on his condition, what they heard was "He's in surgery right now. It could be a while."

They were directed to the waiting area by the kindly but busy woman behind the desk and took seats, though within seconds Brian was up and pacing. Hospital staff passed to and fro and friends or family of other patients came and went, often collected by aides while Callie and Brian were left to themselves.

Brian, his adrenaline eventually worn down, sat on the stiff plastic couch beside Callie. "I hate hospitals," he said, his hands clasped over his knees.

"Not my favorite place either," Callie agreed.

"I mean, I really hate them."

She looked over at the intensity of his tone.

"My brother was sick a lot when I was a kid."

"Your brother?" This was the first Callie had heard of a brother.

"Yeah. He died when I was twelve. He—Pauly—was only eight." Brian's voice wavered slightly, and he cleared his throat noisily.

"That must have been tough."

Brian nodded. "There were so many hospital stays. Starting when he was just a baby. Each one longer, none of them doing any good, at least as far as I could see. It got so I hated the smells that hit you when you first walked in. I can't stand the smell of antiseptics to this day. It brings it all back."

"I'm so sorry." Callie put a hand on his arm and felt the tension in it. She understood, now, why he'd asked her to come. He wouldn't have wanted to put Annie through a similar reaction.

She remembered the hospital visits to see her dad during those final weeks. She'd been older than Brian was with his brother, almost seventeen, which probably made it easier. Although easy wasn't exactly the word she'd choose. Still, being nearly grown up was better than twelve. She wasn't about to bring any of that up, though.

"Would you rather wait outside? I could call you as soon as I hear something."

"No. I'll be okay. Just thought I should explain why I'm so jumpy. That, plus worrying about Elvin."

Callie searched for some means of distraction. The TV mounted on the wall spouted news that they'd already heard three times. The months-old magazines scattered around weren't going to do it. "Would you like to tell me," she asked, "how you manage to come up with some of the amazing specials on your café menu? Things like the veggie sandwich on nut bread. Are they state secrets, or can you talk about it?"

Brian looked over, his eyes showing awareness of what she was doing. But she saw appreciation along with a spark of interest.

"So you really liked the veggie?" he asked.

"Loved it. And the nut bread. Where do you get that?"

"There's a great bakery ... " he began, and was soon off on the tale of its discovery along with his many after-hours experiments with various meat and vegetable combinations. "I eat a lot of trial-and-error dinners," he said, smiling by that point. "Some of them not so great. But the good ones go on my menus."

He talked about the sauces he mixed up, tweaking recipes he sometimes found online or in one of his many cookbooks. He'd moved on to salads when a man in green scrubs stepped into the room.

"Brian Greer?" he asked, and both Brian and Callie jumped up from their seats.

The surgeon introduced himself. He'd just worked on Elvin, and, looking serious, he talked about multiple fractures, severe head injury, and a drug-induced coma. "Necessary until the brain swelling goes down. The next several hours—or days—will be critical. We'll just have to watch and wait."

"Can we see him?" Brian asked.

The surgeon nodded. "Through the IC window only, for now. An aide will come get you in a few minutes," he promised. He then shook their hands and left.

"How did this happen?" Brian asked, running a hand through his hair. "What was Elvin doing riding an ATV in the woods in the middle of the night?"

"He'd stolen it," a voice answered, and Callie turned to see that Jonathan Harman had stepped into the waiting room. "From Duane

Fletcher," he added. He waited a moment as they dealt with the shock of his news before asking, "How's he doing?"

Callie shared what they'd been told by the surgeon. "How do you know Elvin stole the ATV?" she asked.

"It was on the local news," Jonathan said. "That's how I learned he was here. Elvin was supposed to come by and finish some work today." He held out a hand to Brian and introduced himself. "You're Greer, right?"

Brian nodded and shook Harman's hand, but he looked numb from his news. "Stole it? Elvin doesn't do things like that."

Jonathan shrugged. "You might know better than me. But that's what they said. I assume it came from the police report."

"Elvin doesn't even have a driver's license," Brian said, "though I guess that wouldn't be his biggest concern. I suppose those things are fairly easy to handle?"

"Probably," Jonathan agreed. "He did talk a little about wanting to try things like that."

"ATVs?" Callie asked.

"Those and other sport vehicles like mopeds, go-karts, jet skis. He might have been lucky not to have chosen a jet ski. Who knows but that he might have drowned before anyone got to him."

"That just sounds so unlike Elvin," Brian said, still grappling with the news.

Callie thought of her last encounter with the man, outside *Stitches Thru Time*. His last word to her, out of the blue, was "Why?" One word didn't tell her much, but she did remember the anxiety that had flashed across his face. Tabitha would say it was premonition. Was it just coincidence?

An aide came to invite the three of them back to the ICU, and they followed the woman, Callie bracing herself for what they might see through the visitors' window. It was as distressing as she expected. Elvin was barely recognizable under the bandages, slings, and IVs.

Brian let out a small groan, and she squeezed his hand. Jonathan, she saw, did the same to Brian's shoulder before moving over to her side. After a few minutes, Jonathan asked if she intended to open her shop and if so, did she need a ride back? With a shock, Callie realized she'd forgotten all about getting back to *House of Melody* for its Sunday afternoon hours.

"Brian, will you be staying?" she asked.

Brian looked over at her and then at Jonathan. He'd obviously heard Jonathan's offer of a ride. "No," he said. "I need to open up the café. I can take you back, unless you'd rather ... "

"Actually, if you two are leaving," Jonathan said, "I think I'll hang around. I don't have businesses to attend to. I can let you know if there's any change."

"That'd be great, Jonathan," Callie said and Brian nodded. They left then, quietly, and a glance back by Callie saw Jonathan watching them and giving an encouraging thumbs-up. But it was going to be a gray afternoon.

Twenty-Four

That afternoon Callie opened her shop to a steady influx of customers, which she was more than happy to see for reasons beyond possible sales. Keeping busy would help keep her mind off Elvin. Beside worrying about his injuries, there was the fact that he had actually taken Duane's ATV. It made Elvin a confirmed thief, which was bad enough. But that in turn made him a prime suspect as her burglar, and beyond that, possibly Aunt Mel's murderer. She hated that last thought and tried her best to reason it away. But too much kept her from completely doing that. She was left only with the hope that when Elvin awoke he would have an explanation for everything.

From occasional glances out her window, Callie saw that the Keepsake Café was as busy as she was, despite it being past the usual lunch time. Many people were leaving with cold drinks or ice creams in hand as the weather continued warm and sultry. Once she spotted Delia coming out with a tall drink, but she went directly back to *Shake It Up!* without a glance toward *House of Melody*, which made Callie sigh. As soon as she got a chance, she would try to make things right between them.

"My daughter loves anything to do with Broadway musicals," a tall woman said to her. Her wedge sandals added more inches to her height, and Callie craned her neck to meet the woman's gaze. "Her birthday is coming up, and—"

"I think I have something she'd love." Callie led the way to her shelf of higher-end music boxes. She brought one down that made her customer gasp. The ornately framed shadow box held a scene from *Phantom of the Opera*, showing Christine in her white dress being transported in the phantom's boat to his underground lair. When Callie moved the switch, the overture from the musical played. Her customer clapped her hands in delight.

"It's perfect! She'll love it." The woman didn't even ask the price but simply followed Callie to the counter to complete the purchase, a satisfied smile on her face.

About mid-afternoon, Callie was surprised to see Laurie Hart walk in but assumed the toy shop owner wanted to ask about Elvin. Laurie waited patiently until Callie was free to talk, then said, "You heard about Elvin, didn't you?"

"I was at the hospital this morning and saw him." Callie shared what the surgeon had said and about the drug-induced coma.

Laurie shook her head sadly. "I don't know what he was thinking. But unfortunately Elvin's reasoning process isn't the sharpest." Her expression turned to disgust. "That creep, Duane, is more upset about his ATV than Elvin's injuries. I couldn't stand to listen to him going on and on about it and had to just walk away. Why does he need an ATV anyway? From what I hear he just bought himself a boat. The ATV was probably going to just rust away from non-use."

Laurie lifted the lid of one of the music boxes and listened to its tune: "Edelweiss." "Pretty," she said, smiling. "Listen," she said, turning serious again. "We have to pin this guy down before he runs off with the rest of our money. Have you thought any more about sup-porting an audit on the association books?"

Callie had probably thought about a million other things lately, but she considered it now. *Why not?* she asked herself. Aunt Mel had had her suspicions, and her own had grown too. "I'll back you up," she said.

"Great! That will bring us within four votes of a majority! Thank you."

"You're welcome. If it settles the debate, one way or another, it'll be worth the cost."

"Absolutely. But I think no one will regret it when they see what it turns up."

Laurie seemed more interested in listening to additional music boxes than in getting back, so Callie decided to ask for a favor.

"Would you mind watching my shop for a few minutes? There's something I need to discuss with Delia in person, and I'm afraid she might disappear if I wait until closing time."

"Sure, no problem," Laurie said. "Bill's fine without me for a while."

"And if something comes up, of course, just call." Callie patted the phone in her pocket. "I can be back in a flash. Thanks so much!" She hurried off, hoping to catch Delia in a receptive mood and grateful that Laurie asked no questions. This talk would be very personal.

She waited outside of *Shake It Up!* until she was sure Delia was alone. Then Callie took a deep breath and headed on in.

"Oh!" Delia said, looking up from a lower shelf she'd been straight-ening. "Hi, Callie." It came out weakly, her usual broad smile appear-ing forced. "I heard about Elvin from Brian. So heartbreaking."

"It is," Callie said. "But I didn't come to talk about Elvin right now. I might have only a couple minutes," she said, glancing out the win-dow. "So I'll have to get right to it."

Delia didn't look exactly open and eager to hear anything, but at least she wasn't stopping her. So Callie plunged in.

"Duane and I are *not* seeing each other. What you saw last night—the two of us sitting together—was totally unplanned. I'd come to the diner to meet with Karl Eggers's nephew, and it didn't go well. Duane just happened to be there and came over to commiserate. That's all there was to it."

"Oh!" Delia's face reddened. "It really was none of my business—"

"I wanted you to understand. How you feel or don't feel about Duane is none of *my* business, but it's important to me that we're good."

"Of course we are!" Delia cried, her eyes filling. "I never for a moment thought anything negative toward you, Callie. It was just... I was caught by surprise last night, and I behaved very stupidly."

"I probably would have done the same. If it makes you feel any better, I'm pretty sure Duane never caught on."

"Men!" Delia grinned ruefully. "They never do, do they?" She reached out to give Callie a hug. "Thank you for coming to tell me this. You're Mel's niece, for sure." She dabbed at her eyes with a tissue and laughingly said, "So, tell me about this date with Karl's nephew!"

"No date," Callie said, laughing along with her. "More of an attempt at smooth talk that quickly morphed into an arm wrestle."

"Sounds like fun!"

"He actually suggested splitting my shop down the middle—half music boxes, half model trains. Wouldn't that be a combination!"

"Oh!" Delia shrieked. "What would you call it? *House of Musical Trains*? Customers wouldn't know what to expect! Can you imagine trying to run a half-and-half shop like that? If he's anything like Karl, what a delightful partnership that would be!"

"More like penance for all my sins. But he seemed to think it was perfectly reasonable. Or maybe he hoped I'd wear down after six months of such togetherness and hand the whole thing over to him."

"If you lasted even that long."

Delia thankfully having returned to her usual self, Callie said she'd better return to her own shop. "Laurie Hart agreed to stay and watch it, but I should let her get back."

"She was here a little while ago," Delia said, walking Callie to the door. "She wanted me to agree to an audit on Duane's bookkeeping. I told her I couldn't do that."

Callie nodded but didn't mention that she had. It might have to come out later, but if things turned out the way Laurie expected, Delia could be looking at Duane a little differently by then. Callie just hoped it wouldn't hurt too much.

❦

Late that afternoon, Jonathan called. He was still at the hospital.

"There's been no change," he reported.

"You've been there all this time?"

"I had some paperwork in my car, so the time passed quickly. A couple of people I knew came by, so that helped. I just thought I'd let you know in case you or Greer were thinking of coming to visit tonight. The doctors say nothing's likely to change very soon."

"That's helpful to know. I'll pass it on to Brian. It was really nice of you to hang around, Jonathan."

"Well, I felt sorry for the guy. I got to know him a little while he was working for me. Sounds like he was managing the best he could under difficult circumstances. We can only hope if—uh—when he comes out of this that things won't be even harder for him."

"I spoke to Elvin very briefly the day before he was hurt. He mentioned that you'd invited him indoors to take a break and cool off."

"Right. The heat was pretty grueling for that kind of work."

"The last thing he said to me was one word: 'why?' Nothing we'd said had led up to that, so I didn't know what he meant. But I wondered if it had something to do with the job he was doing at your place. Would that make any sense?"

Jonathan seemed to be mulling it over. After several moments, he said, "I can't think of anything he'd be referring to. I told you how he'd talked about his interest in ATVs and jet skis. I had no idea at the time, of course, what he intended to do, but I might have said something like 'not worth the money' or 'they can be treacherous.' I don't remember exactly. That's all that comes to mind."

"Well, maybe he'll be able to explain it to me himself before too long."

"Let's hope so."

They hung up, and Callie was distracted from immediately calling Brian by customers coming in. It then slipped her mind altogether until after she'd closed up shop and gone to her cottage. She grabbed her phone, fingers crossed that she'd catch him.

"Brian!" she said as she heard his voice. "You're not on your way to the hospital, I hope."

"No, still cleaning up here at the café."

"Good. Jonathan called a little while ago and said there's no change in Elvin and doctors don't expect any for quite a while. It sounds like there's no use going back tonight, in case you were thinking of it."

"I was, but I'm also pretty beat. I wouldn't mind putting it off. So Harman hung around that long?"

"Yes. I was surprised, because he barely knows Elvin. I don't know. Maybe he feels a bit responsible."

"Responsible?"

"Well, perhaps for not talking Elvin out of that sudden interest in sports vehicles? I don't know. Maybe he's just a nice guy."

"Mmm. Well, thanks for letting me know. I'd better go."

Callie hung up, feeling like something had been left unsaid. She rubbed Jagger's head absently as he nudged her for attention, then realized she was hearing Grandpa Reed's music box playing softly once again. She hadn't heard it in a while, and it startled her. What set it off this time?

She'd just been talking with Brian about Elvin. Did it have something to do with that? Or, she thought, standing up with an impatient shrug and heading for the kitchen, maybe it was simply that a speck of rust dropped off the mechanism and stirred it?

"If you're sending messages, Aunt Mel, a text would be a whole lot more helpful!" Callie said into the air. She pulled out her diner leftovers and popped them into the microwave to warm up. "I didn't hear anything after that long phone chat I had with Hank last night. What was up with that?"

She punched in the time on the keypad and hit the start button, then looked over at Jagger, who sat watching her from the living room with rounded eyes. Hank, she reminded herself, hadn't posed any real threat during their chat. She had shut things down the moment they took a wrong turn. So what did that mean, in relation to tonight's conversation? Since she had no idea, Callie decided that the music box's playing didn't mean a thing, and that was the end of it.

Her microwave dinged and she pulled out her steaming meal. Jagger hurried up at that point, his nose quivering.

"Uh-uh," she said. "Cats eat cat food and people eat spaghetti and meatballs." She sat down and proceeded to do just that.

Twenty-Five

Tuesday morning, Callie had just finished a conversation on the shop phone when Tabitha arrived, dressed in what Callie at first thought was normal clothing on another one of Tabitha's "rest" days. Then it struck her that she'd worn a denim mini skirt back in high school just like the one Tabitha had on. A similar tank top as well. Had her own teen years become vintage? A scary thought, but she didn't have to find out for sure as Tabitha launched into distressing news concerning Laurie and Bill Hart's shop.

"A town crew has ripped up the entire sidewalk in front of *Kids at Heart*. Nobody can get in!"

"Why did they do that?"

"Somebody apparently reported that the edge of one section was lifted up and a danger to pedestrians. Our mayor has been scared to death of lawsuits ever since the town lost a ton of money over a sinkhole that opened up a couple of years ago. A guy got hurt along with car damage."

"But I've walked on that sidewalk more than once and never noticed any problem."

"Laurie said one corner was raised maybe an inch from a tree root. And it was over to the side where nobody goes, anyway. She said they'd filled it in themselves with a little grout, just to be safe. They were keeping an eye on it and would have called for a repair themselves if they thought it needed it. And arranged for a much better time, like, maybe a Monday? When the shops are closed? The crew charged in this morning and tore everything up without any warning. Bill and Laurie are tearing their hair out."

"How awful. You said somebody reported it?"

"Yeah, after the sinkhole debacle, Mapleton has a hotline for calling in problems like that."

"And they consider an inch of sidewalk rise as an emergency?"

"Crazy, isn't it?" Tabitha slipped her colorful, yarn-fringed purse behind the counter.

"I keep forgetting that Keepsake Cove is not its own town. That we're a section of Mapleton."

"You'll remember if you get slapped with a fine for breaking one of Mapleton's town ordinances. Mel got one when she didn't clear the snow out front soon enough."

"Really?"

"Yeah. It snowed on a Sunday night but she put off taking care of it, figuring Tuesday morning would be okay. But she got fined." Tabitha tucked her rib-knit tank top a little tighter into her skirt. "She always suspected that Karl turned her in, though she couldn't prove it."

"So who reported the Harts' sidewalk?"

"Good question. I'm sure Laurie and Bill would like to know."

Callie's eye was caught by movement across the street, and she was surprised to see Annie lowering the Keepsake Café's awning.

"Oh yeah," Tabitha said. "Meant to tell you that, too. Annie's handling the café today. She said Brian is sick."

"Oh my gosh! I wondered why I didn't hear anything from him yesterday. You know about Elvin being in the hospital, right?"

"I sure do. Poor guy. And I heard you went to see him Sunday morning."

"I did, with Brian. He seemed fine then. Brian, that is. I wonder what's wrong?"

"I forgot to ask. Want to run over and find out?" Tabitha asked.

Callie nodded. "Be back in a minute."

She stepped outside and checked around for approaching customers. Seeing the coast was clear, she trotted across the street and found Annie, now inside the café and bustling about.

"I just heard about Brian," she said as she went in. "How sick is he?"

Annie, looking just a bit frazzled, shrugged. "It's some kind of flu. We dragged him to a clinic late last night, and they're pretty sure that's what he's got. Fever, aches, stomach problems—the whole enchilada, if you'll pardon the expression. All they could prescribe is bed rest and lots of fluids. He thinks he picked it up at the hospital, but then he's ready to blame anything on hospitals."

"Yes, he told me how he feels about them and why."

"He did? Good for him. Brian tends not to talk about that. But you're okay, right? I mean, you were there and didn't catch anything?"

"No, I'm fine. But I remember Brian saying on Sunday evening that he felt pretty beat. I'd guess he was coming down with whatever he has by then and must have caught his bug much earlier."

"I'll tell him that. When I get a minute, that is. Right now, I'd better do a few million things back in the kitchen."

"Think you'll manage okay?"

"I'll be fine. I've taken over here other times. But usually with a lot more notice, so that I had time to arrange things at home—like where the kids will go after the school bus drops them off. I just got off the phone with a friend who'll pick them up."

"If there's something Tabitha or I can do to help, let me know," Callie said. Not wanting to hold Annie up, she wished her luck and left, hoping the café's business would be light that day and that Brian would be back in charge soon.

She could see a bit of the *Kids at Heart* sidewalk situation in the distance. A glance toward her own shop told her that Tabitha was fine, so Callie headed over to the vintage toy shop.

Bill was pacing just beyond his shop, and as Callie drew closer she saw that he had put up a large sign directing customers to the back entrance. The sidewalk spanning the entire front of the store had been turned into rubble. Several orange safety cones and tape roped it off.

"I heard," Callie said to Bill as she drew near. "Where's the crew?"

"That's what we'd like to know!" Bill said, waving his hands in frustration. "They turned our perfectly good concrete into this, then took off. Laurie's on the phone now trying to get answers."

"I'm so sorry. At least you have your back entrance. Are people using it?"

Bill shook his head. "They see these cones and the mess and cross to the other side of the street before they get close enough to read my sign. I'm out here, ready to assure anyone that they can still come in, but no one's even coming near. I don't know what else we can do!"

He ran fingers through his thinning hair, and Callie could see his plaid shirt had darkened with sweat and was sticking to his back. *Kids at Heart* got the morning sun, which was already blazing. "If this doesn't get fixed soon, we might be in trouble. One day, I can handle, but I don't know how much longer. Somebody's got to get back here and work on it!"

"I heard about the hotline report. Any idea who called it in?"

Bill shifted uneasily. "Laurie thinks it was Duane. That he heard about her audit efforts and was getting back at us. She's always ready to think the worst of him, but I don't know. I can't see it. My guess is it was some cranky customer who stubbed a toe or just enjoys causing trouble."

Duane could be pretty cranky over what he'd consider Laurie's harassment and want to cause trouble, Callie thought. But like Bill, she didn't really know. Troublemaking shoppers were just as good a guess. "I hope Laurie will stir some action," she said before turning back to *House of Melody*. Before going inside, she stopped to examine her own sidewalk and was relieved to spot nothing that could cause any alarm. But who knew? Maybe that hotline system didn't ask for proof, and an anonymous claim was all that was required to set things in motion.

On that uncomfortable thought, Callie entered her shop. The mail had come, and Tabitha was sorting through it. She held up a large envelope for Callie.

"This looks like the estate sale Mel was interested in. I think it's this week. You might want to look into it."

"An estate sale?"

"Yeah, Mel enjoyed going to them. She sometimes picked up unique music boxes that way."

That sounded intriguing to Callie, and she opened the envelope. "It's on Thursday evening," she said, reading. "In a place called Mullica Hill in New Jersey. A long drive?"

"Probably over two hours," Tabitha said. "But it's worth it, from what Mel always said. She went there a lot. She'd stay overnight and check out the antique shops before heading back. There's a lot of them, she told me. I could close up for you on Thursday and open up Friday morning if you want. I used to do that for Mel once in a while."

"Did you? Then that would work. Let me think about it, though."

"Sure. I don't need to know before Thursday. Look over their brochure and see if you think it's worth the trip. But I know you'd love Mullica Hill, just for itself."

Callie smiled, liking the idea of a get-away that could also be good for her shop. But she still had a lot to consider. "Thanks, Tabitha. As usual, you're a font of information."

Later that afternoon, Callie looked up from the brochure she'd been studying to see Jonathan walk in. She felt a bit guilty for not having thought about him since his report on Elvin on Sunday and doubly so when she learned he'd spent a large amount of time at the hospital since then.

"It wasn't that hard for me," he insisted. "I have other things to do in the area, and I can bring my work with me to the hospital, unlike you." He tilted his head toward her music boxes with a smile.

"How is Elvin?" Callie asked.

"They tell me his brain swelling is slowly going down. They can't say much about his prognosis. It's still a wait-and-see situation."

Callie shook her head. "Brian is hoping to get to talk to him." She grinned wryly. "I think he wants to scold him. But only because he likes Elvin and worries about him. Brian would have been at the hospital too except he's come down with the flu. His sister has been running the café."

"I wondered why I didn't see him. That's too bad. In that case, I'll make a point of stopping in at the hospital again tomorrow. I think somebody should be there for Elvin. Even if he isn't aware of it."

"That's really nice of you."

"Well, as I said, I got to know him a little and can't help feeling sorry for him. The only thing is, that hospital cafeteria food is pretty bland. I have a meeting tonight with a new client and will have to work in the stop at the hospital tomorrow between a couple other things. I'm always eating on the run lately, which gets old pretty fast. But," he said, shrugging, "I'll survive."

"Why don't I fix something tomorrow night?" Callie said.

"Oh, no, I didn't mean—"

"I'd love to, really! I've hardly cooked since I've been here, and, you know, I kind of miss it." Callie felt, too, that she owed it to Jonathan for the dinners he'd taken her to, as well as all the trouble he was going to for Elvin. "It would be a treat for me, honest."

"Well, if you're sure?"

"Absolutely. Does seven o'clock work for you?"

"That would be perfect," Jonathan said. "Thank you. I'll look forward to it."

Jonathan took off, and Callie watched, already mentally scouring through the short list of company-level dinners she was capable of fixing and beginning to worry that Jonathan's tastes might be much more discriminating than hers. Then she shook herself. She could definitely put something together that would top *hospital cafeteria,* so that would be her starting point. Anything after that would be gravy, so to speak.

She smiled, and decided she was also looking forward to what would be her first hosted dinner at the cottage.

Twenty-Six

The next day, while Tabitha was there to take care of the shop, Callie drove the several blocks to the supermarket to pick up what she'd need for her dinner that night. She'd decided on baked salmon as something she could fix in the limited time, along with vegetables and a store-bought dessert.

"I won't be long. Just a few things on my list," she'd promised her assistant, omitting the part about who exactly she was picking up the dinner items for. Although she was comfortable with her reasons for issuing the invitation, she wasn't sure Tabitha would interpret it that way, and she wasn't in the mood for either a teasing or a lecture.

Callie quickly found what she wanted at the store, pleased that everything looked nice and fresh, and was heading back within minutes. While driving past *Kids at Heart*, she noticed a crew working on Laurie and Bill's sidewalk. Good, she thought, until she realized the crew was pouring wet cement, which would take several hours to set. That meant no front door use for the toy store's customers at least until the next day. She grimaced and hoped the Harts could deal with a second day's major business slow-down.

Annie was running the Keepsake Café for Brian again, but hopefully having had more time to plan had made it a little easier for her. The thought of her two neighbors and their difficulties made Callie grateful for her current comfort and ease, though she should probably knock on some music box wood once she got back. Things could change in the blink of an eye, as she was already keenly aware.

She had decided to drive up to Mullica Hill the next day for the estate sale and smiled as she anticipated that trip. Tabitha had described the quaint town with its multiple antique shops enticingly, and though it would mean some hours on the road, the get-away, with its justifiable purpose of shopping-for-the-shop, sounded great.

As she drove past the Keepsake Café, Callie spotted Annie catching a breath of air, and she tooted her horn lightly and waved before turning left to park off the main road. She made a U-turn to bring her car to the closer side of the street, then grabbed her bagged groceries and carried them past *Car-lectibles*, carefully avoiding any glances into Karl Eggers's shop. She then followed the path along the fence to her cottage, where she stowed away her perishables. After throwing together a cheese sandwich, Callie checked around the living room as she ate, looking for any missed areas of tidiness from her previous night's clean-up, Jagger following at her heels.

"Guess I'll have to brush off the seats again before tonight," she said as she spotted a circle of gray cat hair on a sofa cushion, but she reached down and scratched the cat's head affectionately as she spoke. Jagger had been a great antidote to loneliness during her evenings in the cottage, and the extra work he required was well worth it.

She filled two glasses with iced tea, then, and carried them across her small yard to the back of *House of Melody*, one glass intended for

Tabitha. As she walked in, she could hear her assistant guiding a customer through the many music box choices available to her and tossing out questions that might help narrow them down, queries such as *Does your sister like classical music? Where would she keep the music box? In her living room? What style of furniture does it have, and would she want her music box to blend in?*

An older woman's quavery voice answered each point, sometimes firmly, sometimes uncertainly, and Tabitha eventually led her toward choosing between two boxes: a rather expensive glass-topped box that played *Hungarian Rhapsody*, and a medium-priced, ivory-inlaid box that played *Pachelbel's Canon*.

Callie stayed out of sight, not wanting to disrupt the serious thought going into the purchase. The woman, after a long silence, finally pronounced, *"Hungarian Rhapsody."*

"Great choice," Tabitha pronounced, and Callie smiled. What a gem of a saleswoman she'd inherited. The ultimate proof, of course, lay in the sale remaining final, but so far Tabitha had scored a hundred in that respect.

When Callie heard the door close behind the customer, she stepped out of the office and congratulated her assistant, handing her the modest reward of an iced tea.

"Thanks," Tabitha said. "She was a sweet old thing. She wanted the perfect gift to celebrate her sister's milestone birthday. Turning ninety! Luckily for us, *Hungarian Rhapsody* had a special significance."

"Lucky indeed."

Callie told Tabitha of having seen *Kids at Heart* getting its new sidewalk poured. "I don't know how fast cement dries, but I'd guess it won't be walkable before tomorrow."

"That's too bad. Well, at least it'll be done. Maybe they can run a special sale or something to make up for it. Got your food okay?"

"Oh, sure."

"So who's the lucky guest?"

"Um..."

"No, let me guess. Jonathan! Am I right?"

"Tabitha, you really are psychic, aren't you?"

Tabitha laughed. "Didn't need to be, this time. The only other choice is sick in bed."

"I might have invited Delia, you know."

Tabitha thought about that. "Yeah, you could have. But the vibes I was picking up didn't fit Delia."

"No vibes," Callie countered. "Just a home-cooked meal for a guy who's been generously looking after Elvin when the rest of us can't."

"Okay. Whatever." Tabitha's words and casual shrug may have implied acceptance of the explanation, but Callie wasn't fooled. She didn't have to be psychic herself to guess what was going through Tabitha's head.

"I've decided to drive up to Mullica Hill tomorrow," she said, changing the subject. "Are you still okay with putting in the extra time?"

"Sure, no problem. While you're up there, you might keep an eye out for music boxes with a little history. Jonathan loves those."

"That's right. I remember he said something about that."

"Mel picked one up once—not at Mullica Hill, but somewhere else—that had been owned by one of the Roosevelt daughters. He went totally bonkers over it."

"Really? Which Roosevelt?"

"Huh? Oh, gosh, did they both have daughters?"

"Uh-huh, but Teddy's was more well known. Alice."

"That's the one." Tabitha grinned, adding, "I think."

"I'll keep that in mind—something with a history, that is." Callie glanced out her windows. "What's the weather going to be for my drive up there? Any idea?"

"I don't need to be psychic to know that, either. Hot, humid, with a chance of thunderstorms in the late afternoon. Just like they've been saying nearly every day lately."

"It does get old, doesn't it? Thank heavens for air conditioning," Callie said, adding as she saw two women heading toward the shop, "which might keep people at home too much, but once they're here, they hurry into our nice cool shops. Good afternoon!" she greeted the women as they came in, setting down her iced tea and getting back to work.

❧

Tabitha had been gone for a while when, during a quiet time, Callie suddenly realized she'd forgotten to buy one item for that night.

"Bummer!" she cried, knowing she wouldn't have time to run back to the supermarket and still get herself and her food ready. Then she thought of the Keepsake Café and grabbed her phone.

"Annie? Got a minute?" Getting an okay on that, Callie asked, "Do you have any dinner rolls I could buy?"

"Dinner rolls? No, the only rolls we keep on hand are the sandwich type." Callie's groan was swallowed when Annie then asked, "Would nut bread do?"

"You have nut bread? That's great! Can I run over for it right now?"

"Sure. The place is empty. I was getting ready to close up."

Callie said she'd be there in a flash and grabbed her keys to lock the shop's front door, just in case. As she trotted over, she could see Annie coming out of the kitchen holding the tasty bread.

"Thanks so much," Callie said, hurrying in.

"Glad to help. Expecting company?"

"A last-minute thing. I thought I had everything. How's Brian?"

"Getting grumpy, which probably means he's improving. Still pretty wiped out, though. I convinced him to let me run the café one more day."

"That must be a dilly of a virus. I hope you won't come down with it next."

"I've taken precautions," Annie said with a small grin.

"You're sliding his food through a slit in the door?"

"Not that drastic, though I did consider it. With my boys starting summer vacation soon, I can't be down and out. Have you inspected your front sidewalk, by the way? You know what *Kids at Heart* got hit with, right?"

"I do, and I did. Laurie Hart has suspicions about who might have caused it all."

Annie pondered a bit, then said, "Duane Fletcher?"

"So you've heard about all that."

"Some. I've only met Duane a couple of times, but something about him put me on edge."

"Oh?"

"Yeah." Annie leaned a hand on her counter, thinking. "It might have just been me. I tend to be a little suspicious of overly friendly people at first. But there's something else about him." She shook her head. "I don't know. It's hard to pinpoint."

Callie wanted to ask if Annie thought Duane capable of the things Laurie was accusing him of, but since Annie had just said she'd met him only twice, she let it go. Sometimes, though, first impressions were spot on. Just the fact that Annie had strong reservations about the man …

"Well, here's your bread," Annie said, interrupting Callie's thoughts. "I've got to lock up and check on Brian before I take off."

"Of course. Give him my best, and thanks so much!" Callie tucked the wrapped loaf under her arm and left, realizing as she stepped outside that three women were peering through the glass of her shop door and probably wondering why the lights were on but the door was locked.

"I'm coming," she called out to them, and hurried across the street as soon as the traffic allowed. As she opened the door and waved the trio in, she glanced at the clock. It was five thirty. She'd hoped to close up a little before six o'clock to give herself a few extra minutes at the cottage. Would that still be possible?

"Were you looking for anything in particular?" she asked but got discouragingly vague answers as the three wandered off in different directions, clearly in a browsing mood. At two minutes to six, one of the women finally brought a child's musical snow globe to the counter. Callie was ready to ring it up when one of the younger women said, "Mom, Ali's not into unicorns anymore."

"She isn't? Then what does she like?"

The two conferred as the unicorn globe was put back, and Callie watched her clock's minute hand move ahead. The third woman suddenly showed interest in one of the better musical jewelry boxes, which Callie didn't want to discourage, but the potential customer remained indecisive for several minutes while the other two dithered about Ali's likely preferences.

In the end, woman number three went off with a promise to think about the jewelry box a little more, and Callie rang up a ten dollar purchase of Disney's *Frozen* characters in a musical snow globe. The last two customers were barely out the door before she swiftly turned the lock and pulled the shade.

Within minutes she was dashing out her back door and into her cottage, hoping Jonathan would be either late or not starving. What, though, with the way things were going, was the likelihood of that?

216

Twenty-Seven

After throwing some cat food in Jagger's bowl, Callie hurriedly brushed cat hair off the sofa cushions. She jogged upstairs to freshen up and change, then rushed back down to wash and trim her vegetables, mix up the sauce for the salmon, and get the salmon ready for the oven.

In the middle of all that, she heard Grandpa Reed's music box playing from inside the roll-top desk. She tried to ignore it, hoping it would soon stop, but as the time crept closer to seven, the music box continued to play in spurts. Finally Callie threw down her towel. She'd had enough.

"Sorry to whomever or whatever is causing this, but I have a guest coming. I can't have this bringing up questions I can't answer."

She unlocked the desk and lifted out the music box, then wondered where to put it. If she simply moved it upstairs, the sound would likely carry. Then she thought of the blanket chest at the foot of her bed.

"My apologies," she said as she carried it there. "But it won't be for long. After all, you brought it on yourself," she chided. She set the music box on her bed, then lifted one thick blanket and a pillow out of the chest. She nestled the box on top of a puffy quilt at the bottom of the chest and covered it with the blanket and pillow. That, she thought, looking down with satisfaction, should surely muffle any music that might play during the evening.

She'd barely trotted back down the stairs when her doorbell rang—precisely at seven—and she opened the door to Jonathan, standing on her doorstep with a bottle of wine. He was wearing a sports jacket over a shirt and tie with slacks, which made Callie feel instantly underdressed in the blouse and capris she'd changed into. But Jonathan quickly put her at ease.

"I didn't have time to go home and change. Mind if I shuck the jacket and tie?"

"Please be comfortable." Callie pulled a hanger out of her closet, then took the bottle of wine from him with a smile.

"Had a few meetings with clients today," Jonathan explained, slipping out of his jacket. "But I managed to stop in at the hospital, too. Elvin's still being kept in the coma, so there's no change." He looped his tie around the hanger, then undid his top shirt button and rolled up the sleeves. "Anything I can do to help?"

"Not a thing until it's time to open the wine." Callie realized she didn't know if she had a corkscrew, never having had a need until then. "How did you know to bring white wine?" she asked from the kitchen as she began scrambling through the tools drawer. "It's perfect for what we're having, which is salmon, by the way."

"Sounds great, and I have a confession to make. There's a bottle of red sitting out in my car, just in case. I must have had a premonition about the white when I picked it to bring in." Callie glanced over, thinking she was close to overload on hearing about anything psychic-related. She saw Jonathan take a seat and reach out coaxingly toward Jagger, who'd jumped down from another chair. Jagger paused to allow a brief head scratch but then continued on his way up the stairs. Jonathan leaned back comfortably. "Nice place," he said.

"You've never been here?"

"Never had the pleasure."

"As you can see, it's space-challenged. No dining room, so we'll have to eat in the kitchen, I'm afraid." Callie's fingers landed on a corkscrew amidst the spatulas, whisks, and peelers, and she pulled it out triumphantly. "But you won't have to break into the wine bottle with a screwdriver!"

"That's good news," Jonathan said, grinning. "And kitchen dining is fine. I'm so grateful that I'd be willing to sit on your stairs with a plate on my lap." He glanced around. "All this was Mel's, I take it?"

"A hundred percent. I had some of my things sent down, but only clothes and such. Mel's furnishings were perfect as they were."

"I don't see her music box. Didn't you say you moved it here from the shop?"

"I did." Not wanting to admit where she'd banished it to or why, Callie simply said, "It's tucked away for now." She tested her vegetables and the salmon, which had been steaming and baking. "Almost ready here. Would you like to open the wine?"

Jonathan came over to handle that, and Callie pulled out two wine glasses and set them on the small table next to Aunt Mel's pretty, floral-patterned plates. She'd found a white tablecloth the night before, which she'd hoped to top with a centerpiece of flowers from the garden. Time had run out on her for that, but she saw there wouldn't have been room, anyway. All in all, she was happy with her table and only hoped the food would live up to it.

They took their seats and passed serving dishes back and forth. Fairly soon, Callie could see that Jonathan was enjoying everything, as was she, and she relaxed.

"Love this sauce," Jonathan exclaimed, dabbing a little more of it on his salmon. "What's in it?"

"Top secret," Callie said, then laughed. "It's simply dill, lemon juice, and capers mixed into plain yogurt. And a little salt and pepper. It's my mom's recipe."

"Delicious. And your mom lives where?"

"A small town in northern California."

"That's where you grew up?"

"More or less. We moved there when I was ten. I left when I was nineteen."

Jonathan nodded and seemed on the verge of asking about the later years. But perhaps picking up that Callie would rather not get into that, he instead said, "I've been to northern California a few times. Beautiful area."

"It is. Have you always lived here on the Eastern Shore?"

"Just for the last few years," he said. "It was cities before that, but I like the peace and quiet and privacy here." He seemed to stress the word *privacy* a bit, and Callie, appreciating his restraint regarding her past history, returned the favor. She did wonder about family or other relationships, which Jonathan had barely mentioned so far, but she was fine with waiting until he chose to share more.

"Elvin mentioned your impressive collection of music boxes," she said. When Jonathan looked up in surprise, she explained, "This was after he worked on your tree. When you brought him inside to cool down."

"That's right. I remember him looking at them, rather puzzled. There are a lot. But you know about how my grandparents got me started on that."

"I do. Tabitha said you particularly like ones with some history attached. She mentioned that because I'll be traveling tomorrow to an estate sale."

"Are you? Where?"

"A town called Mullica Hill in New Jersey. It's apparently quite a focal point for antique lovers."

"I've heard of it, though I've never been there. A long drive?"

"Long enough to make it an overnight."

"Probably a good idea. Yes, I do like music boxes with a story attached. It makes the music that much sweeter, to my mind. But it's still the music that resonates with me."

"Yes, I remember that you like Strauss and his era," Callie said, thinking of the music box Mel had ordered for Jonathan that was delivered with *Ode to Joy* instead of *The Blue Danube* that he'd wanted.

"It's a special favorite."

"So, in Mullica Hill I'll keep an eye out for anything from that time period."

Jonathan smiled.

Callie mentioned how she'd decided on the last-minute trip partly because of the stresses of the last two weeks. "I'm hoping the time on my own, short though it is, will help me recharge."

"I know what you mean. When there have been too many days in a row with difficult clients, I like to decompress with a quiet stroll along the cove. Nothing more relaxing for me than watching the wildlife on the water."

"Well, I hope you don't have that spoiled from now on by Duane Fletcher buzzing by with his new boat, as happened to me a few days ago. He apparently has his own way of relaxing. I did appreciate running into him the other day at the diner." Callie paused. "But that's a long story." When Jonathan assured her he'd enjoy hearing it, she told him about Karl Eggers's nephew trying every trick he could come up with to get her to sell her shop, then stalking off furiously when she resisted. "Duane rescued me from sinking into solitary embarrassment," she finished.

"He can be quite the people person," Jonathan agreed.

"I wasn't sure, but he seemed to imply that you'd been to his house once to discuss financial planning. Was that right?"

"Hmm? Oh, right! That was some time ago." Jonathan took a sip of his wine. "Nice place, if I remember. He'd added a sun room to the back of it."

"Lots of glass collectibles around?"

"Some. What really caught my attention was the sheer volume of art he had on his walls."

"Oh? What kind?"

"All kinds. Oils, watercolors, modern, old. No particular taste or theme that I could see."

"That's interesting." Callie remembered Duane saying that Jonathan had struck him as too interested in his belongings. Maybe he'd just been trying to understand them?

"They all looked quite good," Jonathan said. "Seemed like originals, not copies."

"Sounds expensive."

"Possibly. But it was the amount of what Duane had that was, well, overwhelming."

That *was* interesting.

When they'd finished, Callie suggested they have their coffee in the living room, and she shooed Jonathan out of the kitchen instead of letting him help clean up, pointing out how the small space allowed for only one worker. But she'd also noticed the beginnings of a headache—a rarity for her. She put it down to the pressures of the day and hoped that it would go away now that things had wound down. Jonathan had turned down dessert, and she was glad. She wasn't the least bit hungry for it herself, and it wasn't as though she'd gone to any trouble over the small cake beyond choosing it at the store. Besides the headache, she was fairly tired and didn't mind at all having less to deal with.

She brought out the coffee, then, and found herself glancing surreptitiously at Aunt Mel's wall clock, then chastising herself for it. Jonathan had been a perfect guest and she shouldn't be so eager to see him go. But unfortunately, she was.

So when she offered a refill on his coffee and he declined, Callie was relieved, but then felt instantly guilty. It wasn't his fault that she was tired and her head ached. She might have hustled those last dawdling customers along a little better and given herself a few minutes to relax.

"This has been great," Jonathan said after retrieving his sports jacket and tie and slinging them over his arm. "You're an excellent cook."

Callie smiled but shook her head, knowing how simple her menu had been. "Your wine made all the difference. Thank you for that."

"You're quite welcome," Jonathan said. He stepped out the door, then paused to look up. "No motion detector lights yet?"

"I haven't had the time."

"I can look into it for you, if you like. It's been a while since mine were installed, but I might still have the name of the firm or could track down a new one."

"That would be great, Jonathan. I'd appreciate that."

"As I've appreciated tonight's dinner. Thank you again."

Callie waited at the doorway until Jonathan was out of sight, then tiredly closed and locked it. As she turned, she saw Jagger coming down the stairs.

"Well, weren't you the gracious host," she began to mock-scold, but he rubbed against her legs so engagingly that she leaned down to pet him. That, however, caused a rush of pain in her head. Callie straightened, carried the used coffee cups to the kitchen, checked that there was food and water in Jagger's bowls, and then dragged herself off to bed. Two aspirin and a good night's sleep, she assured herself, would fix her up for the next day.

Twenty-Eight

Despite her hopes, Callie woke the next morning feeling as though she'd barely slept and that her head was stuffed with cotton. A strong cup of coffee was definitely needed.

She discovered she'd never turned on her dishwasher the night before or even added the dirty coffee cups to it, so she finished that job, then downed a glass of juice while the dishwasher chugged and her coffee perked. By the time she'd showered and dressed, she felt slightly better but not very hungry—which she put down to her later-than-normal dinner of the night before—and she passed on breakfast and instead carried a mug of coffee with her to the shop.

After opening up her shop, Callie sank onto a behind-the-counter stool, feeling as energized as an elderly slug. A few customers wandered in but browsed as lackadaisically as she felt, and she attributed that to the ongoing hot weather and humidity that tended to sap the life out of one. When her customers had gone off without buying, she was pleased to see Delia heading toward her door. But once her friend walked in, Callie saw signs of distress.

"Laurie Hart got Krystal Cobb to call an emergency association meeting tonight," Delia said.

"Emergency? Why?" As soon as it came out, Callie knew.

"Laurie is pushing a vote on paying for an audit on Duane's bookkeeping. It's horrible. It's terribly insulting. Duane doesn't deserve such an action. Will you come and vote against it? I told Duane I'd round up as many association members as I could to come and support him."

Callie gulped. What could she say? She'd already told Laurie she'd back her up on voting for an audit, but she hated to disappoint Delia. Then she remembered.

"I'm afraid I can't be there. I'm leaving this afternoon to drive up to an estate sale. I'll be gone overnight."

"Oh! Perhaps you can phone in your vote, then? Though Duane was hoping to have a large presence of supporters. There'll be a discussion ahead of the vote, which could make all the difference. He'll be sorry not to see you there." Delia was nodding to show acceptance of Callie's answer though she was clearly disappointed. "I'll tell him about your trip. I'm sure he'll understand."

"I'm sorry," Callie said, feeling more regret over Delia's feelings than Duane's. But there was always the chance that the examination of the books—if it came to that—wouldn't turn anything up. For her friend's sake, at least, she hoped that would be the case.

"I've got to run," Delia said. "Lots more shops to get to."

Delia hurried off. She'd barely disappeared from sight before Callie's phone rang.

"Emergency meeting at the library tonight. Seven o'clock." Callie recognized Laurie Hart's voice.

"I heard. I'm sorry, but I can't make it. I'll be out of town."

"No! Can't you postpone?"

Callie drew in a breath. She could postpone, but she didn't want to. Choosing between putting herself in the middle of the association fight where she was bound to offend somebody and a quiet, solitary drive to a quaint town to scope out vintage music boxes was a no-brainer. "I'll call in my vote, Laurie."

"Well, okay. But I wish you could be there too. Wish us luck. Gotta go."

The call disconnected as Laurie likely moved on to contact other shop owners. Callie realized her headache had reappeared, and she wondered if Aunt Mel had kept any aspirin in her office. She was searching through desk drawers when she heard the shop door open.

"Miss Reed!" an all-too-familiar voice boomed out.

Callie groaned, grit her teeth, and went out to face her much-less-bearable next-door neighbor, wishing she could instead swivel and head out the back door.

"Mr. Eggers."

"You need to move your car. Now."

"My car? Why? It's not blocking your shop." Callie knew she'd parked around the corner the previous day after coming back from the supermarket. It was on Eggers's side of the street but definitely public, not private parking.

"A delivery is coming. Your car is sitting where they have to park to bring my orders through the side door."

Callie sighed. A truck couldn't park a few feet farther down? The delivery was presumably of model cars, not pianos. But she decided it wasn't worth arguing about.

"I can't run out right now. But I'll be bringing my car in front of my shop this afternoon before I leave for New Jersey. Can it wait till then?"

Eggers glared. "New Jersey." Callie watched his thick eyebrows dance as a keen look came to his face. "You're moving?"

Oh Lord. "I'm driving up for one day," she said, emphasizing *one*. "My car will be out of your way for twenty-four hours."

"Don't block any of the space in front of my shop before you go," Eggers warned before turning his back and marching out.

What next? Callie wondered as the door slammed shut behind him.

But what came next was infinitely more welcome. Tabitha arrived, dressed in the tie-dyed shirt and bell bottoms that she'd been wearing the day she and Callie first met in the supermarket.

"I wondered when you'd start repeating," Callie said. "I was beginning to imagine a huge closet filled with a year's worth of costu—um, outfits."

"Oh, I just mix and match by my mood. This is one of my favorites. Did you hear what's going on at *Kids at Heart* now?"

"You mean for tonight's emergency meeting? What, has Laurie plastered her windows with posters about it?"

"No, I mean what's happening outside the shop. It's being picketed."

"Picketed! What on earth for?"

"A group of moms—I think—believes *Kids at Heart* has been selling real-looking toy guns. There's a lot of sign waving and shouting. They're mad!"

"Are they? I mean, have the Harts sold authentic-looking toy guns?"

"I never saw any. And Bill and Laurie swear up and down that they never have. But nothing they say seems to get through to the picketers. It's like someone's totally convinced those moms what the truth is."

"Someone?"

"Don't ask me who," Tabitha said. "I tried to talk to a couple of the women marching up and down with their signs, but they wouldn't stop chanting long enough to let me get a word in."

Another day of business disruption for *Kids at Heart*, Callie thought. And just as Laurie was working to gather votes for an audit on Duane Fletcher's books. Coincidence? Callie doubted it. But proving it might be another thing. She rubbed at her throbbing temples.

"You don't happen to have some aspirin on you?" she asked. "I couldn't find any in the office."

"Afraid not," Tabitha said. "Got a headache?" She looked closer. "You look a little flushed, too."

"I'll just run over to the cottage. A couple of aspirin and a tall glass of something cold should take care of it. Want anything?"

Tabitha shook her head, and Callie turned toward the back but then remembered about moving her car. Might as well do it now. She went out the front door instead and around the corner to where she'd parked. But by the time she'd started the car up and pulled forward to the intersection, a black Land Rover had grabbed the space in front of her shop. She grimaced, having wanted her own car nearby to load her things for her trip, but there was nothing to do about it.

She drove directly across the street and slipped into an empty spot just beyond the corner. The walk to her cottage in the scorching heat upped her fatigue and achiness, so that the ice-filled glass she was able to press against her face once she got indoors was a blessed relief. She downed her aspirin, slipped the bottle into her pocket, and topped off the glass to carry back to the shop with her.

"That looks inviting," she said to Jagger, who was dozing on the sofa. He barely lifted an eyelid before snuggling his nose deeper between his furry paws. She was on her own, he seemed to say. He had already claimed that cushion.

Callie sank onto a nearby seat for a minute. She sipped her water, then pulled out her phone in case she'd missed a text from Tabitha. She hadn't. But she did have a new email. It was from a Patty Wilkens, a name that sounded vaguely familiar. Then it hit her. This was the woman who'd organized Aunt Mel's reunion, the woman who might know about the mysterious Tom! Callie opened the email with high hopes.

Dear Callie, it began. *I was so sorry to hear of the loss of Melodie. Thank you for letting me know. I do remember Melodie well and regret having lost touch with her over the years. She was a wonderful person. I remember Tom, her boyfriend, too. You could hardly see one without the other back then. We were all so sure they would eventually marry. I've written to Tom about your search for him. I'm sure he'll contact you very soon. I'll also put an announcement about Melodie's death in our…*

The email continued, but Callie had stopped at *I'm sure he'll contact you.* She'd asked Patty for information about Tom, not to have her request forwarded to him. She now realized it was foolish not to anticipate this. Patty Wilkens, after all, knew—or used to know—Tom, but she didn't know Callie. What this might mean for herself, Callie didn't know.

She closed the email and stood, Patty's words—*I'm sure he'll contact you*—running through her head. She'd definitely need to think about that more, but later. Right then, she had to get back to the shop. She headed over, wearing a small frown.

From the shop's office, Callie could see Tabitha waiting on a customer as a second woman browsed. She drew a deep breath before joining them, offering assistance to the browser, which was declined, and then sank onto her stool. She sipped at her ice water and mulled over Patty Wilkens's message, though *Kids at Heart*'s troubles and Duane Fletcher's situation vied for her attention as well. None of it did much to improve her continued weariness.

About an hour and several customers later, when things had quieted down, Callie admitted to Tabitha, "You know, I'm not feeling so good."

"I wondered." Tabitha put a hand to Callie's forehead. "You've got a fever. No way should you go on that drive to Mullica Hill."

"That's what I was thinking."

"I bet you're coming down with the same virus Brian caught."

"I hope not. That bug has put Brian out of commission for days."

"Maybe it won't hit you as hard. But you should definitely go lie down. Right now. I was going to stay late today anyway, so I'll close up. And I'll be here first thing in the morning, like we planned. Don't even think about dragging yourself out of bed tomorrow if you don't feel well."

Callie nodded, not having the energy to protest. "You're an angel, Tabitha," she said.

"So I hear," Tabitha said, grinning. "Need any food? I could drop some off tonight, no problem."

"No, I'm good." What Callie really meant was that food was the farthest thing from her mind right then. Bed, on the other hand, was the closest.

She thanked Tabitha with all her heart and trudged off, confident that she was leaving *House of Melody* in good hands. Once inside the cottage, she closed her draperies, made sure that Jagger had what he'd need to survive, and dragged herself slowly up to her bedroom.

She'd just laid her head on her pillow when she heard her cell phone ring. She'd unthinkingly left it on the end table near the front door when she came in and put her keys away. No way was she about to run back down to answer it. The call could go to voicemail.

No sooner had the cell phone stopped ringing than the cottage's landline began to sound. Callie groaned but again let it go, this time to Aunt Mel's answering machine. She thought she heard someone leaving a message but couldn't distinguish the words. Nothing that can't wait, she told herself before drifting off to a welcome sleep.

Twenty-Nine

Troubling dreams disturbed Callie's sleep. In the last one, she clung to the sides of Duane's boat as he zoomed around the cove; she protested futilely over the roar of the motor that it made her seasick. She woke actually feeling queasy—aware, though, that it was likely due to her virus.

She pulled herself out of bed to see if she had any ginger ale, remembering her mother's antidote for an upset stomach, and found a bottle on the bottom shelf of the pantry. She poured herself a glassful over ice. That and a couple of soda crackers calmed her stomach enough to let her take a shower. She'd fallen into bed fully dressed except for shoes, and she'd been sweating. The tepid shower refreshed and soothed her, and the change to fresh nightclothes raised her hopes for a more restful sleep.

When Callie climbed back into bed, Jagger jumped up to join her, though she warned him things might be a little bumpy. It wasn't long before she proved that to be accurate, as her next dream had her running after Elvin as he zigzagged between trees on Duane's ATV. When she woke from that one, Jagger had moved to the far corner of the mattress.

She managed to fall into a deeper sleep after that until once again, her brain grew agitated. This time she traveled down a much darker road; she watched Aunt Mel come out of the guest bedroom, where she'd slept that final night, and, wrapped in her robe, head toward the stairs.

"Don't go down," Callie pleaded, but her aunt shook her head and silently put her finger to her lips.

Callie tried to rush after her, but she'd become so tangled in the bedclothes that she was in effect tied to the bed. She thrashed, trying desperately to free herself, and heard the cottage door downstairs close behind her aunt as Grandpa Reed's music box played. "No!" Callie cried out in her dream, upset enough to wake.

She found herself sitting upright, her sheets scrambled, blinking into the darkness. She continued to hear the music, though faintly. Was she still dreaming? Then she realized the sound came from inside the blanket chest, where she'd left the music box, forgotten as her illness took over. The muffled music stopped, much to her relief.

Then she heard the noise.

Was that Jagger? Had he gone downstairs and bumped something? But no. As her eyes adjusted to the darkness, she saw the large cat at the foot of her bed, not curled in sleep but on his feet and staring alertly toward her door. He had heard the thump, too.

Callie held her breath. She hadn't imagined it. But what had caused it? Maybe a tree branch had fallen onto the roof? She didn't hear any wind blowing outside, but dead branches sometimes dropped of their own accord, didn't they? She realized she was trying hard to convince herself that all was well. Then she heard the second noise. The creak of a downstairs floorboard. Someone was in her house.

Callie patted frantically on the nightstand for her cell phone until she remembered she'd left it downstairs. Her heart sank. What could she do? At least, she told herself, get out of bed and not wait there like a sitting duck! She slipped out as silently as she could manage and grabbed onto the nightstand as a wave of dizziness swept over her. When that passed, she thought about what she could use to defend herself. The lamp over the nightstand had been clamped to the wall, and her tugs couldn't release it. She eased over to the open closet, holding her breath that no floorboard squeaks would betray her. Was there anything heavy and weapon-like in the closet? Her mind raced, picturing the currently invisible contents. No crowbars or hammers, unfortunately. Nothing sturdier than a boot or a wooden hanger came to mind, and she wasn't willing to stake her life on either.

She grabbed the robe that hung on the door and wrapped it around her thin pajamas, an automatic action that only seemed to highlight how vulnerable she was. Then she remembered the can of pepper spray she'd bought back in Morgantown, for the nights she came home late from work. She'd last seen it in her winter purse, the one she carried when she wore her long puffy coat against the bitter West Virginia winds. But where had she left that purse?

Callie reached for the closet shelf, trying hard not to accidentally knock something down and alert her intruder. Why hadn't she organized her things by now? Nearly everything lay in the jumble they'd fallen into as she'd unpacked her many boxes, putting off doing a better job until later on. What was that procrastination going to cost her?

Not finding the purse on the shelf, she lowered herself to the floor to run her hands through the heaps of shoes. Would the purse have ended up among them? She heard a scraping sound from the living room and froze. What was that? The downstairs closet? Was her intruder searching it for valuables?

Knowing there was nothing worth stealing there gave her no comfort. He wouldn't likely stop with one room. Did whoever it was believe the cottage to be empty, keeping lights off and moving quietly only to avoid alerting neighbors? She had planned to be away overnight. Who would have known about that? Too many people, Callie realized, but she didn't have time to think about it. She needed to find her pepper spray.

Her search on the closet floor turned up only shoes, a bag of yarn, and a small pocket umbrella, none of which were of any use. She leaned back onto her heels and scoured her thoughts. Where was that purse? Suddenly an image of a hook at the back of the closet appeared. Of course! She'd hung it there!

Callie stood to reach between her hanging clothes, beneath the shelf. Her hand landed on a hook that had two leather straps over it. Jubilant, she followed the straps down to the top of the purse, recognizing the shape and feel as the one she'd been looking for. She eased the zipper open and slipped her hand inside. She immediately felt the bulge in an inside pocket and pulled out the small can. She clutched it in relief but knew she'd still need to think and act fast. And her illness was dragging her down.

One worrying sign was the dizziness that had struck when she'd risen from the closet floor, causing her to reach out to steady herself. Something on her feet might help. She searched with her toes for the pair of slip-on, rubber-soled shoes that she usually kept near the front, and finding them, slid her bare feet inside. Then she considered her options of where to stand if—make that when— her intruder came into the bedroom.

The closet was too cramped and stuffed to try to hide in. Behind the bedroom door would be better. She would wait there, Callie decided, letting him come all the way in before firing off the pepper spray. Firing too soon would mean he could block her escape. Cool though it all sounded, Callie trembled at the thought, keenly aware of all the things that could go wrong. Chief among them was her own lack of full control.

She heard another sound come from below, which she identified as the lid of the roll-top desk being raised. She'd left it unlocked after moving Grandpa Reed's music box and knew that little else of any interest remained there. Thank goodness her growing fatigue had caused her to forget about bringing the music box back downstairs. If she'd returned it to the desk, she doubted the flimsy lock would have held against much force.

She began to hope that the intruder, not finding anything, would be discouraged and leave. Aunt Mel had no silver to steal or other items of obvious value. But then she saw a flash of light swing under her door, which could only mean one thing, and she braced herself as she heard the first footfall on the stairway. He was coming.

Her eyes had adjusted enough to the darkness to see outlines of the bedroom furniture. She scoured the area for any signs of Jagger, but didn't find any and assumed he'd hidden under the bed. A strong desire to join him arose, but Callie knew she was better off upright, ready to attack and to run. She drew a breath and waited.

A step creaked, this one higher up, informing Callie he'd nearly reached the top. The light from his flashlight was stronger, and she pictured him only feet away in the short hallway. She heard him cover that distance in seconds, pause between the two bedrooms, and then put a hand on her doorknob.

She watched the doorknob turn. There was a soft click and the door began to open. She raised her pepper spray and waited. A dark figure stepped into the room, preceded by the light from his flashlight. Callie stood motionless, afraid to breathe as he passed within inches of her. Then he turned slightly, and the brightness of the beam was enough to illuminate his features. Callie gasped and he spun around toward her, the light hitting her eyes.

She pressed down hard on the valve of the pepper spray can, aiming blindly and not caring that it was Jonathan, the man who'd been to her home for dinner just the night before, the man who'd seemed to offer nothing but friendship. He'd broken into her home in the middle of the night, and that was all she needed to know. The can hissed weakly, then stopped. It was dead.

Jonathan knocked it from her hands, keeping his flashlight aimed at her eyes. "You said you'd be gone!"

Callie tried to rush past him, but he grabbed her arm. "I don't want to hurt you," he snapped. "Just tell me where it is and everything will be okay." His clutch on her arm was vise-like.

"Where is what?" Callie asked, struggling against his grasp and still grappling with the shock of his being there.

"The music box! Don't be stupid. Where is it?"

"It's not here."

He threw her to the wall, and Callie's head cracked hard against it. Any hope that this was some kind of awful mistake instantly fled. The room spun for a moment, and she thought she was passing out. But he caught her before she fell and held her. Jonathan wanted information, and her only hope was to keep that information from him as long as possible until she could escape.

"Where?" he demanded.

She managed to look anywhere but at the blanket chest. "I ... it's back in the shop. I wanted it where Tabitha could watch over it."

Jonathan stared at her for a long time, deciding if he could believe her. Callie hoped she looked frightened enough to blurt out the truth. The frightened part wasn't hard—she was truly terrified. But she was also stalling. Any time she gained, though, would run out when he didn't find the music box in the shop. What would she do then?

After a full minute, Jonathan nodded. "Show me," he said, his voice low and menacing. He pulled her to the door, his left hand gripping her upper right arm, the flashlight in his other hand. "Don't try anything dumb. I have a gun. Be good and you'll live."

Callie doubted that, but the longer she could drag things out, the better chance she might have. She moved forward awkwardly, angled sideways by his grip on her, and they inched their way together down the hallway and the stairs.

"I'll need my keys," she said. "They're in the table by the front door."

He pushed her forward, keeping the beam of his flashlight aimed at the floor as they wove around other furniture toward the end table. Callie reached for the drawer pull with her right hand, Jonathan still gripping her arm tightly but leaning with her, and she shuffled through the drawer even though her fingers had instantly landed on the keys. Her goal was to distract Jonathan from noticing her left hand, which covered the cell phone lying dark and hidden in the shadows on the table top. She noisily pulled out the keys while slipping the phone into her robe pocket.

"How did you get in here?" she asked as further diversion.

"Your lock is easy to pick."

"Is that how you got into the shop? That night you killed Aunt Mel?"

"Never mind," Jonathan said gruffly and yanked her toward the front door. "Open it," he ordered as he turned off his flashlight.

She did, and they faced the blackness of the yard until gradually shrubs and the back of her shop grew visible in the pale moonlight. He began walking her across the yard, warning closely against her ear, "Don't even think of yelling for help. No one will hear, but even if they did, you'd only be bringing them to their death. I won't hesitate to shoot."

"Why?" Callie asked. "Why would you kill for a music box?" She stumbled on one of the raised bricks of the walk and Jonathan wrenched her upright.

"Just unlock the door."

Callie took her time fingering through several keys on the ring to find the shop key, listening, as she did, for any sounds of life—of *help*—nearby. But could she actually call for that help after Jonathan's promise to shoot? She knew she couldn't, so her only hope was that someone might have seen or heard them from a window. But what was the likelihood, at that hour?

She felt for the keyhole with her left hand and slid the key inside. The lock turned and she opened the door. Inside, with the door closed behind them, Jonathan turned his flashlight back on but once again kept it aimed at the floor.

"Where is it?" he demanded.

"First, I need to understand," Callie said. "Why is my grandfather's music box so important that you would kill for it? You did kill Aunt Mel, didn't you?"

"It was her own fault."

"How can you say that!"

"She surprised me that night, but she didn't know who it was since I had a hood and scarf covering my face. I would only have stunned her enough to get away. But stupidly she fought and pulled down the scarf."

And so you killed her, Callie silently finished for him. *As you'll kill me once you get what you want.* Though gulping back fury at his cold-blooded statement, she needed to keep him talking. "And the music box? Why do you want it so badly?"

To her shock, Jonathan started chuckling. "You fools, all of you, having that magnificent piece for so long and never understanding what it was. *Whose* it was."

"Tell me."

"It was Sophie's." He fairly breathed the name.

"Sophie?"

"Duchess of Hohenburg," he clarified impatiently. "Married to Archduke Franz Ferdinand. You know who that is, don't you?"

Callie scoured her memory for the name, glad at least to be getting some kind of explanation. If she didn't come up with the right answer, though, what then? But her years-ago World History exams rushed back to her and she remembered. "He was assassinated, right? It started World War I."

Jonathan nodded. "Some years before they were killed, he gave her that music box. Sophie wrote about it in her diary. She treasured it, as I do, for its music and because he gave it to her."

How did Grandpa Reed acquire it? Callie wondered. She could only hope to have the chance to find out. One very important thing she did discover as Jonathan spoke was that he wasn't actually carrying a gun as he'd claimed. The only pocket in his dark clothing that held anything significant bulged in a flat, rectangular shape. She guessed it might be his lock-picking tools. It was definitely not a gun.

That, while being a relief, didn't totally put her out of danger. Jonathan had killed Aunt Mel with a blow to her head, and he still had his heavy flashlight in hand.

"Enough of this," he said, turning Callie roughly toward the shop area. "Where did you put it?"

Callie started to walk blindly, not knowing what to do next, when her cell phone suddenly rang. It startled them both but Callie recovered first, which gave her an instant to pull the phone from her pocket and press *answer*. "Help! Call 911!" she screamed, then spun out of Jonathan's loosened grip and ran for the back door.

She only managed a few feet before Jonathan's flashlight crashed against her skull. Callie staggered, but Jonathan's aim had been slightly off, only grazing her, since unlike her aunt she'd been prepared to duck. Before he could strike again, she rushed forward, making it to the door and slamming it open. She made it out but then felt him grab her hair, yanking it hard. Callie cried out, falling back, and feared the worst until she heard a new voice order, "Stop right there."

They both froze for a moment until Jonathan pushed Callie hard toward the voice. She stumbled against the man she now recognized as Brian. He caught her as Jonathan ran toward the path.

"Are you all right?"

"Yes! But he's getting away!"

"No he isn't," a gruff voice near Aunt Mel's tall fence said. Callie heard a cry and a heavy thump.

She picked up the flashlight Jonathan had dropped and aimed it toward the fence. Karl Eggers stood, scowling, with one heavy-booted foot pinning Jonathan to the ground.

"Where did you two come from?" Callie asked, astonished. But with blood running down her head and sirens sounding in the distance, she had to wait a while for her answer.

Thirty

Callie looked up from her hospital bed at the three faces gathered around and was touched by the concern she saw. Her head was bandaged and it ached, this time not from her flu virus but from the crack Jonathan had given it. She'd also been hooked up to an IV "for dehydration," she'd been told.

"Don't look so worried," she pleaded. "I'll be fine. They're just keeping me a few hours for observation, then I'll go home."

"Where you should still take it very easy," Delia said.

"And you three should get some sleep," Callie said. "But first I need some answers. How did you two," she asked, glancing from Brian to Karl, "manage to show up just when I needed you?"

The two men looked at each other, then over to Delia, who squirmed.

"I called them," she said.

"But how—?"

"I'm not really sure." Gathering her thoughts, Delia sank onto a chair. "All I know is that I woke up suddenly in the dark with a strong feeling that something was very wrong. At first I thought it was something to do with my house, and I got up and checked around. But everything seemed fine. That awful feeling, though, wouldn't go away. So I stepped outside."

"And saw Jonathan's flashlight in my cottage?"

"No, I didn't see any light. But I heard your voices, yours and Jonathan's, though I didn't recognize his."

That must have been when we were crossing the yard or at the back of the shop, Callie thought. But they'd kept their voices so low, Jonathan warning that he'd had a gun. How could Delia have heard? Did the still summer air carry voices that well?

"I was sure something bad was happening," Delia continued. "I worried that the police couldn't come quickly enough, so I called Karl, then Brian."

"Then you called my cell phone?" Callie asked, thinking of the ring that had startled both her and Jonathan and given her the chance to run.

'Your cell phone?" Delia asked. "No, I called the police next."

"But—" Callie began, but Karl interrupted.

"I'm normally a very sound sleeper," he said. "My wife used to—" He stopped to cough. "That is, I have to set two alarm clocks to wake myself in the morning. But Delia's rings got through to me somehow."

"And to me," Brian said. "Luckily, we both got there in time."

"And I'm very grateful to all of you," Callie said. "Jonathan would have killed me, just as he killed Aunt Mel."

"Over a music box?" Brian asked.

"It's a very special one, in a way none of us realized but Jonathan did. Valuable."

"Still … "

"I can only guess that he had an obsession that went way beyond a collector's passion," Callie explained. "I think Elvin may have picked up on that a little when he was in Jonathan's house. How is Elvin? Do you know?"

"Much improved," Brian said. "They've said the brain swelling has gone way down."

"I'm so glad!" Callie mulled a few moments. "Now that I think about it, I wonder if Jonathan had something to do with Elvin's accident? When he told me he'd hired Elvin, he said that he wanted to get to know him. Once he realized that Elvin sometimes hung around Aunt Mel's cottage, maybe he feared Elvin saw him the night of the murder. Perhaps he goaded Elvin into taking Duane's ATV."

"Let's hope Elvin will be able to tell us something about that once he's recovered," Brian said. "One thing I do know—Jonathan didn't spend all the time at the hospital that he claimed he did, watching over Elvin."

"No?"

"The staff said they never saw him after Sunday morning, when he told us to go home and said he would stay. All those updates he had on Elvin probably came from simply calling in."

"If Jonathan had any concern at all," Delia said, "it must have been about what Elvin might say when he woke up. He could have intended to show up then and convince Elvin about what he did or didn't remember."

Callie shook her head. "He managed to convince me that he was being so kind and thoughtful."

"Jonathan fooled us all," Delia said. "So don't be too hard on yourself."

But I invited him to dinner, Callie wanted to say. *He sat at my table, and I cooked for the man who killed my aunt.* She shook her head again and then winced at the pain, her hand shooting up to the bandaged spot.

"We should let you rest now," Delia said, getting up.

"Give me a call when they're ready to release you." Brian reached down to squeeze her hand.

"Thank you," Callie said, smiling. "I will."

The three left and Callie closed her eyes, ready to let whatever pain meds they'd given her get to work. She was surprised in a moment to hear a soft tap at her door and see Karl's head poke back in.

"I have something more to say. May I come in?"

"Of course."

He walked to the end of her bed, looking highly uneasy, and Callie thought if he'd had a hat in his hands, he'd be twisting and fingering it. She started to brace herself for whatever was coming.

After a few throat-clearings and a hand run through his hair, Karl finally said, "I need to apologize."

"Oh!"

"I had no idea what happened to your aunt. I believed she'd simply fallen. I was angry and thinking only of my nephew, who needed work. I was hard on you. I'm sorry."

Callie was astonished enough to be at a loss for words for several moments. Then she smiled. "Thank you, Mr. Eggers."

"Karl."

"Karl. What you did for me tonight makes up for a lot, believe me."

He nodded, saying nothing.

"I learned only recently that you'd lost your wife," Callie said. "I'm sorry for that."

He cleared his throat some more. "I miss her," he said. "She was good for me. Kept me in order." His lips twitched upward. "More than just waking me up in the morning."

Callie smiled at that.

"I did come to Mel's funeral," he added. "But I came in after everyone was there and stayed in the back. Funerals are hard for me."

"I can understand," Callie said. "I'm sure Mel knew and appreciated it."

"Well," he said, "I just wanted to say that. I'll go now. I hope you'll feel better."

"Thank you, Mr.—Karl. Thank you very much. You get some rest, too."

Callie watched him leave, carefully closing the door behind him, and stared at the door for several minutes. She reached for a tissue to swipe at her eyes, then switched off her light, thinking this was surely a day of surprises.

Some a lot better than others.

Thirty-One

Callie returned to *House of Melody* after several days of rest, still a bit shaky but eager to be out of her cottage and back in the world. She'd been fussed over by Delia, for which she was very grateful, but she was doubly grateful to learn that she hadn't, in fact, suffered a concussion from Jonathan's flashlight. Her flu virus, in addition, seemed to be a less virulent strain than Brian's had been, so she didn't need to further impose on Tabitha, who'd been generously putting in extra hours at the shop. Callie raised her shade, opened her shop door, and took a deep breath of fresh air, thinking, among many other things, how great it was to be alive.

Brian was outside his café, lowering the awning, and he noticed her and waved heartily. She waved back and would have trotted over to chat except that she saw customers heading his way, probably wanting their morning coffee. Brian had brought her home from the hospital, and they'd had a good long talk along the way. She'd begun thinking that maybe she was ready to start dating again. Once everything settled down, if he asked her out she would very likely accept.

Settled down. It was a questionable concept after what had happened. There was so much to still grapple with. Elvin had come out of his coma and told his story about the night of his crash. Apparently, as Callie had suspected, Jonathan had told Elvin to take Duane's ATV that night, claiming Duane had bought it from him but never paid. He'd convinced Elvin not only that the ATV was legally his but that Duane had swindled many of Elvin's friends as well, and that this would be the start of setting things right for them, too.

The only thing Elvin couldn't quite wrap his head around was why, if Brian had been swindled by Duane, Brian hadn't asked directly for his help in retrieving his property—possibly the "why" Elvin had asked aloud when Callie had run into him that afternoon in front of *Stitches Thru Time*. He would have done anything for Brian after Brian's steady kindness to him. Jonathan had probably picked up on that and used it to manipulate Elvin.

Elvin also said that Jonathan had asked him several times about the night Mel died. Elvin had been confused by the questions and in the end simply confirmed everything Jonathan already suspected—in other words, that he'd witnessed enough to put Jonathan in jail. That had nearly led to Elvin's death.

Callie had had time to think a lot about that night, too, and decided that Aunt Mel had seen or heard something coming from *House of Melody* that had concerned her enough to check out, but not enough to call the police. A fatal mistake, as was her not following up on the suspicions she must have had when she'd started, but never finished, the email to Callie about something worrying her. Callie would never know exactly what that was, but she could guess that it was something to do with Jonathan. Looking back, she realized that the music box had played several times when Jonathan was present. But she'd been distracted by other things happening at the same time, which had caused her to misinterpret the warnings—if, in fact, they had been warnings.

One of the less shocking but still disturbing things that had occurred during Callie's convalescence was the blow-up between Laurie Hart and Duane Fletcher. When confronted by Laurie after she'd pried incriminating information from one of the leaders of the picketing group, Duane admitted having been behind both the sidewalk disruption and the protest. He claimed he'd been highly offended and hurt by Laurie's insinuations about his bookkeeping and said that she deserved to know how it felt to be wrongly accused, at least by the picketers. He also insisted that he'd been able to afford his few luxuries because of wisely investing the money he'd inherited from his mother along with her glass collectibles—"not that it's anybody's business," he'd added.

Laurie told Callie, and probably everyone who would listen, that Duane had revealed his true character through his spiteful actions and that she still believed the audit that had been voted for would reveal many irregularities.

Unsurprisingly, Delia's feelings for Duane had cooled considerably after hearing what he'd done to the Harts. "He's not the person I thought he was," she said, though Callie heard that Duane still had several supporters. Apparently charm and charisma carried one a long way, but time would likely tell.

Tabitha had offered to come in early again that day, but Callie assured her she was ready to return to the usual schedule. She was glad, though, that customers so far had been few. The woman who'd kept her late the night of her dinner with Jonathan returned to buy the musical jewelry box she'd been looking at, so that definitely made up for it.

"I told my husband he could consider this my birthday gift," the customer told Callie as she watched her pack up the jewelry box. "He was happy not to have to come up with anything himself and didn't even ask what it cost."

As the woman left, clutching her package protectively, Callie saw Orlena approaching and went to meet her colorfully dressed neighbor at the door.

"Thank you, my dear," Orlena said as she floated in wearing another multi-colored caftan, though her mood didn't seem to match its brightness. "I noticed you were here and wanted to see for myself that you are all right." She held Callie by the shoulders and inspected her earnestly before crushing her in a great hug. "I was horrified to hear what you went through," she said, "but so relieved to see you're well. You are, aren't you?" She held Callie out again at arm's length.

"I am," Callie assured her. "The flu might actually have been worse than my injury, and I can't blame that part on Jonathan."

"Evil man! If he had been to my shop, I might have seen him for what he was and been able to warn you. But we never came face to face."

"He was clever at keeping his true self hidden," Callie said.

Orlena paused. "I did want to make sure you're well, but I came here for another reason also," she said. "To explain myself."

Callie waited.

"I held back my true thoughts about Duane Fletcher when you asked about him, and also when Laurie Hart begged me to vote for the audit. I had my reasons, and I'm sorry to say they were not unselfish."

"Oh?"

"It wasn't for myself," Orlena assured her. "But family is next to one's self, is it not? It was for my baby sister. Alyshia needed Duane's goodwill to start up her restaurant. He has been considering investing in it, which is absolutely necessary. How could I say anything against him when my sister's future lay in his hands?"

"I understand."

"I have never had a good feeling about him, but not concerning his honesty. What I have seen and never liked was what just came out in his actions against the Harts—his deep-down, petty meanness. But he has money to invest, and I convinced myself to overlook a lot if he would help my baby sister reach her dream. Though I did warn her about his other side."

"And she's okay with it?"

Orlena nodded. "Alyshia said that if his check cleared, everything else between them after that would be through the bank. He would only be a silent partner while she ran the restaurant. And it will be a good restaurant, believe me! But," she went on, "I tell you this in confidence, you see, because maybe people who don't like Duane won't come to my sister's restaurant if they know he is involved with it, and that wouldn't be right. But I know I can trust you. You are a good person. I wanted you to understand my silence."

"It was totally reasonable," Callie assured her. "When I asked you about Duane, you know, I had in mind a much worse crime than disrupting someone's shop. It turns out he wasn't guilty of murder, so no harm done. What kind of restaurant will your sister have?"

Orlena smiled broadly. "Caribbean, of course! Ackee, callaloo, curry shrimp! It will be wonderful."

And won't compete with Brian's café, Callie was pleased to realize. "Sounds intriguing. I'll be looking forward to it."

"Looking forward to what?" Tabitha asked as she walked in.

"To my baby sister's new restaurant," Orlena answered. "But it won't be ready for a while. In the meantime, Tabitha, you and I must be sure to watch over our friend after what she has suffered—you with your cards, me with my third eye. We will keep her safe from now on."

"Great," Callie said. "Just wrap me in bubble wrap right now and keep me from talking to any strangers for the rest of my life. Sounds like fun!"

Orlena laughed heartily and gave Callie a farewell hug. "No bubble wrap, dear one. But you will have to listen to our warnings. Right, Tabitha?" she asked on her way out the door.

"Well," Tabitha hedged until Orlena had moved on, "I guess it would help if the warnings were more specific. I thought someone might be a danger to you, but I couldn't point out exactly who or how."

"That's pretty much the way everything is though, isn't it?" Callie asked. "We get hints and clues, but it's up to us to put it all together. I know I'll be a lot more alert from now on."

Tabitha nodded. "On another note, Laurie and Bill's sidewalk is fixed and they're good to go."

"And that should be the end of any other problems caused by Duane."

"And by Jonathan," Tabitha added, "now that he's in custody. With solid proof to keep him there." She paused. "Has Mel's music box been quiet?"

"It has. Ever since it woke me up in the middle of the night when Jonathan was in the house. Maybe I've heard the last from it."

Tabitha cocked an eyebrow but made no comment. "You're keeping it, right? I mean, now that you know how valuable it is, you could ... "

"That music box has more value to me in a whole other way," Callie said. She would never part with it, but she hoped she'd reached the end of any more "messages" from it, and, in particular, the need for them.

She thought about how her phone had rung that night in the shop, just as her ability to stall Jonathan was about to run out. Delia, who'd frantically called Brian and Karl, said she hadn't tried to call her. And later, when Callie checked, there was no record of a call to her phone at that time.

That didn't completely surprise her, after all that had already happened, but she decided to keep it to herself. Some things, she felt, were best left unsaid.

～～～

That evening, Callie was checking emails on her phone while curled up on the sofa with Jagger when she saw one from a name she didn't recognize: Thomas Hodder. She stared at it for a moment until it came to her. *Tom.* She opened it.

Dear Ms. Reed, it began. *Patty Wilkens informed me you were interested in contacting me in regards to your aunt, Melodie Reed. I would be very happy to speak with you.*

He gave a cell number and invited her to call that evening.

Callie stood and walked around her small living room for several minutes. What would she say? What would *he* say? Finally, she made the call.

"This is Callie Reed," she said. "Mr. Hodder?"

"Yes, this is Tom. Thank you for calling. I wasn't brave enough to speak to you at Melodie's funeral. But I'm ready now."

"I think I have most of the answers to the questions I had, Mr. Hodder. You were someone very special to my aunt. I don't need to pry any further."

"No, you have the right to understand, Ms. Reed. I think Melodie would want it."

Callie waited while Tom cleared his voice. "Melodie and I were very dear to one another back in high school. But we were young, things happened, and we foolishly separated. We found each other again at the twenty-fifth reunion. Twenty-five years! So much time, and yet it was as if no time at all had passed. Nothing between us had changed. We knew we both felt the same. The problem was, during those years I had married."

Yes, Callie thought that might be the case.

"You might ask, Ms. Reed—"

"Callie, please."

"Callie, you might wonder why, if I felt such love for Melodie, why didn't I divorce my wife so we could be together? It wasn't, however, so simple. My wife, you see, has suffered for several years with severe mental illness. She's been hospitalized much of the time. None of this is her fault, of course, but I simply couldn't leave her. I'm all she has, the last thread connecting her to reality."

"I'm so sorry."

"Melodie understood," Tom continued. "And when I sometimes weakened under the stress and vowed I would free myself, she wouldn't let me. She said our time would come. I don't know what I would have done without Melodie during some of the worst times. She helped me through them and kept me sane. I miss Melodie terribly," he said, his voice breaking. "I was at the funeral, as I said, but I blended in as one of the many who were there. I needed to say that final goodbye."

"I'm glad you were there. I wish we'd met."

"I wish things had been different, and Melodie and I had never parted all those years ago. What's that quotation?" he asked. "The saddest words are 'what might have been'?"

"Something like that." Callie's heart ached, not only for her aunt but for this man whose life might have been so much happier had he made the right decision at the right time.

"Well, that's my story, *our* story. Thank you for letting me tell it. I won't take up any more of your time."

"I have plenty of time," Callie said. "I'd be very happy to meet, Tom, if you'd like."

"Let me think about that," he said. "I'll get back to you."

"Please do." They said goodbye and Callie sat, stroking Jagger lightly and thinking of all she'd just heard. The music box, she realized, had remained silent during the call. Did that mean Aunt Mel was at peace? She hoped so.

After quite a while, her phone rang, and Callie smiled as she saw that it was Brian.

"Hi," he said. "I wondered how you were doing. How did your first day back in the shop go?"

How did it go? Callie thought about her early skepticism about things "settling down." In some ways, though, they had. Orlena had explained her mysterious reticence, and Tom's phone call had answered her remaining questions. But talking with Tom also stirred up plenty of the emotions concerning her aunt that Callie had only just begun to deal with.

"Fine, but tiring," she said.

"Too tired to go for a little walk? There's a gorgeous sunset right now. And I've got ice cream."

"Ice cream?" Callie smiled, thinking that sometimes the right decisions at the right times were a lot simpler. "See you out front."

As she started to pull the cottage door closed behind her, she paused to listen. Not a sound came from inside the roll-top desk.

"Good night, Aunt Mel," she whispered. "And, thanks."

THE END

Acknowledgments

No book reaches publication through the efforts of one person alone. My thanks go out first to my husband, Terry, for his ongoing support as well as the countless times he helped me out of the tight spots I'd written myself into. I'm also grateful to the members of my critique group—Shaun Taylor Bevins, Becky Hutchison, Sherriel Mattingly, Debbi Mack, Bonnie Settle, and Marcia Talley—for catching problems but also sharing their enthusiasm. Many thanks to Terri Bischoff, Sandy Sullivan, and the entire Midnight Ink team for their final, careful molding of my loose pages into a polished book. And of course to Kim Lionetti, whose agenting skills got the whole thing started.

© Angela Powell Woulfe

About the Author

Mary Ellen Hughes is the bestselling author of the Pickled and Preserved Mysteries (Penguin), the Craft Corner Mysteries (Penguin), and the Maggie Olenski Mysteries (Avalon), along with several short stories. *A Fatal Collection* is her debut with Midnight Ink. A Wisconsin native, she has lived most of her adult life in Maryland, where she's set many of her stories. Visit her online at www.MaryEllenHughes.com.